A KINGDOM BY THE SEA

Arthur Butt

A Kingdom By The Sea

Arthur Butt

Dedication

As always, to my wife Susie

Chapter One

Seventy.

Eighty.

The needle on the speedometer brushed ninety before Kenya realized how fast she was driving.

"Shoot."

She slowed to a respectable seventy-five miles per hour. *I need to escape and relax, get my head together. A traffic ticket isn't the way to do it. Cops love to pull black women over for speeding.*

The GPS on her phone informed her the exit she wanted was approaching. Kenya slowed further, checked over her shoulder, and eased into the right hand lane, making a long curve down the exit ramp to a secondary road.

The tension did not leave Kenya's body. This was the first vacation in four years since graduation from high school. First, she worked at the diner, and then bartending at night. The guilt of inactivity caused a knot between her shoulders.

The gas gauge read one-quarter. Across the road stood a convenience store and pumps. Kenya drove over, filled up her tank, and entered the store, passing three girls in green uniforms behind an aluminum table stacked high with cookies. She winked at the girls and walked inside.

Twenty minutes later, she was back on the road. Four boxes of chocolate mint cookies sat on the passenger's seat, while an open box nestled between her legs. A bottle of water rested in a cup-holder.

She kept telling herself she wasn't running away, but rather to something. She wanted—what?

Too dumb to have a scholarship for college, too rich to get a grant.

She felt like a rat in a maze, a hamster on a treadwheel. Kenya knew the dream. Sing. Write music, all kinds, any kind. She could sing anything from gospel to rap.

Off to one side of the highway the faint crashing of ocean waves on beach resounded as she drove along a country road. To the right forest loomed, dark and foreboding.

On the left, sea oats reached to the sky, packed as tight as sugarcane. Kenya passed a green sign saying a university lay ahead. *Must be close, Inn advertised with pictures of a college.*

The GPS said her turn lay ahead, and then chattered as she missed it.

"Damn."

Kenya slammed on the brakes and backed up. In between the sea oats, she spotted a one-lane strip of asphalt, hidden beneath drooping leaves. To the GPS she said, "How is anyone supposed to find this place, huh? You'd think they'd keep this stuff cut back." She gunned the engine and sped through the offending foliage, adding, "Better concentrate on what I'm doing. Daydreaming can wait until I find the inn."

Kenya had a lot to think about, and she realized she did. What about JT? Everyone said they were the perfect match. He was clean, worked steady, and went to church, but did she want to get married?

The beach was close; the sound of waves and wind beyond the grass echoed in the air. Kenya passed a pile of rubble, and she slowed to look.

She could make out the tip of a crumbled tower above the oats with supporting masonry, blocks of stone stretched to the road.

Lighthouse? Castle? Have to check the place out while I'm here. Might be interesting to explore. A wave of vertigo swept over her. Hazy images of another time, place, people. Kenya slammed on the brakes until the dizziness passed. *Again? Lord, I know I need a vacation.*

The Twin Oaks Inn was another quarter mile up the road. Kenya pulled into the parking lot with a crunch of tires on gravel and dragged her luggage to the front porch. Peering through the screen door, she saw a desk. She entered and took a cautious step into the darkened interior.

"Hello? Anybody here?"

"Right here, dearie," a voice called from behind the desk. Kenya stepped forward and saw an old woman sitting in a rocking chair shucking peas. "Can I help you?"

"Yes. I have a reservation. I'm Kenya Williams."

"Oh, yes," the woman cut her off. "I've been expecting you." She stood. Kenya wasn't sure if the chair creaked or the woman herself. "Sign our guest book, dearie, and we'll find your room." She glanced behind Kenya. "You're alone?" The woman scanned Kenya suspiciously.

"Yes, a short vacation. Wanted to get away and relax."

"Well, no loud music, no guests in the rooms after nine p.m.. No noise after ten. We have no guests right now, but doors lock at ten o'clock."

"Of course. All I want to do is rest and think." *What does she think I am, a hooker?* "Is there a problem?"

The old woman shook her head in denial. "Oh, no. We usually cater to young couples and families, that's all. Don't think we've have a single person here in two, three years." She pushed a leather bound ledge forward. "Oh, by the way, my name is Kay."

Kenya scribbled her name. "The pile of stone I passed, Kay, what is it?"

"Oh, the ruins." Kay waved a hand in dismissal and pulled down a room key. "Old castle—been there forever."

She passed the key over. "I serve breakfast from five to eight. You're on your own for lunch and supper." She stepped out from behind the desk. "Follow me. You're on the second floor."

The old lady climbed the stairs, Kenya trailed behind, bumping her luggage on the steps as she went. "It's a walk," admitted Kay, pausing to catch her breath, "but you have the balcony. Lucky you're the only guest here at the moment. Good view of the beach."

The room *was* nice. Kay bustled around pulling up shades and throwing back drapes on windows to let the afternoon sun shine in.

"Do they give tours?" asked Kenya, sitting on the bed and watching Kay buzz around.

"Tours, dearie?" Kay jerked heavy drapes apart, revealing French doors. "Oh, you mean of the castle? No, it's a pile of rubble. We have terrible storms here during the winter. At one time, they did, but the government put the place off limits. In fact," she surveyed the sun lite room in satisfaction, "students from the archeology department from the school explored the ruins underwater. They're not sure if the ruins are a castle, or what the structure was. The place has been here so long."

"That old? Really?"

Kay nodded and dusted her hands off. "Really. If you need anything else, I'll be downstairs." She eyed Kenya's wavy black hair and slender figure. "This is a college town, though. If you're looking for things to do, there are plenty of restaurants and bars in town. If you want a quick bite, we have a diner a mile up the road."

After Kay left, Kenya bounced on the bed. The mattress was hard which she liked. She stood, strolled to the French doors and threw them wide. A cool breeze flooded the room, blowing the drapes. She walked out on the balcony to see whatever was there.

The scene was beautiful, Kenya admitted. From her vantage point, she could see over the sea oats and cane to the beach and ocean beyond. Waves dashed on the sand, and she had a clear view of the castle. She understood now, what Kay meant by a "pile of rubble". Combers lapped around stone washing in and out. Farther in the water, the tip of a breaker wall protruded as the waves peaked and broke. On top of the wall she spied a stone statue of what she thought of as a bird, its wings lifted. She noted for further use a path weaving through the cane to the beach.

For the first time that day, Kenya smiled. Maybe this wouldn't be so bad. A chance to gather her thoughts. When she broached the subject of her music, and the idea forming in her mind, most of her friends looked at her as if she'd gone insane. "Girl, black women don't sing country western music." When she'd tried to explain this was exactly why she wanted to try, she'd received eye-rolls in return. Sure, Kenya knew of some black country singers, but not many. The field was wide open.

Singing professionally was such a big step, though. She'd have to quit at least one of her jobs, maybe move back in with her parents. Travel to nearby towns, beg to sing her songs in bars, send out recordings. The thought scared her.

I am such a coward. Wish I had the nerve to try something new in a big way. Could I really make a life as a performer?

On impulse, she opened her suitcase and took out a hairbrush. Kenya giggled to herself. *I am such a fool.*

She held the brush to her lips, started to dance and sing.

"City boy, take me away,
back to the country
where I belong.

Fishing at the old creek,
sitting on the back porch,
drinking beer and talking,
playing a song.

My grandpa use to tell me,
'Beware those city folks, hear me?
There ain't no fields of cotton.
No acres of corn.'

City boy, take me away,
back to the—"

A loud banging on the door halted Kenya abruptly.
"Miss Williams? *Miss Williams.*"

Kenya opened the door. Kay stood outside, plainly aggravated. "Yes?"

"You are being much too loud." Kay peeked inside the room. "I don't remember a radio in here. What were you playing? Your phone?"

"Uh," Kenya grinned sheepishly. "Sorry. That was me. I was singing."

Kay looked at her in new interest. "I didn't know you people liked country western music?"

"Huh?" *You people?* Kenya drew back slightly.

Kay saw her reaction and said hastily, "I mean, you young people. Especially around here. I doubt there's a country western station on the radio."

"Oh. I love all sorts of music. I want to be a singer and composer."

"Really? Have you ever had anything published?" Kay appeared intrigued.

"No, not yet," Kenya admitted. "But I'm trying."

"Good luck with the music, but keep it down." Kay turned and left.

After the woman disappeared down the stairs, Kenya walked back into the room and debated whether to drive into town and find lunch, or take an afternoon nap, something she had not done since high school. To her surprise, the nap won out and she ran to her car and retrieved her boxes of cookies and water. *Yeah, adulting.* Kenya snacked, took a quick shower, sat on the bed and finished another box of cookies.

Wonder if the dreams will start again?

She'd dreamt the last few nights of a place where her music was real. Not a nightmare exactly, or a good dream, but a place where she was happy, doing what she wanted. Kenya had put the nightly visions aside, marking them up to the stress of working two jobs, dreaming of one day being a singer, and she wondered if today, a day of relaxation would provide different images.

Kenya stretched out on the mattress and suppressed a deep yawn, curling into a ball on her side.

A damp breeze and the faint ring of music and laughter woke her some time later. In the dark, she groped for her phone. Three a.m.? How did she sleep so long? Kenya staggered to her feet and bumped her way out to the balcony to see what the ruckus was about outside.

Down on the beach a bonfire raged. People flicked in and out of the wavering light and back into shadows, completing circles of dance as they frolicked and sang with joyous abandonment.

Damn, they're having a party down there.

The more she gazed at the dancing figures the more her anger grew. She'd driven to the inn for peace and quiet, was even chewed out by Kay for singing too loud. How dare they wake her up out of the best sleep she'd had in her life. Drunken college kids, no doubt, remembering Kay saying this was a college town.

Kenya marched into her room, snapped on a lamp, rummaged through her luggage and pulled on a jacket, shoving her phone in her back pocket. Stalking out the door, she stamped down the stairs.

The drone of someone humming echoed from a back room. The smell of fresh bread filled the air. Kay doing early morning baking. Kenya hesitated, wondering if she should complain, then decided whining would do no good. This wasn't the woman's fault, and from her brief acquaintance with Kay, she'd probably protested to the school many times. Instead, Kenya walked out into the parking lot and looked around.

A lone street light provided scant illumination, but good enough to locate the path to the beach. Again, Kenya stopped. Maybe she should have brought a flashlight, the tall cane and sea oats cast dark shadows in the moonlight. The sounds of laughter made up her mind and Kenya plunged into the cane, using the faint light from her phone as a guide.

Her eyes adjusted to the gloom and she walked on following the twisting turns of the path. She did not remember the cane and oats being this deep to the beach when she'd surveyed the vegetation this afternoon from the balcony, and shied each time she heard a rustling noise, imagining snakes and lizards lying in wait to leap out and attack. With hurrying steps, Kenya kept walking faster until she almost ran in terror.

A noise rustled behind her, and then a low grunt. She stumbled into a clump of sea oats and fell. Scrambling up, Kenya cast a look behind and discovered the path again. Her heart raced in her chest and breath snorted in short gasps.

So engrossed was she with checking behind, she did not realize she ran onto the beach until the firelight played shadows on the dark sea oats. The dancers twisted in her direction and for the moment, the music stopped.

Kenya froze and tried to understand what she saw. This was no drunken college party, unless the gathering was a type of frat turnout. The women dressed in ball gowns of bright colored silks, the men sported tunics to match. All wore masks and hats with feathers pluming skyward.

Practicing for a Renaissance Fair? Looks like a gathering of the Macaroni Society.

The music started again and the couples resumed their dance. An unattached watcher with a weather-beaten face, topped with sandy-brown hair, wearing a forest green tunic drifted over to her.

"M'lady, you are late in joining us." He surveyed Kenya dressed in jeans and t-shirt with a grin. "And you have forgotten to array yourself for the occasion, but, shall we dance anyway?" Emerald eyes stared at her.

For the first time in her life, Kenya didn't know what to say. She forgot why she'd walked to the beach, forgot everything except those green eyes boring into hers. Before Kenya regained her composure, the stranger clasped her around the waist and whisked her away into the circle of dancers.

"Who—who are you people?" Kenya giggled, not sure why. The other women surrounding her smiled, nodded, and laughed.

"Tonight we are the host of Evertree, and merry-make to its branches, spreading life to the sky." He laughed at her confusion as they spun in a circle around the clearing.

"No, really….What is all of this?" Kenya laughed so hard she found her mirth hard to control. *This is ridiculous. A troop of entertainers' maybe, practicing for a play at the school?* "Be truthful—who…who are you?"

"I?" The stranger chuckled. "My name is Marcos. We are the chosen few who are allowed to dance tonight in celebration of life on the longest day of the year." The music stopped. "And you, m'lady? What is your name? I have never seen you before. Have you journeyed here to dance in joy of life, too?"

"I...."

A tankard thrust into Kenya's hands before the sentenced finished. By reflex, she took a sip.

Thick, with a taste of honey and cloves, and Kenya suspected high in alcohol content. She took another taste and allowed the liquor to claw its way down her throat and erase what remained of the anger for being awakened.

"Your name, m'lady?" Marcos held a tankard also. The man took a large gulp and wiped his mouth with the back of a hand. "Or should I call you mystery woman from the unknown?"

"Oh, sorry. My name's Kenya." The drink made a warm spot in her stomach, spreading a sense of well-being through her body and leaving a dizzy feeling in her head.

"Are you here to salute the joy of life also? This is the Summer Solstice. The longest day of the year. Enjoy the light and warmth, for winter soon approaches."

The joy of life? Kenya never thought of life in those terms before. She was too busy living on the treadmill of responsibility to worry about joy.

Kenya looked around and found herself ringed by the other dancers, anxious to hear what her reply would be. She knew what they wanted her to say, felt the emotion by the expectant expressions on their faces. Kenya took another swallow from the tankard, wiped her mouth, and grinned back at Marco.

"Well, for today, anyway. What the heck."

Murmurs of approval from the other members of the group arose. Marco leveled a questioning stare at her but said, "Well and good. Come—dawn is breaking soon and we have much dancing yet to do." With those words, he took her in his arms and the two swept out around the barn fire.

The breaking dawn became a blur of events to Kenya with singing, dancing, drinking. The life she fled from faded away in the joy of merriment.

If this morning could only stay like this forever. I'd never go back to my old life. This is the way being should be. No cares, worries, fears.

The music continued to beat into her brain, louder, more demanding, lifting her soul and spirit to heights never felt before.

***

Kenya's head throbbed. With painful grunts, she opened her eyes and sat up. She was in a bed, but not the bed at the inn, nor her room, she was sure. The walls were made of rough stone blocks and the ceiling high-vaulted. Panic gripped her. Where was this place, what happened last night, what was done?

She slipped out of bed and stood, her stomach grumbling. For a moment, her head spun, and she steadied herself on the bedpost. The feeling passed and she staggered to a window to look out. In the near distance, a massive wall stood, and farther, the grey ocean stretched to the horizon. Below, people hurried about their work.

Plenty of pigs, chickens, and goats; carts, horses, and wagons roamed; but no signs of a cars or buses, not even kids on bicycles playing. Kenya turned away from the window and walked to the door determined to learn where she was.

The door would not open.

"Hey, open up," Kenya yelled, rapping on the wood. When no reply returned, she banged harder, slamming a fist on the door. *"OPEN UP, I SAY."*

A muffled reply originated from outside. A few seconds later, the latch rattled and the door swung wide. A wizened old crone stood staring at Kenya. Wisps of white hair framed the wrinkled face, the small body bent over. "I see yer awake now," the woman mumbled. "Food's downstairs." The hag swung about to leave.

"Wait." Kenya grabbed a boney shoulder and spun the woman around. "Where am I? I want…" She thought back to the morning on the beach with the man she danced with at the party. He was the one who must have brought her here. What was his name? "I want Marcos. Where is he?"

The troll stared back at her and nodded. "You stay here." Without saying another word, the woman walked off.

Kenya spent the next fifteen minutes pacing across the floor, drumming fingers on a table, and fuming. In exasperation, she sat on the bed, crossed her legs, and tapped a foot. By the time her companion from the morning arrived, she was ready to bite someone's head off and demand an explanation of what was going on.

Marcos rapped on the door, stuck his head into the room glancing around, and stepped inside. Today he dressed in buckskins looking raggedy but clean; he wore both long sword and short sword. "I see you are up and around," he exclaimed with hands on hips surveying Kenya with a smile. "I thought you slept the sleep of the dead."

Kenya sprang off the bed and stalked to him. "I don't know what you're playing at mister, but take me home—NOW." She took a deep breath. "What are you, a kidnapper?"

Marcos' grin disappeared, replaced by shock. "*M'lady.* You swooned on the beach, and I knew not where you lived. How could I leave you laying there on the sand by yourself?"

Kenya conceded he had a point. She replied, chagrinned, "Yeah, okay, I guess you're right. I want to go back to the inn."

Marcos grinned returned. "Of course, Kenya, but let us eat a noonday meal first before we faint from hunger.

Where is this inn you speak of? I know of none around here."

Kenya frowned. Was this man playing with her, or just dumb. "The Twin Oaks Inn, of course." Some of her anger returned. "How many inns are around here?"

"Not many," acknowledged Marcos with a frown, "and I know them all. We have no inn by that name in this kingdom."

"What?" Kenya scrutinized his face in disbelief, positive the man was lying for some reason. "We were dancing a hundred yards from the joint. What do you mean you never heard of the Twin Oaks Inn? What is this, a looney bin?"

"If you wish I can take you to the spot we dance," temporized Marcos, holding his hands up, "but I assure you, Lady, no such inn exists there."

Kenya walked passed him to the door determined to make her way back to the beach and inn. "Let's go."

They hurried down flights of stairs. Kenya's head kept sweeping back and forth, gazing at the strange tapestries hanging on the walls, along with ancient weapons and shields. They exited by a side door into a courtyard, her eyes widening in amazement as the massive building loomed behind her. The place wasn't an insane asylum. More like a medieval castle complete with staff. Outside, Kenya confirmed her suspicion by the people walking, dressed in tunics and the odor wafting in the breeze.

Marcos kicked a flock of pecking chickens out of the way as they passed over a wooden drawbridge and under a wrought iron gate, heading for the beach. A twenty minute walk along the shore brought the two to the site of a burned out barn fire. The signs of shoe prints showed where people danced, and a forgotten tankard half buried in the sand gave testimony a party happening in the recent past.

Kenya couldn't discover the path through the cane and sea oats, although the location was clear in her mind where the trail *should* be, directly opposite the site of the party, as an hour trudging up and down the beach with Marcos following her like a puppy, showed her. Kenya tried forcing a trail through the cane until she was red in the face and dripping sweat. Marcos drew his sword and kept hacking at the tall grass until they reached a spot clear of green leafy foliage, which allowed a clear view of landscape covered in meadows and then dense forest beyond.

Kenya gazed around in bewilderment, her mind filling with panic. "Where—where—am I?" Mounting terror swelled inside her threatening to cloud out all sense of reality. She swung in a small circle, but no inn, road, nothing to indicate civilization, rose into view. "The house must be here," she muttered to herself, starting to walk toward the woods, determined to search to the ends of the earth if need be to find a familiar landmark. "How?"

Marcos reached out and grabbed her shirt. "M'lady Kenya, even this close to the castle, it is not safe to wander about unless in a large group. You are unarmed, and I only carry my sword. Wild animals roam in these forests that would gladly dine on us if able."

Tears of frustration clouded her vision. Kenya wiped her eyes and spun around. Framed against the horizon was the massive castle perched on a small peninsular, and beyond, the stone wall, the savage ocean crashing forward. The scene reminded her of the old pile of rock by the inn.

The castle? It couldn't be. Kay said the weather destroyed the pile of stone ages ago, no one knows how long. Kenya took a long, hard look at the wall. On top perched the stone edifice of a bird, an eagle, facing Evertree with wings raised—and then nothing made sense anymore.

Chapter Two

They trudged through the sand to the castle.

It was impossible. IMPOSSIBLE. Events such as falling asleep and waking up in another world didn't occur in real life. What was happening in her mind must be one of those wild dreams she'd been having lately, too much worrying about what was happening in her life, what career she'd have after a decision. Kenya felt sure the thoughts were escape into a fantasy world, a realm where everyday problems did not matter. Soon this Marcos would sprout wings, break out into one of her songs she tried hard to compose, float in the air like a soap bubble, and take her hand. They would drift over the landscape seeing familiar faces of people they knew but couldn't place, swooping and diving as if they flew in the air.

Marcos walked beside her and watched her face reflect the horror she felt. "Sometimes, M'lady Kenya," he said, uncertainty in his soft voice, "when you dance to joy under the moon on the Summer Solstice, strange things happen to your soul."

Joy? In my soul? The dream wasn't playing out as her fantasies usually did. Joy, yes, but the joy hadn't happened yet, only confusion and growing fear creeping up from her stomach to lodge in her chest and spine. Kenya's eyes flickered from the grey sea to the stone fortress and she licked her lips nervously, tasting the salt from the ocean air on her mouth. *Wish I'd wake up. This dream is turning into a nightmare. So real.*

"I'll be happy when I can learn what's happening and how to return to the inn," Kenya snapped back. She eyed Marcos with an air of suspicion. "I still think something fishy is going on."

Marcos replied matter-the-fact as he attempted to distract Kenya from her fears, "What is it you do, Kenya for a living? Do you have any useful skills you trade for money?"

"Huh?"

Do? Skills? I'm not an expert in anything. I serve drinks and food. No actual skill in that. Makes me money, yeah, not very much though. If this were the real world and I was role-playing my real jobs, I'd call myself a tavern wench or barmaid. In my dreams, I was always a singer and composer. A person who made beautiful words and weaved them into wisdom of life to entertain and instruct. What would be the word to describe what I want to be? What the heck, this is only pretend.

A crazy idea entered her mind. "I'm a wordsmith," Kenya said at last.

Marcos' eyebrows rose in curiosity and he pursed his lips running the title through is mind. "I have heard of such an occupation," he admitted after a long pause, "but I confess I know not what they do. In my memory we have never had such of your profession at Evertree, even under the old king."

Kenya reached back into her mind and pulled up a saying remembered from an English book during high school. "A wordsmith draws letters from the crucible of chaos and beats them into a sword of prose or poetry."

Marcos nodded in understanding. "I see what you mean. We will discuss your ability with my uncle. Perhaps he has need of a wordsmith, or perchance knows of a lord in one of the kingdoms who desires such as you with your ability. We shall see." He gestured with a finger across the sandy ground to the middle of the cape. "We will go this way, it is quicker and the walking is not as hard as in the sand." He cut up the beach with his long legs eating the distance. Kenya hurried to catch up, taking two steps to his one. They hit a cobblestone road running through the middle of the cape with the front of the castle looming before the two.

When they reached the highway, Kenya halted. For the first time, she was able to scan the vista spread out before her while spinning in a slow circle, with the fortress at one end of the cape, and peninsular disappearing into the dark forest on the other.

I've seen this castle before. Not the same but…déjà vu? I know I've never been here before. Reality merging with my dream.

Kenya broke off her concentration of the landscape and swung her attention back to what Marcos said. "Your uncle? Who's your uncle, Santa Claus?" she joked, calling out and walking again toward the castle.

Marcos waited until Kenya caught up, puzzled. "Santa Claus?" he said, strolling slower so she didn't have to hurry. "I know him not. No, my uncle rules in Evertree." He gestured to the fortress.

"Really?" Kenya looked at him sideways, surprise mirrored on her face. "Is he a king or something? Does that make you a duke or prince? Do you have a castle, too?" Maybe this dream wasn't so bad after all. She'd always thought about dating royalty. Kenya giggled to herself. *Well, maybe not dating, but at least hanging out with the high and mighty. Maybe get an autograph.* Images of women dressed in fancy ball gowns with their hair done up, and men in tuxedos with swords by their side, dancing in a circle, flooded her mind with an orchestra playing soft music in the background.

This brought a chorus of chuckles from Marcos, and he leaned closer to Kenya. "My uncle is a king, yes, but I am the second son of a second son. Long on titles of nobility, but short on gold coins or other wealth, and not even a tower to my name. I am liegeman to my uncle pure and simple, and I fear, not a good one."

"Second son? You have a brother?"

Marcos walked slower and studied the ground beneath his feet. "Somewhere. He traveled North and West three years ago searching for adventure, and no one has heard from him since, nor has anyone brought news of him. My uncle sent riders out onto the plains two years ago when he did not reappear, and they returned with no information. I fear he will never make his way back to Evertree now. Too much time has passed."

Kenya tried thinking of something to say, but instead clamped her jaws tightly shut. She'd never lost a sibling, but knew nothing she might express would replace the loss of a brother. *Why do I feel so sad for Marcos? I didn't even know his brother.*

The road ended in a small village of one and two story buildings surrounding the castle's walls. They sauntered through a patch of wooden hovels, which in Kenya's judgement, needed tearing down, or better yet, never erected with their raggedy appearance in the first place. She felt sure a strong wind would make the shacks tumble down on the inhabitant's heads.

The people weren't in much better shape. Dirty ripped clothing, downcast eyes, and a shuffled walk was the mark of dwellers in this hamlet. They reminded Kenya markedly of pictures with people fleeing disasters in war torn counties having no other place to live.

The acid odor of wood smoke fill the air in a grey pallor over their heads, and the reek of garbage covered with flies was everywhere. The insects created a swirling black mass, with the low hum of buzzing echoing in Kenya's ears as they picked their way through the street.

Besides the sorry looking homes, a few better-built structures stood clustered in one section of the village on the edge of either side of the street next to the castle's gate. Each one carried a plaque or sign indicating what the proprietor sold inside the shop. One she knew from reading in school, a bush hanging upside down by the door. A tavern. Kenya kept gazing inside each place of business, curious to see if anything occurred of interest. They passed an open-air smithy, what might be a wheelwright and a shop with plants and jars displayed in the window, an apothecary. Kenya kept looking left and right taking in the strange smells and sights until they stood before the castle's walls.

Marcos continued to walk with his head bowed, and Kenya saw by his eyes he still thought of his loss. "Sorry to hear about your brother," Kenya muttered, knowing something needed to say something, but words wouldn't help. She tried to sound upbeat and added, "You never know, he may return any day. Stranger things have happened." The man beside her attempted to perk up with a wan smile and a nod. "Perhaps so, Lady. As you say, he has not returned, but then again, there is not word of his death either."

Kenya changed the subject before he fell into a flunk again. She surveyed Marcos's lean, hard body and boyish grin. "But what about you? You look okay to me. Why do you say you're a lousy follower of your uncle? Not trying to plan a coup and overthrow him are you?" she joked, only half-sure it was a joke.

Marcos drew his head back, mouth dropping open in surprise. He saw Kenya grinning, and suppressed the smile lifting his mouth at the corners when he realized she was teasing him. "Of course not. What would I do with a kingdom? I can barely control my horse." He said seriously, "In this kingdom one must be a complete man. I have some small skill with the sword, it's true, maybe more than small, but I cannot command the forces of the ancients as the great lords can. Watch." He stretched out his hand toward a pile of rubbish and closed his eyes in concentration.

At first, nothing happened. Then, from the top of the pile, a broken plank shook itself free and drifted upward. The wood hovered for a moment suspended in the air. By its own accord, the wood moved sideways, trembled, and fell next to the heap onto the ground with a clatter.

Kenya frowned, perplexed, and blinked. Had she seen what she thought she saw? Kenya rubbed her eyes, sure this was some type of trick. The plank wobbled as the wood settled into a new position. Kenya looked around at the other side of the mound to assure herself someone wasn't hiding there. The space was empty. "How did you do that?"

"Not well," Marcos admitted embarrassed by his poor performance. "I told you, the spirits dwelling in the nether regions favor me not." He shook his head, pretending his shortcoming meant little, but Kenya heard the bitter tone in his voice; saw the disappointment in his eyes, and the slump of his shoulders. "To be a king, prince in truth, or even a captain, and command troops, one must have the favor of the gods and the strength of magic in his arms. True, a few of the warriors follow me, for I am of royal blood and usually correct in my judgements. Most view me with scorn, however, especially my uncle the king, and it is he who I must impress most."

"Well, it's pretty impressive to me. If I could do that, why…" Kenya left the rest of the sentence hanging, thinking of what this man Marcos did. With the ability he'd shown, what couldn't he accomplish if he put his mind to the task?

No sign of the awe Kenya felt showed in Marcos's tone. "Of course, the true mark of a wielder of vast power is how great he can make his sword flame," he continued, matter-of-fact. "Again, I can make my sword blaze, but not as much as a true adept can, or as long. My brother always chided me for my lack of confidence since we were small children learning the trade of warrior. I fear he was right, even though he stood over me and explained what I did wrong over and again."

Kenya bit back a remark. *This one has a problem, and it's not how much he can make some piece of metal flame or lift a piece of wood. There's more to being a ruler than tricks. His ability to make people believe in him, his wisdom, his vision of the future for the kingdom and the subjects he rules.* Kenya studied Marcos. *Having your big brother hovering over you criticizing your every effort doesn't help, I bet. Made him nervous as heck. I wouldn't be able to do my best either.*

While they talked, a small group of dirty-faced peasant children gathered around the two gazing at Kenya in her strange clothes and listening closely to Marcos talk. The brats showed no astonishment at all by the small miracle Marcos performed by levitating the plank, but were more interested in the sword at his waist and Kenya's appearance. Excited whispers shot back and forth with a few giggles in between.

They passed an open-air shop where a man busily spun a bowl on a pottery wheel, a hot kiln throwing off heat behind him. More people wandered passed Kenya and Marcos along the street toward the beach carrying nets. "What do all these people do?" Kenya asked. The group of children clustered around Marcos and Kenya grew larger, hands out, begging for a treat.

"Most are fishermen," Marcos said and waved to the water where the men loaded their nets into small boats. Each craft had masts laid to rest inside. "Others are the families of soldiers who protect the castle, but do not have high enough rank to live inside. These," he pointed to the craft shops, "provide for their needs and those of the fortress, which are not manufactured within. We have a happy little town here. Most of our wants we provide for ourselves."

From the expression on the sullen faces, Kenya doubted the people were cheerful.

Marcos fished around in a leather pouch hanging about his neck and withdrew a stained, rectangular package covered in parchment. He unwrapped the parcel. Inside the animal skin was a hard brownish cube. Marcos broke the material into small bite sized bits, and passed the fragments out to the children. With eager cries, the morsels disappeared from dirty fingers into waiting mouths. "Emergency provisions," Marcos said when Kenya gave him an inquiring stare. "Pounded and dried honey, berries, nuts and meat. The brats love them and rations are a nice change from the fish and grains they usually eat."

With a friendly wave of the hand to the youngsters, and a promise for more if they behaved themselves, the two tramped over the drawbridge covering a moat, reentered the castle's walls as a bell tolled ringing the hour.

Marcos grabbed Kenya's fingers. "Come, it is time to sup, and we have yet to break our fast," said Marcos. "The dance continued to the wee hours of the morning and we slept over long." He transferred his hand to Kenya's back, guiding her through a large cobblestone courtyard into the castle proper. "I fear we drank too much also," he admitted with a gruff chuckle. "We must fill our bellies to rid ourselves of the sour feeling in our stomachs."

Kenya realized the cookies eaten the night before were a long ways off, and her stomach confirmed the fact with a loud grumble. *He's right, whether this is a dream or not, I'm starving.* The queasiness felt before was gone and she was ravenously hungry.

The main hall of the castle was set with tables along either side of the walls, some higher than others, and leaving a large vacant space in the middle where people congregated with muted conversation. At the apex of the benches, a large man sat on a carved wooden chair, the figures of sea hawks staring out from the armrests in bold relief. Flanked on one side was a woman Kenya's age dressed in gold and white silks. Her vision immediately fell on Marcos and Kenya as they entered the hall, the sides of her lips twitching upward in a smirk Kenya was positive was one of distaste, either for Marcos, or her, or both.

The man resembled Marcos superciliously, with hair a sandy brown, receding up his forehead, and speckled in grey streaks. The long tresses fell in curly waves around his powerful shoulders. His face, however, showed soft flesh and sagging jowls from lavish living. The piggish eyes roved from his plate to the diners below as if counting the food consumed and weighing the gold to pay for each person to dine. As Marcos and Kenya strolled into the hall, the man switched his attention from the feasters to track Marcos and Kenya's movement as a cat might follow a mouse before the feline pounced and devoured them.

Marcos ignored the stares and took Kenya's hand drawing her to one of the lower tables less occupied, and where space remained for two on one bench without having to squeeze between others. Food passed around the long bench and the chewing and slurps of the hungry diners mingled with the dinner talk filling the room. Marcos grabbed two empty trenchers resting on the end of the table and a platter of roasted fowl. He handed one of the bowl-like plates to Kenya and dropped the platter within easy reach.

"Here you go Lady Kenya, eat your fill. My uncle sets a good table this night." With two hands, he ripped the fowl in half, and placed one piece in her trencher. Drawing the short sword from his scabbard, he made a long arm and retrieved bowls of boiled tubers and vegetables sitting in a dark gravy, speared some with the blade like a Shish Kabob, and scrapped everything onto her plate.

Kenya looked around for knives, forks, or at least a napkin. Seeing none, she glanced at the other people nearest at the table. Fingers were the choice of cutlery with an occasional knife for cutting larger pieces of meat. Kenya examined her fingers with disdain. Her hands were filthy, nails encrusted with dirt, and under other circumstances, she would have felt ill eating like this.

Oh, well, a little dirt never killed anyone.

Her stomach growled again and hunger won out, however, and she tore into the food until all that remained were a few well-picked bones and a savory memory.

Kenya was chasing the last bits of gravy in her trencher with a chunk of black bread covered in butter when a voice called out. "Ho, Nephew. Who is this you have brought to my table to dine without asking first? Is my hall then thrown open to ever wanderer who chances by?" The voice was that of the man at the head table. He had finished eating and leaned back, picking his teeth and staring at Marcos with interest.

The young man hastily wiped his mouth on his sleeve and stood. "I ask you pardon, Uncle. I fear my stomach thought before my brain did." This brought a few chuckles from the rest of the eaters. Marcos grinned in return. His uncle did not. "This is the Lady Kenya. She danced with us last night and this morning to the joy of life at the Summer Solstice and now asks for a boon in return if you will find it in your heart to grant a request."

The king's bushy eyebrows rose in amusement as he surveyed Kenya in her ripped clothes and he replied, "So? And what favor would this be Nephew? A new wardrobe perhaps?"

The girl sitting next to him broke out in loud guffaws and whispered something to the king who chuckled back.

"Employment in your service, Uncle."

Marcos uncle's eyes widened even farther and he laughed, whispered to the young woman on his left in return. The girl tittered a reply and shook her head in the negative.

The king composed himself and said seriously, "You now scour the countryside in search of people to work for me, is it, and by her dark appearance you traveled all the way to the southern regions to locate this woman. Well, and good, at least you are some help and try to do the duty to your liege." The king placed two fingers to his lips and said to himself, but loud enough for all to hear, "And what would I need? A serving wench? Scullery maid? I believe the castle has all of those for now." He addressed Marcos again. "What is it this woman does? Cook? I confess I do not see a need for anyone at all." He turned to the girl beside him. "My dear, are you in need of another lady-in-waiting? A seamstress perhaps?"

The girl's mouth bent down into a frown and she glared at Kenya. "One such as her? The creature is so dirty I am afraid to go near the woman, not even to handle my clothes."

The king nodded again and fixed his stare on Marcos waiting for a reply.

A hush settled on the diners. Kenya took a swift survey of the people around them. Wolfish grins shone on their faces. *This is a game they've played out before. I wonder if the king really means what he says? And as for you, girl, I wouldn't sew your clothing if my life depended on it.* Kenya took a deep breath. *Calm. I gotta stay calm though. Maybe they're teasing Marcos.* A tentative smile flickered on Kenya's lips, matching those of the people as she waited for the man to say something.

These remarks did not anger Marcos in the least. He replied glibly, "The lady is a wordsmith, Uncle—known far and wide in the land for prose, poetry and wisdom of her words and songs."

Kenya handed Marcos a sharp sideways glance. She'd listened to this exchange with first amusement, and then growing agitation at their comments about her appearance, especially the woman's snide remarks. Kenya had not told Marcos she was famous, and certainly not possessing any knowledge about poetry, or smart. As for the dirty clothes, it wasn't her fault, and she never asked Marcos to beg a job for her in this castle anyway. On second thought, however, Kenya conceded if she were to live out this dream, she needed a job.

"Hmmm....A wordsmith is it?" A low babble started up and ran through the guests. New glances shot Kenya's way. Marcos's uncle paused, uncertain, taken aback by this answer and scratched the stubble on his chin in thought. "I have heard of her profession, but never thought of employing a person of such trade. I have little need for one such as a weaver of words," he mused. "I am a man of action, not verses." He clapped his hands together and arrived at a decision. He said to Marcos, but looked at Kenya, "Nevertheless, I am a man of compassion and forethought. I can at least allow an audition for the position even though I need her naught. If she is a wordsmith, let her stand and speak for herself." The king waved his hand. "Up girl. You have been silent all this time while we discussed your fate. What do you have to say on your behalf?"

All eyes fixed on Kenya as she stood. She refused to answer their stares, and instead kept her gaze steady on the king. "Your Majesty, if you please, I would like a job," she stammered.

Laughter rippled through the crowd. The girl sitting at the high table covered her mouth and turned her head. The king said, "Not too glib for a wordsmith, are you girl? Well, maybe you save your best work for when you compose. Impress us with this wisdom of yours and wit my nephew Marcos tells us about. I am not a person to buy a horse without checking its teeth first. My minstrels have run out of fresh tunes and tales to amuse us. Let us hear a verse. Something new we have never listened to before and perhaps we will consider hiring you."

Kenya's face burnt as she desperately thought of what he asked. *He wants me to make up a poem or song here and now. Right on the spot without rewriting and fine-tuning? How in the world...?* Her stomach knotted in panic. The amused eyes staring, jeers ringing in her ears from the people at the tables, didn't help the nervousness. Kenya frantically searched her mind for something, anything, old or new she'd written, read, to recite. She closed her eyes, concentrating.

"There once was a king from Evertree,
Who went in search of his enemies.
He looked high and low
Found naught who was foe
Still they pushed him back to the Emerald Sea."

The king leaned forward, shock mirrored on his face. *"Did Marcos put you up to this? How...?"*

"Sire—I did naught." Marcos was as horror stricken as Harold.

At first, the hall fell deathly silent. Then low babble arose turning into a growl as the people yelled to each other and the king. Kenya heard her name shouted in anger and blanched at the thought of what they said.

Kenya clasped her hands over her mouth.

"SILENCE." Everyone swung to stare at Harold. He in turn gazed at Kenya with uneasiness as if she'd looked into his mind and located a secret thought he'd hidden and been unwilling to express out loud.

Where had those words come from? An Emerald Sea? Was that the ocean surrounding the fortress? Kenya was sure she had not uttered them on her own, never heard of a sea, didn't know about any enemies. She never composed limericks, bawdy, funny, or otherwise. It was as if some outside force entered her body and possessed her voice, using her vocal cords for its own sinister purposes. Kenya trembled as the king's face reddened, wondering what he would say or do.

Harold took a deep calming breath, visibly controlled himself and nodded to Kenya. "It appears you are a wordsmith in truth, girl, whether for good or evil I cannot say." He clasped his hands together as he made up his mind about her place in his court. "So be it. Marcos…" He fixed the young man by eye, "I place you in charge of this woman. See to it she has proper clothes, and a room readied. In addition, whatever else is necessary for her personal appearance or comfort within reason. The lady shall be the court wordsmith until proven otherwise."

The girl-woman sitting next to the king gasped in disbelief. "Father, I do not believe you are allowing this person to stay, and giving her a place in your court? This is the most ridiculous thing…"

Harold replied sternly, "I will hear no more. This is my responsibility and decision, not yours." He stood, as did the rest of the hall. "I grow weary. Stay if you wish and eat your fill, but I am returning to my chambers to rest. I bid you all good day." With those parting words, he stretched his arms wide in a yawn and nodded curtly to the girl sitting next to him, standing and strolling out of the hall.

Talk started again. A minstrel walked about the hall playing on his lute, but not so loud as to be intrusive on the conversations going on. Servants circulated, removing empty platters and putting away vacated benches.

A few people sauntered over and introduced themselves to Kenya, some she recognized from the morning dance, and smiled shyly back while trying to associate name to face for future use. The rest the diners drifted away to attend to their own business. The young woman who sat at the king's table mingled with the remaining crowd, making a slow journey toward Kenya and Marcos while not appearing to do so, greeting people with a quick smile and wave of the hand as she wandered closer.

"Well, cousin, let me inspect further what you have brought to us this day," the woman remarked when she stood before Kenya and Marcos. Her head tilted slightly, making the raven black hair sway, and examined Kenya from head to toe, as if a steward inspecting a piece of butchered beef deciding to buy or not.

This slut I am not going to like. Has the look of a vulture in her eyes. I've see the look before. Deception in her voice and stance, in every movement of her body. She thinks she is everything and people exist on earth to be her plaything. Why is she so nasty?

As if to confirm Kenya's thoughts, the woman gave Marcos a sickly grin and said, "I do not know if my father was right or not in his decision, but he was correct in one thing. Find new clothes and a bath, too." Her nostrils flared with distaste. "Your new lady smells like a pigsty. No better than the grubbing scum who live outside the castle walls." The princess nodded to herself, and Kenya, as if she'd solved a problem plaguing them both with her blessing. With a flip of her perfumed hair, and a flutter of manicured fingers in their faces, the girl wheeled away on the tips of her toes, waving at a couple about to leave the room, and hurried to them before they left.

Before Kenya could make a remark, Marcos said in way of apology with a weak smile, "My cousin, Jessica. She can be, well, how would you say it—outspoken at times, and does not always consider how words affect others. Think nothing of her attitude." He watched his cousin titter at a remark by a passing noble. "She treats most people the same way unless needed for some reason."

Kenya swallowed hard and calmed herself enough to admit between the alcohol of the morning, sweat of the afternoon, and dirt from *everywhere*, she needed a good scrubbing. She reeked. Kenya inhaled and could smell the odor of her body, and dreaded what the reek would be when she took off her shoes and socks; but she did not need to hear how filthy she was from that one. Kenya tried to temporize and commented, "Well, maybe your cousin is right. Some people are outspoken. They say what they think."

Marcos leaned forward and pretended to sniff. "I smell nothing wrong with you. Do not all wordsmiths smell of the land, lust, love and passion? These are the tools of your trade, no?"

He's right. This is what a songwriter deals with, and not only songs either. A fear grew in her mind. She called herself a wordsmith, but what did a wordsmith do, other than make songs and write poems? Especially a wordsmith to a king. Dimly Kenya remembered troubadours carried news, dealt with political issues, sometimes, instructed the people or nobles on new concepts. She knew this evil witch Jessica would watch for any mistake, any uncertainty on her part, others also for how she carried herself, said and did. One wrong move, a bad song or a missed cord, and life here in Evertree was finished, and they'd cast her out into forest by herself.

Dream or not, I must learn what this woman's game is. If I am to stay here until I wake up, I must know who my friends and enemies are, the dangers which stalk this land. "Why was there no queen sitting with your uncle? Is she sick? Dead?"

"No queen rules with Harold at this time. The Lady Wanda, concubine to the king, is the closest we have to a queen, but does not dine with us," Marcos waved a thumb toward the higher levels of the fortress. "The lady has her own servants, cooks, who wait on her. I doubt you will ever see Lady Wanda."

"Doesn't like people?" Kenya asked.

Marcos glanced around the chamber, almost empty now, and lowered his voice. "After his wife died Harold never married again. Wanda is bitter, but," he shrugged, "what can she do? The woman lives on the sufferance of the king, if the lady displeases him, where would Wanda go? The closest thing we have to a queen right now is Jessica, and even my cousin fears the king's wrath when he is angry. So the Lady Wanda sits and broods, perhaps plotting a scheme to elevate herself over my cousin. This castle is full of plots."

Just as I though. They all work their own angles. "I take it they never had children?"

"None. I think Harold does not want a possible successor to the throne." Again, Marcos's lips bent down. "My brother, William, was being groomed to marry Jessica. It is in my heart he still waits in hope my brother will return."

"Really? I thought she's your cousin. Isn't marriage, uh, dangerous? I mean with defective kids and all?" Kenya recalled the hemophiliacs of European nobility.

Marcos acted as if this was of no concern. "My uncle and father had different mothers. The queen and my mother were no relations. The chances of a deformed child are slight." Marcos shrugged. "Besides, an alliance between the two would keep the bloodline secure. And the army always feels better with a man they know leading them." Marcos's attention focused on a banner of crossed swords hanging from the rafters. "There are few of noble birth outside our kingdom who are unmarried or seek a wife. Our customs would allow it, but in that case Jessica must choose for herself."

"Your brother is luckier than he knows. Missing, yes. But if he returned he would have been worse off being married to a shew like Jessica."

Marcos threw his head back and laughed. "Now I know you are a reader of the past as well as a wordsmith. Being second in line for the throne, the king would wed *me* to Jessica if it were not for my poor ability in magic. This is why I believe my uncle ridicules me, for his disappointment. Jessica and I have hated each other since we were small children, but still fears her father will make us wed. For this reason she looks down upon me also."

A surge of jealousy lodged in Kenya's chest. "You wouldn't marry that woman would you? Your cousin is a terrible person."

Marcos heard the resentment in Kenya's tone. "Why, Lady Kenya, when have you grown so protective of me?"

Kenya realized how her words must sound and blushed. "I—I mean you should have someone better, who loves you, or at least *likes* you. You said you've hated each other since childhood, right?"

"Well, this is not up to me, nor to Jessica, but up to King Harold and whatever he decides. Who knows, he may seek for a political alliance with the few nobles he can find and who are acceptable to Jessica. Perhaps I will be lucky after all and find a woman whom I love and who loves me back. I must see who I can whisper to in the court."

Marcos plays games too. Feints, within feints, within feints. A dangerous dream world indeed.

Kenya ran this information through her mind and decided she had much to learn about the inner workings of this kingdom, took a deep breath of resignation, and wrinkled her nose in disgust. *Phew! I can sure smell myself.*

First things first. She needed a bath. Definitely, a good scrubbing was in order, and time to think, sleep. Yes, sleep—gloriously sleep. Kenya released a huge yawn. Today was a horrible day and showed no signs of getting better in the next few weeks. The dream was turning into a nightmare with no end in sight. "Your cousin is right. I'm filthy dirty, and my clothes," she grimaced gazing down at herself, "if I wasn't wearing them, I'd burn what I have on. Do you think…?"

Marcos noted the weariness in Kenya's voice. "Of course, Lady," he agreed taking her by the shoulder. "Back to your room and make yourself comfortable for now. Relax, and rest assured, I will arrange everything and have it brought to you immediately."

Before Kenya knew what was happening, she was back where she started in the morning. Four husky men carried in a large wooden trough, and hot water hauled by the bucketful to fill the tub. The men left and Kenya gratefully disrobed, slipping beneath the warm water with a sigh of relief as the liquid eased her aching muscles. The old hag appeared, this time with a crooked smirk on her face addressing Kenya as "Wordsmith" and snatching away her dirty clothes, returning to replace ripped t-shirt and crusty jeans with a plain gray dress. The harsh yellow soap provided by the men before they left would have been better used on the floor for scrubbing, but Kenya didn't care. Even though the soap stung the scratches on her skin, the lather washed away the dirt and left her smelling good and feeling clean. She rested in the water up to her neck, felt the cares and the grime from her body washing away.

I will survive. This cannot go on forever and even the most horrible nightmares arrive at a conclusion. Somehow, I will survive.

Chapter Three

The next few weeks in castle Evertree were both monotonous and busy. Kenya's duties were light, but her status as "Wordsmith" was still uncertain to the king and the court surrounding him, also to herself. She was called to "give words" at the end of each evening meal before the king retired for the night. The voice possessing her did not return, and Kenya found herself spouting speeches, phrases, or poems by memory she learned in school, from reading, or made up on the spot as circumstances dictated. She hung around the main gate of the castle waiting for merchants or travelers to arrive, pumping them for news, and rephrasing the gossip for the amusement of the nobles. After one late night session with the king where she recited Poe's 'Raven' by memory, Kenya found herself laughing. *I'm Sherehezade. I hope these people never realize I haven't the slightest idea what I'm doing. Hope I can keep it up, though. Otherwise, I'll be back serving hash and beers.*

Even though she had her days to herself while the king was busy with affairs of state, and wandered the castle at will investigating every corner until she knew the structure by heart, the king still required her to leave her whereabouts with one of the guards at the main hall in case he wished to summons her.

In the beginning, however, Kenya was afraid to leave the castle, but as the days melted together, she took long walks on the beach, watching the fishermen haul in their catches, drying the fish on long strings erected on the shore where the wind was the strongest to keep the flies away. Sometimes she investigated the stores in the small town and became acquainted with the shopkeepers.

She grew familiar to the servants, mostly by having to ask directions every time she made a wrong turn in the maze of twisting corridors in the pile of rock she found herself living in. Nevertheless, they appeared guarded, afraid the castle gossip, which was their primary entertainment, would get back to the king, and they in trouble. Kenya listened carefully, though, and by things not said, or subjects avoided, began to compile an outline of the true castle hierocracy and problems facing the kingdom.

The women of the court and upper class residing in the castle avoided her totally, and Kenya began to suspect the obvious snubbing was on direct orders of Princess Jessica until her status in the king's court was firmly established. Kenya took every opportunity conceivable to veer away each time the princess walked her way. During the first days of residence the princess would put her nose in the air, sniffing as if a dead animal was resting in the corridor when Kenya wandered by. The first time this happened Kenya's face burnt and she hung her head down, mortified, scurrying away as fast as possible. But after a while she tended to disregard the slights, kept her head raised and ignored Jessica. Kenya knew the princess did this for no other reason than to be mean, especially when her friends, or ladies-in-waiting accompanied Jessica, and she heard the tittering as the gaggle disappeared down the hallway with excited whispers and glances over their backs.

Of Marcos, Kenya saw little, except at the evening meals. When she did see him, however, he rushed to her, the sides of his mouth lifting up in joy, eyes twinkling. On those times the slights of the day melted into nothingness, and she poured out all the frustrations to him. He always nodded, attempting to quell her aggravations as best he could. He confided she was the bright spot in his day also. "We ride, leagues at a time, patrolling the kingdom, sometimes in groups, sometimes alone. You are my sole pleasure."

On one occasion after a particularly nasty run in with the princess she asked him, "Your cousin Jessica, if I ever catch her alone in a dark alley....You said she was to marry your brother. Is she..." Kenya groped for the right phrase, "a wielder of great magic, too? Jessica acts as if she doesn't have a brain in her little empty head. Do you know what she did? Bumped into me on purpose, started coughing, and told one of her cronies a dog must have gotten loose and," Kenya ground her teeth in frustration, *"IN THE HALLWAY."*

Marcos's eyes widened in surprise and he broke out into deep guffaws, slapping his thigh in delight. "That sounds like something Jessica would say or do. Nevertheless, what you guess is true, she possesses great magic, and wields the power when need arises, although to watch you would never know Jessica is more than a plain woman. My brother and my cousin were trained together, so was I until I proved a poor student, and then my instruction lagged." Marcos dropped his hands onto the table and clutched the edge until his knuckles shown white. "William," he breathed deep, remembering, "Always the wanderer, seeking new places, new vistas to see. Much like my father, I think. He was a match for Jessica, not in temperament, but more than able to put her in her place when she grew out of line." Marcos's eyes took on a faraway look and he appeared sad. He stretched his arms over his head. "I am tired and sleep now, Lady Kenya. The morrow comes early and I must be off on the king's errands."

These meetings with Marcos were days apart, but Kenya waited for each one, counting the minutes until he arrived. King Harold kept him busy riding the kingdom on patrol, checking outposts, surveying the savannah, which was the breadbasket of the realm, and collecting intelligence. By bits of information overheard while waiting on Harold, and whispers of the servants when they thought no one listened, she pieced together a countryside under siege by dark evil forces. Kenya heard tales of strange creatures half seen in the night, of outlying villages sacked and burnt to the ground, and travelers vanishing without a trace and only their luggage surviving to show they ever existed.

One evening she managed to corner Marcos before he went to sleep and quizzed him about the dangers overheard constantly, whispered at every conversation with increasing fear. He pounded in long after the evening meal finished accompanied by a group of dusty riders and sat by himself, wolfing stewed meat and washing his meal down with swells of wine. His shoulders slumped, eyes half closed from fatigue, cloak covered in dirt from long, hard riding.

"What keeps you out late every day?" Kenya spotted him as she was about to leave the main hall. She hurried over and sat next to him watching the gloom of weariness covering his face. "I hear rumors of evil...are they true?"

Marcos swallowed and his lips flickered up at the corners weakly. "I will tell you the truth, my lady. If you hear tales of strange powers let loose on the land, and stranger events beyond the kingdoms borders, then yes. We ride..." he took a deep breath and straightened up, wincing from an unseen pain in his back, "and seek for the culprits, but we are always too late. Today we happened upon a hamlet incinerated until the sole trace was the ashes of the building blowing in the breeze. The inhabitants gone without a sign they ever were. Seek as we might, however, we located no sign of bodies or tracks no matter how far we circled around the scene of destruction. Our legends tell us this was commonplace in the days of old when evil fought with good for supremacy of this world. I am afraid, myth stalks this earth again."

Kenya sensed the desperation in his voice and grew aware the few people still in the hall close to where they sat stopped talking to listen. "What did these tales say? Didn't they hand you any hint of how to combat whatever monsters you're hunting," Kenya said. "You must have folktales of the events. A hero who saved the day. A kingdom standing triumph and how the people vanquished the enemy?"

Marcos took a deep breath and rubbed his temples. "A few stories have passed down to us from history." His voice trailed off and he gestured with his fingers toward the sword on his hip. "You think the magic I and my fellows control is great? In the beginnings of time, the ancient lords commanded such magic as we can only dream of today. In their greatness, they created both good and evil creatures for whim or amusement. A war broke out between those who would do good with their magic, and those who wished to do evil and bring harm to the land. These two forces clashed in epic battles across the whole of this world in a seemingly never ending struggle for domination. Eventually the wickedness was defeated and thrown down. Destroyed or banished to other worlds not on this plane of existence."

Other planes of existence? Different dimensions? Is this what happened to me? Maybe? "I'm not sure what...."

Marcos saw the confusion in Kenya's face, and mistook the expression for bewilderment of the present situation. He held his hand up. "Do not worry. No one understands what happened to the elder people or where they are now. Our legends say some of the evil lords left voluntarily, through doors they'd opened during their experimentation, taking the misshapen creatures they'd created with them in a grand accord with the victors. The ones who followed good faded also without a trace over time. Some feared their descendants might turn back to evil and so start the wars again. Others growing weary of this

Earth and wishing to seek new adventures. Our legends tell not where they went only that it was not of this world."

"But doesn't someone—King Harold, know...." Kenya groped for the words, "where the evil went, what was left behind? Surely as king he must have studied...."

Marcos gave his head a tired shake and gulped thirstily from his goblet of wine, as if his tale left his throat parched. "We are his eyes and ears. What we know, he knows. For years, the evil has slept and we thought died for good with the masters who created the beasts. Now something, or someone, has awakened and summoned the wickedness back. Perhaps recreated the monsters from old writing forgotten, but still surviving from the past. Perhaps unknowingly this happened, but the malice once dissipated roams again on the land. We are sure of this one point." Marcos placed his hands behind his head and settled back, stretching his weary muscles and twisting his shoulders to relieve the tension lodged in his neck. "The person, or people, who have opened this world again to the foulness of the past, are unknown to us. I myself hope this is some natural force and we do not fight against active evil, for an innate product of the environment will fade away in time. If this is the work of some entity...."

Kenya drummed her fingernails on the table thinking about the implications of monsters from a dim past of history of this land roaming unchecked, destroying homes and killing people. In her mind, a dark lord raised his hands and demons appeared out of a black mist. She asked, "What is the king planning to do about the situation? Do you have any idea?"

"What can he do until more is known of what plagues us?" Marcos pushed himself away from the table with a groan. "He has asked for a conclave of the other Kings of the East to discuss these matters and exchange information. We here at Evertree are far removed from the rest of the kingdoms of this land, and perhaps others know more of what transpires than we do. In three days hence we troop to the castle at Cliffward to meet." He clasped Kenya on the shoulder in a light grip. "Mayhaps he shall bring you along to make a speech for him. My uncle is a brave and fearless warrior, bold when the war trumpets blow and men ride to battle, but he is not known for his eloquence when addressing his peers."

"Me?" squeaked Kenya, looking startled. The thought never occurred she would someday be thrown into danger. Although she'd heard rumors of a conclave, Kenya always assumed what she did now, compose songs in the safety of the keep, was what she would continue to do. "Didn't you say something about a hamlet being burned and the inhabitants disappearing? Is it wise to take people who can't defend themselves on an extended trip across the plains? What if the party is attacked? I mean, in a pinch I can fight I guess, but if what you're telling me of the danger is true, I will be more of a hindrance than a help." She pictured herself fighting a ghoulish monster jabbing the creature in the face with no more than a quill pen and a rolled up piece of parchment.

"Not to worry, m'lady," Marcos assured her, ignoring the fear in her tone. "We take a large force of warriors with us, too large for even a beast of legend to dare attack. Many of the other women from the castle will be traveling, too, in our party—even the Lady Jessica wished to venture on the journey. There will be feasting aplenty and games, meeting of old friends and making new ones at castle Cliffward. You will enjoy yourself I assure you." Marcos grinned sheepishly and scratched the back of his neck. "Perhaps I have overblown the hazards of the savannah with my own concerns to impress a pretty woman with my courage. The plains are not as dangerous as I have made the region out to be."

He thinks I'm pretty? Nah, he's saying that to be polite and soothe my fears.

Long after Marcos left to sleep, Kenya sat at the table and thought about what he said. Monsters? Legends? Had her mind fallen into the Land of Oz with lions and tigers and bears, Oh, My? If the women of the castle were going, the trip must be safe. Harold wouldn't put his own daughter in danger. Nothing to worry about as Marcos said. Still....

So Kenya wasn't surprised when the following evening King Harold told her at the end of the evening meal, "Wordsmith, you will hold yourself in readiness for our journey to Cliffward. Ah, compose a welcoming speech and, uh, perhaps remind the lords it was I who called the conclave for the protection of the land." The king paused, "Oh, yes, maybe an epic poem or song about our journey across the great plains and the dangers we faced." He saw Kenya blanch and added in a loud whisper, "Do not worry. No danger, but the tune will play well with my fellow monarchs, I think." He winked at her.

Three days turned into over a week with every petty noble in the kingdom riding in from the outlying areas requesting to venture along on the trip. During the wait, while the lords sorted out seniority among themselves, wagons and carriages exited the castle into the town for decorating and painting, stores packed away in watertight containers for the journey, and festive clothes seldom used aired and cleaned for the approaching occasion. Growing excitement filled each evening in the main hall as the residents of the castle gathered to eat and discuss the upcoming trip. Kenya found herself caught up in the enthusiasm in spite of the scowls Jessica and her ladies-in-waiting threw at her; laughing, joking, and speculating what adventures Cliffward would hold in store for the inhabitants of Evertree and herself.

On the day of the expedition, carriages drew up before the main gate of the castle and the nobles and wives piled in as King Harold's chief steward called their names.

Kenya waited in the rear of the throng to see which one of the coaches would be hers, and then decided perhaps her name was called and hadn't hear the man among all the babble of the waiting people. Kenya sauntered to the front where the king's multitude of advisors and women of the court waited patiently for one of the gaily-painted wagons to draw up before them. Jessica entered her own private coach with a few chosen friends, and Kenya breathed a sigh of relief. Marcos sauntered over and touched her on the shoulder.

"You will ride in the supply wagons with the other servants, Lady Kenya," he said. "They assemble at the rear of the procession."

"What?" Kenya glared at him in indignation. "Whose idea was this, Jessica's? I bet she's the one to suggest it, right?"

Marcos's face remained blank. "The king's orders," he replied without further comment.

"Well, back of the bus for the wordsmith? It figures." Kenya was not too disappointed, though. Traveling with the advisors or ladies of the court, who still refused to speak with her, was almost as bad as riding with the princess. She never made any friends with the women, nor did they make any overtures. During the weeks in the fortress, Kenya discovered she possessed more in common with the staff of the castle, than the frivolous Ladies—especially Jessica, who was forever worrying about her clothes, hair, and nails. In fact, when she wasn't busy exploring the keep, or attending to the king, Kenya spent much of time in the kitchen, watching the cooks and swapping recipes. Kenya grew enthralled with the working of the stillroom where everything from herb drying, bleach production, to vinegar making occurred.

Kenya picked up the small amount of gear she was bringing packed in tight bundles for carrying, trudged to the last wagon in line, an old unpainted cart someone forgot to add grease to the axles, and climbed in as the wheels protested with squeaks and groans. She made herself comfortable on one of the wooden bench seats and tucked her gear under her feet for safety so the clothes wouldn't be jostled out of the cart by the bouncing.

Before the caravan started, Marcos rode up to Kenya's wagon and peered inside. "Here, take this and secure the strap around your waist." He tossed a sword belt, and scabbard, with short sword inserted, to her.

Kenya picked up the belt and looked from the sheath to Marcos in apprehension. "What's this for?"

"My uncle has put me in charge of you, remember?" the young man hesitated, finally replying, "I would feel better if you were armed and able to protect yourself if we have need. I found you. I do not want to lose you."

Some of Kenya's foreboding returned about the trip they took and the danger. "Do you think I'll need a weapon? You said you exaggerated about the danger. So did Harold."

Marcos shrugged and attempted to make light of the sword. "I hope not, but nevertheless, I would be amiss in my duty if I did not do my best to keep you safe." He murmured gently, "Wear the sword for me, Lady Kenya, so I will not worry." He added in an even lower voice. "You are precious to me."

Kenya's attention focused on his eyes and saw the pleading there, heard his words. Her face blushed deep. "You are such a liar," she chided, pleased by his words. "Oh, well, if you insist." She wrapped the belt around her waist and buckled it securely, while Marcos watched. She wrinkled her nose at the warrior. "There. Happy?"

"Quite." One of the soldiers galloped up calling out Marcos's name with an impatient wave of his arm. Marcos lifted his hand in acknowledgment. "I am called and must leave you now, but I shall return from time to time to see how you fare." He surveyed the wagon Kenya's rode in and added with a faint chuckle in his voice, "I hope you have a comfortable trip."

During the first day, Kenya kept a constant vigil, attempting to search in five directions at once for danger at the first sign of a strange sound issuing from the dark forest they rode through. She saw lurking monsters in every shadow and felt sure the caravan was about to be attacked at any moment by demons from some long distance past of this world.

From her place in the rear of the line, Kenya watched Marcos riding in an out reporting to Harold during the course of the day. True to his words, before he rode off again he'd swing by checking on Kenya. "All is well, Lady. The savannah is quiet, the forest empty, as I told you. How do you fare here?"

"Okay, I guess," Kenya admitted glumly. Her mood wasn't made any better by the rest of the passengers in the wagon who remained quiet and cast their vision straight ahead in mute silence. By the time nightfall covered the land in darkness, Kenya had drained herself and ate a scant meal, falling into a dreamless slumber from nervous exhaustion sitting upright in the cart. Even when Marcos found the opportunity to swing past her wagon and attempted to wake her gently, urging Kenya to lay down under the cart by the campfire, he was unable to. Finally, he lifted her bodily, and carry Kenya to the fire, laid her down and wrapped her in a blanket.

The second day's journey was better, although Kenya noticed the older wagons in the rear of the procession lagged, breaking down with broken wheels and axles. This happened to the wagon she rode in, and the repair took almost an hour before the mechanics banged off the old hub and hammer on a replacement. This caused part of the party to arrive later at the prearranged camping sites each day and in parts, the convoy of wagons and carriages stretched out for miles during the march.

No other problems besieged the caravan, however, and seeing, nor hearing any signs of danger approaching, Kenya settled down and enjoyed the landscape they traveled through with scattered woods and the occasional farmhouse, surrounded by acres of grain crops, and pastures for herd beasts, fruit orchards laid out in straight rows, and trees heavy with nuts. Along the road during the early morning hours, the long procession trekked between a field of tall yellow flowers with huge buttons of seeds in the middle, which took Kenya's breath away with their beauty as the plants swayed in the light breeze. Marcos rode up with a courteous nod and a flash of a grin.

"This is the true strength of Evertree," he boasted, sweeping his arm in a wide circle, which encompassed flowers, earth, and sky. "We are a great seafaring people, none the better. Our ships travel the known world trading at every port of entry. Goods from far off lands pass through the harbor of Evertree, but," he paused and gazed at the brightly colored blooms and inhaled the smoke-free air, "This is the backbone of our kingdom. Our lifeblood, the muscles driving our bones. Without the farmland we would starve and die as surely as if our jaws were bound in wire."

"This is beautiful country," Kenya admitted, pointing at the flowers. "I like those. What are they used for?"

"Some for feed of fowl, or people," Marcos explained as he rode beside the wagon, "but more so crushed for their oil, part of which is prized and sold in the Northern regions where these flowers do not grow," he added in a dry voice, "and, of course, to grace the dining tables of the farmers and nobles."

When she wasn't watching the farms, fields and herds, Kenya passed the time talking to the maids and cooks riding in the wagon, swapping stories of culinary disasters, teaching the women songs, while learning theirs, or listening to the gossip so hard to come by while in the castle, but which flowed easily because of boredom.

On the third day, they arrived at a large swift flowing stream, actually a small river, which ran clear and sweet as the water twisted across their path. In the distance rose the ruin of an old city. Most of the buildings crumbling into ruins, the lofty spires once gracing the tops gone. As the party formed a large circle settling down and making camp for the night, Marcos sauntered over to Kenya as she gratefully climbed out of the cart and stretched arms and legs. "We will be here for two days regrouping and making any necessary repairs to the carriages before we attempt a dash across the Great Plains. If we find danger anywhere we will meet evil there."

"Those ruins I saw in the distance," Kenya asked, "Were they a city at one time? They look huge. Bigger than Evertree and the village combined. What happened?"

Marcos looked up and studied the devastated buildings in the distance. "Balaroon," he replied in a low voice casting another quick glance in the direction she pointed. "At one time the people of the city were a mighty race and ruled these plains in peace with justice. Then in the Great War I told you about the city was utterly destroyed by some force released by the evil ones. All we know was a blinking flash occurred, a cloud rising to the heavens, and heat burning everything in its path. Even now, after all these years the ruins are still death to anyone who ventures within the dark streets and stay too long within its boundaries."

"Oh." *Wonder what the place looks like up close. Must be a mess, but I'm curious if anything survived. Sitting here with nothing to do or see for two days will be boring.* "Do you think we could ride over there tomorrow and take a look? Not long, just a quick peek. If the destruction was so long ago, I can't imagine there's much danger left, do you? I really want a keepsake of this trip." Kenya gave him her saddest little girl face and watched Marcos without much hope.

"Well...." Marcos looked at her drooping mouth, hopeful eyes, and back at the ruins dubiously. "Maybe for an hour," he said at last grudgingly. "I will have to leave word with King Harold, and permission to leave the camp and visit is really up to him. We cannot linger long, though. Remember, all the rumors say entrance means our death if we do."

Kenya threw her arms around his shoulders in a bear hug and pressed her head into his chest. "Thank you," she breathed.

Chapter Four

The following day after a hurried breakfast, Kenya and Marcos set out with instructions from King Harold to remain no longer than an hour. As they rode through the knee-high grass, small buildings first appeared, most burnt to the ground with only foundation stones showing where they once stood. Later, tall wrecks of structures arose missing the top of their roofs, in places the rock itself melted from a great heat. Vacant windows stared like unseeing eyes with dark interiors. Empty doorways leered like mouths with missing teeth. Vegetation refused to grow on the earth, even the tough prairie grass was absent. Evil looking birds fluttered from the black holes in the walls at their passing, mournful cries reverberating off blasted masonry. They reached the city fortifications, tumbled stone blocks spreading in every direction, guarding the deserted remains of Balaroon and the dead inhabitants. They reined in their horses at the beginning of a wide avenue, the central boulevard of the city clogged with debris from above, cracked and heaving pavement under their feet.

"Are you satisfied, Lady Kenya?" Marcos's eyes swept the destroyed buildings and streets. "The city is dead and has remained so for a millennium. Not even the bodies of the inhabitants remain to be seen."

"I guess so," Kenya replied, disappointed. She'd expected to see more than melted rock and rubble. She swung in the saddle. "Let's leave this way," she pointed a finger ahead and to the right where one of the tall edifices partially protected smaller buildings from much of the blast that destroyed the rest of the city. "Maybe something recognizable survived and we can collect a souvenir before we return to camp. I don't want to go back empty-handed."

Marcos nodded without saying anything and they rode to a small building huddled in the shadows. Kenya surveyed the outside and surrounding area. "Wait here. I'll be right back." She dismounted, stepped gingerly between rubble, and peered inside the blown out door.

Nothing. The interior was a single chamber, bare except for bird and rodent dropping and a thick layer of powdery dirt. Disappointed she swung around to leave, and a gleam of metal caught her eye in one corner of the room. Kenya stopped and cautiously strolled over. Beneath her boots, the brittle snapping of dry sticks made it hard to keep her balance. Her tread raised puffs of the dry dirt covering her legs with grit. Kenya kicked the dust away from a long bar of metal and leaped back in fright.

"Marcos!"

The warrior vaulted off his horse and stumbled inside drawing his sword, prepared for battle. He paused at the entrance searching the room for trouble. "What is it, Kenya? I see nothing here of danger or worth keeping."

Kenya shook a wavering finger at the corner. "A body, Skeleton, rather. Over there." She looked down at her legs where her feet rested unsteadily on the sticks. More bones poked upward. "Lots of skeletons," she whispered, eyes wide and staring at the floor.

Marcos strode forward and poked in the dust with the tip of his blade revealing a grinning skull. "Must have been dead a long time," he commented, "but not as long as the rest of the city." He flicked at the shining piece of metal that drew Kenya's attention in the first place and uncovered the rest. "His sword." Marcos sheathed his weapon, bent to pick the blade up by the hilt and studied the runes etched in the grip closely. "This belonged to my brother," he whispered as he cradled the sword reverently in his hands. Marcos switched his attention back to the skull. "William."

He toed the rest of the bones pushing up from the dust and studied them carefully. "These are not human bones, too small." He swallowed, throat dry. "This was not my brother's resting place. This was his final battleground. This room is where he fought his last war against whatever evil attacked him." His fingers tightened around the hilt of the sword until his knuckles shone white.

The silence inside the chamber grew unbearable. Kenya said in a whisper, "We should bury him."

Marcos bent to sort through the larger, scattered bones of his brother mixed in with the smaller ones. From outside a high-pitched squealing echoed down the empty street. He snatched the grinning skull, stuffed it into an inside pocket of his cloak, and raced back to the door, Kenya one step behind him.

Grey shapes flitted from broken doorways to the next, keeping to the gloom, each figure the size of a mastiff. The leader cautiously emerged into the light, stopped and sniffed the air, whiskers twitching, and Kenya got a good look at the creature.

Giant rats.

The head was high-domed, however, and the scarlet eyes spoke of malevolent intelligence lucking within the brain. The creature rose on crooked hind legs, testing the air, paws resembling small hands dangling before the gaunt body. The beady eyes swung in the direction of the building Marcos and Kenya hid and locked onto their horses.

"We must run. These are the shadow people. Our legends describe the creatures of old, but I thought the tales were night stories to scare bad children into behaving themselves." Marcos grabbed Kenya's hand.

"The rest of your brother…"

"No time."

Marcos dragged Kenya back outside to the horses and tossed her bodily into the saddle. The pack leader of the rats released a high-pitched screech when he saw the two emerge for the doorway. Marcos slapped Kenya's horse on the rump screaming, *"Run!"* and sprang onto his mount.

From the ruined doorways, more rats piled out with inquiring squeals, noses twitching in the air to catch the scents of their prey. The street became a heaving mass of grey fur, pink tails, and high-pitched cries.

Kenya's mount raced ahead while Marcos lagged behind, lashing gouts of fire at the grey demons with his brother's sword when they drew too close. His face was set, a grim smile spread across his lips as he bought time to escape.

Kenya looked over her shoulder as one of the giants rats flashed into flame and collapsed, biting itself in pain, and in the process setting others of the pack afire as they leaped over the fallen rodent. In her sight Marcos seemed to swell with power, as if he drew fire from the sun to lay about him. *Oh, god. I never realized the magic Marcos commands!*

The next instant his flame faltered and died.

Kenya slowed. Marcos drew abreast of her. "Keep riding," he gasped. "Straight out to the plain and back to the camp. Hurry, before they catch up to us."

The two sped past the last of the buildings and into the tall grass of the savannah. At the blackened edge of destruction, the giant rodents slid to a halt, snarling and gnashing their sharp pointed teeth in anger as they cast back and forth in fury attempting to continue their pursuit but held in check by an unseen force.

"Some invisible barrier keeps them at bay," Marcos muttered as they slowed their mounts to a fast trot. "Perhaps the same dark magic creating the vermin now holds the monsters captive in this town." A tremble ran through his body. "If my brother only knew they were unable to hunt past a certain point. Instead of making his last stand in that chamber, he could have run to safety and lived."

"I saw you use your brother's sword. I never realized what you meant by making the blade flame. How can you say you are not a great warrior?"

Marcos held the sword out and twisted the blade in his fingers, examining both sides. "If you saw this blaze, you also so me falter when I used it. My brother never doubted his ability when he held this blade."

Kenya was quiet for a long time while they rode across the plain back to the camp. She finally said, "What are you going to do with the sword? Bury it with your brother's remains?"

Marcos studied the weapon, making short jabs and thrusts in the air as they rode. "At first I thought to entomb the sword with his skull as you suggest. Now I think to keep this weapon to remember him by, his strength, and his skill. I felt the power in the weapon although I could not use the magic the blade held; perhaps my brother's spirit still resides within."

They passed the sentries at the perimeter of the camp and rode directly to King Harold to report what they'd seen.

The king listened carefully hearing the truth in their voices. More people crowded around with low murmurs of speculation and a gasp when Marcos lifted the sword of his brother and the skull for all to see. "This I found within the city," he said, "along with the skeleton of William. Many more bones strewn the ground all around him. It must have been an awesome battle before he was pulled down and killed."

Harold placed his hand on Marcos's shoulder. "Your brother was dear to me, almost like a son after your father died. We shall all miss him." The king sighed. "Do you think, perhaps, this city is the source of the demons plaguing our land? The shadow people were thought to have long past this Earth and only exist in legend. Did you see any other monsters of myth?" His eyes switched from Marcos to Kenya.

A lump formed in Kenya throat as she listened to Marcos and Harold speaking about William. Her thoughts wandered to what his last struggle was against the rats, their abrupt halt at the edge of the city, and the dry bones scattered on the floor of the building. She replied hesitantly, "The rats appeared to be trapped within the city limits. I don't know, but wouldn't any other demon from the city be held by the same force?"

Marcos answered with certainty. "We would have seen others of these creatures long before this time stalking the land. As Lady Kenya said, these demons could not exit the place. Whether the magic unleashed years ago in the destruction of Balaroon created them, or they have since changed from what were in the intervening years, they are one of a kind and we saw no others in the city. Perhaps some worker of good laid a geas on them or the city before he withdrew so the evil created would not plague future generations."

"You have left me much to think about," Harold mused. "Go now, you must be tired, and we have a long journey ahead of us."

After their report, King Harold called all the people together and forbid any more excursions away from the camp unless a strong-armed guard was present. Kenya heard some grumbling, but the majority of the people shrugged it off without complaint. Except for the ruins of the city, the empty plains stretched all around without a break in the landscape.

After the two-day rest, the party pushed on again with renewed vigor. The fear Kenya forgot about on the first leg of their journey returned after the attack of the shadow people and Kenya kept a constant vigil, sure from what she'd already seen it was but a matter of minutes or hours before monsters rose out of the waving grass to attack their caravan. The golden savannah showed no end, stretching in every direction with only tall grass and the occasional bird flying overhead, or a stream flowing across the flat earth, to break the vista. When nothing appeared to challenge the party, Kenya relaxed again.

It was not until a week out, while the troop crossed a rocky tree-covered plain with cliffs in the distance, mountains beyond and the journey almost completed, disaster struck.

One of the cook's friends, an upstairs cleaning wench, rode in the cart with Kenya and the rest of the servants today. The woman told a long, intimate story about the strange objects found hidden in Jessica's bedroom under her mattress while cleaning the room. In hushed detail, the maid described devices wrapped in stained pieces of parchment, or stashed behind drawers covered in soiled marks. The cooks were busy paring apples and cackled as they listened, occasionally making comments about the odd ways of ladies. Kenya's mouth dropped and her eyes opened wide as the story continued, and she could hardly contain herself when the woman said, "And the sheets reeked. Old perfume and older sin, I say. What the girl does…"

Kenya giggled and whispered, "Do you mean…?"

The woman nodded sagely and put a finger to the side of her nose. "Both men and women."

So our princess is a little nympho, huh. I should have known. Kenya tucked this piece of information away for further use. She covered her mouth and looked down to stop from giggling thinking up retorts she could make to Jessica's continual comments.

A wild screech above the wagons snapped the occupant's heads up in alarm. Hissing a sick, putrid green vapor, a brown, winged fury descended from the sky in a long glide and landed on the wagon in front of Kenya. The raptor-like talons dug deep into the wooden frame, tilting the cart upward before the boards splintered in its tight grip. With quick stabs of the sharp beak, the monster snatched the passengers out of their seats and swallowed them whole. The mounts drawing the wagon screamed in terror, rearing and broke their harnesses, bolting in panic to escape the screeching horror behind.

The horses pulling Kenya's wagon tried dashing to one side to avoid a collision. The teamster driving attempting to hold the panicked animals back and turn the team around, but the beasts refused to obey his commands. Instead, they halted in confusion, kicking and leaping in the shafts. Finally, with terrified cries, the frightened beasts bucked off their restrains, overturning the wagon in the process and dashing away.

Kenya felt herself going over with the cart and before the wagon crush her under its weight, leaped as far as possible out of the way to land in a heap with a sharp yelp of pain.

Mass chaos reigned in the back of the caravan with screaming horses, cursing men, and shrieking women all attempting to escape the screaming fury.

Dazed, Kenya staggered to her feet. All around a kaleidoscope of confusion beat on her senses. Before her, a woman twisted on the ground. One of the maids who rode in the wagon with Kenya. Trapped, the side of the cart crushed the girl. A splinter from the wagon hung down and jammed into her chest, pinning the woman to the earth.

A broken part of the shaft lay at Kenya's feet. She snatched the pole up and tried to help the maid, jamming the wood under the side of the wagon and heaving, attempting to lift enough for the woman to drag her pinned legs out if she could.

What am I going to do about the wood in her chest? I don't...I can't. The cart barely lifted an inch as Kenya put her full weight on the shaft. The woman's shrieks of pain ripped through the air in high-pitched wails as Kenya's shoulder muscles quivered and the strength in her arms gave out. The bed of the wagon slammed down again. A moment later, the maid was silent, a dark scarlet stain spreading across the front of her tunic.

Behind Kenya, the beat of horse's hooves storming up and the frantic shouts of the warriors drown out the rest of the cries of the dying as soldiers ordered the women to take shelter wherever they could find it.

Kenya stood helplessly and watched in dismay as the rest of the party sped away at a dead run, seeking safety by placing as much distance as they could between the carriages and the monster. The warriors formed a shield of steel between the balance of the retreating wagons and the beast, willing to sacrifice themselves for the ladies and Princess Jessica.

King Harold led this group, face red in anger, his sword out and blazing. Marcos rode close to him, blade out also, dripping fire. *"Sire!"* he shouted waving his weapon in the direction of the fleeing wagon, "you must follow the women and advisors in case more of these creatures lurk ahead. There are more than enough of us to take care of this menace. Their lives must be protected."

The king glared at him, mouth working as he spat on the ground. Kenya saw his jaw muscles bunch as he glanced over his shoulder at his retreating party.

"Go," Marcos urged again. "I—I will stay here in your place."

Harold gritted his teeth watching the monster tear a wagon apart in fury. His mount pranced two steps closer to the demon, anticipating his master's command to attack. The king switched his vision to the sword Marcos clutched in his hand doubtfully and issued a curse under his breath. "I leave this to you, Nephew. See you do not fail me." With a grunt, he wheeled his horse. "You—You—You," he shouted to captains with their men clumped around them,

"Follow me. The rest of you stay here." Refusing to give a backward glance, the king snapped his reins and galloped after the carriages trailed by his men.

Five of the riders gathered around Marcos. He waved the men forward.

Kenya searched around for any other survivors of the attack possibly needing help. Blood was everywhere, and Kenya felt her stomach about to rebel after stumbling over the body of the cook she'd been talking with only minutes before, the face contorted in horror, skin charred black from the corrosive fumes of the flying beast.

A body hit Kenya in the back of the legs and she toppled over in a heap shouting a cry of alarm. She twisted around, groping for the short sword at her side prepared to defend her life if need be.

"Down—stay *down!*" Crawl under the wagon, NOW!"

The person was Marcos. He waited long enough to make sure she found a place to crawl to safety, and then broke out into a run back to his companions, blade clutched in his hand.

The horsemen ringed the creature and drew their swords. Instead of riding in close and hacking away at the monster's scaly body, fire blazed from the tips of their weapons and shot toward the beast. The flames lashed over the animal, engulfed head, and then wings and body, threatening to consume the flesh in a fiery glow of fire.

As the combined blaze died away to nothingness, however the beast stood unharmed, more enraged than ever. The creature responded with another attack of gas. Marcos jerked on his reins and his mount dodged to one side as the gas enveloping the rest of the riders, igniting into fierce red sparks when the fumes touched the glowing tips of their swords. The flashes raced up the blades until they singed the warrior's hands, running up their arms and down their legs. The sparks ignited on the coats of the horses setting the animals ablaze. Mounts and riders screamed in pain and dropped to the ground, withering in agony as black smoke rose from their bodies.

A red blaze erupted from the weapon Marcos held, but died with a flicker. As the gas wafted toward him, Marcos spun his horse and sped away. He wheeled about, and as the other riders ignited in flames, rode back in close, bent low, and swung his sword at the massive leg of the monster.

The blade connected with a meaty *thud.* The beast howled in pain and rage, and its colossal tail whipped around, sweeping Marcos off his saddle. He flung to the sod and lay stunned like a stuffed doll, the yawning mouth and flickering tongue of the monster hovering over him, preparing for the death bite.

"NO!"

Without thinking, Kenya squirmed from the safety of the wagon and sprang up, racing to Marcos. She stumbled, jerking the short sword from its scabbard. Before she went down Kenya hurled the blade at the monster's face with all her strength. The sword flew end-over-end, and by luck, the tip pierced the black tongue, sticking into the lower palate. The creature reared back in alarm, screaming in shock as it pawed at its injured mouth, and took flight with a clatter of wings.

Marcos wavered back to his feet watching the beast circling above the party with angry squawks. Kenya scrambled to her feet, continuing her headlong rush and crashed into him in her haste to reach his side. He threw out an arm around her waist to steady them both before they toppled over and pointed skyward.

"Another creature of legend from the past, a beast used to scare small children who will not go to sleep at night."

"What is it?"

"A wyvern, long thought slumbering in its haunts deep in the mountains or ceased to exist with the passing of time. Be prepared to run, the beast may decide to return and attack us again."

The wyvern was still circling, screeching like an out of control freight train. The creature banked as if to return, and then hesitated, veering off at the last moment as it made a decision. The demon broke from the circle and darted straight as an arrow after the receding caravan.

Marcos wiped his sword on a clump of grass and slipped the blade back in its sheath. "Well, we are safe for the moment." He gazed sadly at the remains of his companions. Smothering bones and the stench of burning flesh was all surviving the attack.

Kenya looked back at the wagons. Nothing moved. No noise rang out. Everyone died when the wagons flipped over. She and Marcos were the only ones to survive the attack of the wyvern.

"Do you think King Harold will dispatch people for us?" Kenya asked, swallowing hard, throat tightening, surveying the death all around.

Marcos issued a dry laugh, eyes assuming a glazed look as he scanned the destruction also. "If the beast catches up to the caravan, they will be lucky to survive themselves. No," he shook his head, "my uncle left me here to kill the beast, and I have failed him. They head for the cliffs where they will be able to locate some protection in caves or overhangs. Harold may send a man back, but I doubt it. When he sees the wyvern, he will assume the beast has dispatched us and be wroth indeed at me for not doing the deed myself as I promised. I am afraid we are on our own for now until we reach Cliffward. Let us pray we have met the worse of the dangers stalking this land for now and the rest of the way is clear."

A cold rush of apprehension sweep over Kenya sending a chill through her body. They were in the middle of nowhere, alone, with no help in sight. The mountains in the distance were two days away. She sighed and tried to push behind the hazards facing the last leg of their journey. "Are you okay?" she asked, looking at his gore-soaked tunic. "You're covered in blood."

Marcos brushed at the stains on his chest with distaste. "Not mine, Lady Kenya. When you pinned the creature's tongue to its mouth, the demon bled all over me. Think nothing of the gore. I am unharmed." He took a deep breath and smirked at himself. "But the monster's blood stinks. I will be an unfit companion to travel with until I can change my clothing." His attitude change abruptly. He examined the scene of carnage once more, the silent plain around them for approaching danger, and reached out a bloodstained hand to her. "Come. We must bury our dead, seek the horses before they wander off too far, and gather what supplies we can find. The sun will soon set. I do not wish to camp here among the carnage of the battle. If not demons, then wild animals will be drawn by the scent of blood from the dead horses."

Marcos ventured off to corral his horse and locate any others wandering loose from the battle. Kenya picked through the debris from the wagons searching for anything useful to dig graves for the warriors, and might be needed for survival, most already squashed or burnt beyond recognition.

Not much. Not much at all. It will have to do.

Kenya kicked a wicker basket half-crushed by the side of the wagon. A handful of pared apples fell out, the remains of the cook's pie she was preparing before the attack. Kenya scooped them up, brushing off as much dirt as possible and stuffed the fruit in a pocket.

After an hour's search Kenya collected a meager amount of food and water, some blankets, and the remains of her scant belongs. No shovels, but she managed to pry two planks from the wagons to dig in the soft earth. With a groan, she began chopping at the sod to create a burial space for the soldiers and passengers.

Marcos returned leading his mount and one of the draft horses that pulled the wagon. When he saw what Kenya was doing he silently grabbed a plank and fell in next to her, helping enlarge the trench she'd started. They dug shallow graves, buried their fellow travelers, back filling with the dirt they dug, and covered the top with what debris from the wagons they could carry so wild animals would not dig into the burial sites.

Afterwards they packed their provisions on the horses. Marcos salvaged a saddle for Kenya from one of the carcasses of the dead warrior mounts so she could ride in comfort. When all was prepared, they rode a mile toward the cliffs in the distance and made camp. "Not much," Marcos admitted as he broke apart one of the bricks of travel rations from his saddlebag and handed half to Kenya, "but unless an animal runs into our path I am not stopping to hunt for game. We still have a long ways to go."

Kenya chewed and swallowed. She refused to believe they couldn't finish their journey. "We will survive," she said simply and pushed the horrors of the trip away.

Marcos reached across the fire and laid a hand on her wrist, his eyes gazing into hers. "I never thanked you for saving my life. It was a brave thing you did." He took her hand and drew it to his lips, kissing her fingers.

Kenya felt her face go warm, blushing in spite of herself. "Well, I couldn't very well let the wyvern eat you now could I? After all," she said, joking, while trying to hide the fluster, "I need someone to guide me to Cliffward. As you said, it's still a long trip. I'd get lonesome."

Marcos broke out in chuckles and released her hand slowly, seemingly embarrassed by his show of emotion. "I will do my best to bring you there in safety. After all, you are the Lady Kenya, the king's wordsmith and I am the one who brought you here in the first place. I must take care of you at all costs, and again, thank you for my life."

They settled down to sleep. Kenya curled herself into a ball close to the fire. She burrowed one side of her head into a rolled up bundle of clothing using the wad for a pillow, draped an arm over her ear to drown out the night noise. What Kenya couldn't stop, though, were the visions of the dead and dying, the attacking monster breathing its noxious gas, or the odor of burning flesh filling the air. She tried focusing her mind on the life she had before in the real world, and found it was impossible to remember details, faces. The world left behind was a dream, clouded in a misty haze. A sudden constriction of horror flashed in her chest and Kenya wondered if the previous existence was all a dream. She still speculated about the past life while falling asleep.

Chapter Five

The next day they broke camp and located the wagon tracks from the convoy, following at a rapid pace in hopes of catching up with King Harold if possible. At mid-morning they rode across the remains of a carriage wrecked almost beyond recognition. Both Kenya and Marcos rose in their stirrups, scanning the landscape for survivors or signs of the beast, or beasts, which destroyed the wagon. The savannah was devoid of life, even the birds usually chirping in the tall amber grass were absent, the signs of a battle showed in the trampled vegetation and black scorch marks on the coach.

"No bodies, no blood," Marcos commented as he strode the area in a wide circle, searching for an indication of what transpired.

"Thank goodness," Kenya replied. "Even if it were Princess Jessica I wouldn't want anyone to be eaten. Do you think they all escaped alive?"

"Hard to know." Marcos scowled. He spoke wearily. "If it was the wyvern that attacked us, the beast could have plucked the people out of the carriage one by one and carried them off, or smashed the coach much as it did when the demon attacked us the first time and the passengers escaped in the other wagons. No way of telling from what I see here."

Kenya swallowed and looked at Marcos.

"Do not be sad, Lady Kenya. No blood on the ground is a good sign, and there is only one carriage destroyed. Let us go, we still have a half a day's light left."

They kept riding for the balance of the day refusing to stop and make camp for a midday meal. As the sun set, they reached the foot of the cliffs with taller alps rising in the background, and located a site to sleep for the night.

"How much farther?" Kenya asked breaking dried brush into kindling for their fire. She stopped, gazed bleakly at the ground and the far landscape beyond, rubbed dirty hands on her filthy tunic and accepted the dried rations Marcos provided, washing the parched morsels down with a sip of warm water from his water bag. Not only was she grimy and tired, but her body ached all over from neck to legs. She didn't remember horseback riding being this hard on her bottom, and after the day was over she could hardly walk. Kenya dropped down on a rock with a groan, clawing feebly at a green insect buzzing around her face, and tried to swat the nuisance away without much success. Her fingers hurt, too. She turned her attention to the peaks instead, hoping they'd grown closer while eating.

Tomorrow. Let it be tomorrow we reach Cliffward.

Marcos saw her studying the dark shapes of the mountains with longing and said, "It will be another three days of good riding through these hills, and then two more through the forest of Milkwood before we attain our destination."

"Five days?" Kenya groaned. "I thought you said two. Isn't there a shortcut or something? Five days?"

Marcos smiled mirthlessly. "I am afraid this *is* the shortcut. Otherwise, we would need to stay on the savannah and travel to the North approaching King Goron's castle from the front. Much faster, but if the wyvern still hunts, the beast will do so on the plains. This will bring us there, but we still journey through dangerous country. If we run into trouble, I doubt the danger will be as bad."

Fear clutched Kenya's chest. "But no more wyverns?"

Marcos shrugged. "Who knows, Lady Kenya. This whole region battled good and evil long ago. This is why King Harold called for the conclave here. The war is fresh in their minds, no matter how long ago the bloodshed occurred. Whatever demons not destroyed in the conflict fled to the heights in fear of discovery, to hide and perhaps to abide their time in the dark crevices in hopes they did not fade away. The thought is in my mind since we encountered one monster from the past already, wyverns and other warped minions of evil still lurk within pockets of these mountains. The wyvern attacking us flew from this region to the plains because of the stench of death. Evil draws evil to it. Good draws good the same way."

Kenya scanned the steep rocks and dark holes fighting with fear. She saw nothing dangerous she could lay a finger on, but….

This is an evil world. I must prepare myself for the worst before it happens.

During the night the dreams started.

Kenya thought she would fall right to sleep. She was exhausted, but the rest desired refused to sweep over her. She drifted in a state between wakefulness and true slumber, tossing and turning in her blanket. She saw light, heard voices talking all around her, doors kept banging open and shut as she remembered from the bar. Objects barely recognizable stretched behind the portals in a never-ending row of shrouded tables disappearing into a white mist in the distance.

Kenya approached one entrance, half-open. She knew something wonderful lay behind the door, something she desired and needed above all else. She tried tugging on the knob, to walk within, but her legs refused to answer. Kenya stood frozen, left hand at her side, right outstretched locked on the handle. The voices shouted in her ears, issuing instructions, but they were a babble of confused noises she didn't understand.

With a start, Kenya bolted upright, gasping for breath while waking. Cold sweat covered her body, and she knew something important happened, but the dream eluded her and faded even as she roused. Kenya lay on the blanket for a long time staring at the stars, and before she knew what happened, dawn broke in the heavens.

***

"I DON'T KNOW."

They rode between towering hills. Kenya tried to explain the dream she experienced during the night to Marcos. He kept badgering for details, but no matter how hard she tried, Kenya couldn't remember but a few fragments, and those only hazily.

"But this is important, Lady," he insisted as he twisted in the saddle scanning for danger in all directions. "You must try." Satisfied nothing lurked nearby he exclaimed, "If these be good forces attempting to contact you, they can be of great benefit to us—if they are of evil...."

Kenya shook her head, trying to clear her mind. It was no use. Nothing would form, and the thought of evil trying to invade her dreams while sleeping.... "Can't a dream sometimes be a dream?" she shot back. "It was probably nothing. Apprehension and worry from the attack and all this traveling."

Kenya heard the doubt in Marcos's voice as he replied, "True, and if we were in a safe place and evil did not stalk this land, I would think nothing of any dream you have." The wild cry of a hunting cat rang through the air, and they both stopped to scan the landscape. Seeing nothing close, Marcos continued, "Nevertheless, spirits haunt this land and disregarding the danger of evil invading your thoughts is never wise, especially when you are vulnerable in your dreams."

I could be a danger to myself and everyone else around me. A spirit took over my voice once. What if a phantom possessed my body? Kenya wrapped her arms around herself remembering the tall tales her grandmother from New Orleans would tell. She always thought they were spook stories... *Grandmother? I don't...?*

To change the subject Kenya said, "Well, at least we'll have a place to sleep tonight." She gestured to the dark entrances of caves on the cliffs. "Nothing can harm us once we hide in there."

Marcos looked at her through the corner of his eyes. "Nay, Kenya. Caves are all right to take refuge in during the day if it is raining. At night, however, they change into the doorways to the netherworld. Who knows what could creep forth from their dark interiors to attack the unwary if one seeks their shelter."

"Oh, great." Kenya shot a glum look at Marcos and the cave mouth beckoning to her. "As if I didn't have enough to worry about right now, you have to put devils from the underworld on me."

Marcos frowned, not understanding exactly what she meant, and then reached out and touched Kenya's arm. "Do not worry, Lady Kenya. You are safe with me as long as I can raise my sword in your defense, whether they be your devils or my demons."

"I meant to ask you about that," Kenya snapped, still disappointed about the cave and the security robbed from her. "What happened back there when we were attacked? Everyone else's swords flamed. Yours sort of— fizzled out. Happened in the city, also."

This time Marcos's mouth dropped. He stared at his saddle and replied, "I told you. Sometimes the power rises in me, sometimes not. This is why my uncle, King Harold, deems me guardsman, errand boy, and nothing more. He does not trust my ability when the need is great."

Kenya immediately felt guilty about her tone of voice. How she said what she did, and what she thought. "I didn't mean, well, I just meant...."

Marcos' raised his head again. He surveyed the sky and cliffs, breathing deep before he replied. "I know what I am, and the limitations the spirits put upon me, but I was the one who struck a blow against the wyvern, not my comrades." He caressed the hilt of his sword. "Sometimes a gift must be achieved through hard work. William would repeat the phrase as he stood over me."

Late in the afternoon, they chanced upon a small trickle of water sandwiched among the rocks, which bubbled up from the brown sand, created a small clear pool of fresh water, ran a few feet, and disappeared again into the dark earth. After drinking their fill and watering the horses, they agreed the little enclave of rock was a safe place to camp for the night.

Kenya huddled by the pool and reveled in its sparkling magic. Water—glorious water. She never realized how good the liquid tasted, smelled, and felt on her body. She scooped up sand and scrubbed her hands, face, and hair until the exposed parts of her ached red from the rubbing, and then rinsed over and again until every inch of her body was squeaky-clean. Kenya was prepared to stay at this oasis of joy for the rest of her life, relaxing and drinking her fill. She pulled her boots off and soaked her hot feet in the pool, stretching her legs out with a sigh of relief. So it was with great disappointment when Marcos insisted they make their camp well away from the precious liquid supply.

"Why?" The aggravation was plain in her voice. All she saw was the circle of water shrinking into nothingness and disappearing before her eyes. *Is he trying to be intentionally mean? I am so tired I couldn't move if I wanted to.* Kenya pointed to the stream. "You—Me— Water—Stay. What's the matter, are you nuts? Why would we want to go anywhere else for the night?"

Marcos shook his head and jabbed a finger at the muddy tracks in the earth surrounding the puddle. "Other creatures use this place to drink besides us, Kenya. I wish to construct a trap and see what we can catch for supper, but they will not approach if we are so close." He paused to allow his idea to sink in. "Also, remember, we are not the only predators with the thought of catching a meal here. If we camp too near, hunter may become the prey during the night. I wish to stay away from this spring as far as possible, and have a restful sleep without worry of an attack."

"Well…" Her mouth watered at the idea of having fresh meat instead of stale bread, moldy cheese, apples, and dried rations. Her stomach rumbled in agreement, and she made a choice. Slowly Kenya pushed herself erect and rose to her feet with a sigh. "Okay, let me fill the water bottles first."

They walked the horses back a hundred yards from the stream then Marcos returned and constructed a trap using rocks, sticks, and a few of their apples for bait with Kenya watching curiously over his shoulder. When he finished Kenya asked, "Do you think this is going to work?" She scrutinized the deadfall dubiously. The trap didn't appear sturdy enough to catch a mouse let alone an animal big enough to be eatable.

"We will soon learn," Marcos replied. "I have built such in the past and they have provided an evening's meal. We shall see. If we catch anything we will hear the rocks fall and the cry of our supper."

The light failed as dusk descended on the world. They walked to their camp and made themselves as comfortable as they could while they waited.

A chill wind blew down from the mountains. Kenya took out a heavy cape from her pack and wrapped the cloak around her, settling by the fire next to Marcos. It seemed they no more began to relax then the tumbling of rocks and screeches of an animal announced a creature fell to Marcos's trap.

Marcos grabbed two firebrands from their campfire and handed one to Kenya. "Let us go and see what we caught."

They hurried to the stream and ran around an outcropping of boulders. Two grey, scrawny legs protruded from beneath the jumble of rocks—Marcos' trap was a success. They strode forward and bent over, tossing the stones to one side.

Short, stubby hands with claw-like nails grabbed Kenya in a steel grip from behind. She twisted in the hold, managed to turn around and a blast of fetid breath hit her in the face. Kenya gagged, stomach threatening to revolt at the odor. She kept struggling, hoping to break free and escape. More bodies emerged from the darkness and piled on top of her back, driving Kenya to the earth and knocking the breath from her lungs. From somewhere nearby Marcos cursed, brilliant flashes of light sparked, and the thud of his blade hitting flesh reverberated as he flailed about in the dark.

Kenya tried to rise, but weight across her shoulders, back, and legs kept her pinned helplessly in the dirt. Hands jerked her arms backward and cord wrapped around her wrists. The weight disappeared and more hands jerked her roughly to her feet.

Red eyes and white fangs ringed her in the semi-darkness. In the light of the dying torch, Kenya made out dirty, gray, furry bodies, the same height as she, but skinny, bone-like structures stretched over silver hides.

They're rats. They tracked us from Balaroon. Huge, monstrous rats blown up into human size. Kenya drew back from the monsters in terror until the clawed hands behind seized her arms again, and then she leaped forward in fright.

More of the horrible creatures dragged a bloody Marcos into view, one eye already swollen shut. "Shadow People." He spat out the name in disgust. "Forgive me Lady Kenya. I did not realize they trailed us to this spot, or hid here already somewhere in these hills. If I knew...."

Kenya looked around at the milling creatures that ringed the two in heated debate, casting malicious glances toward Kenya and Marcos. A chill ran up her spine as saliva dripped down the wicked looking teeth. "What do they want?" She whispered back.

This brought a mirthless chuckle from Marcos. He glanced at the thin legs still protruding from the pile of rocks. "Either revenge or food, maybe both."

The shadow people did not eat or kill the two of them. Instead, they dragged Kenya and Marcos to the mouth of a cave and scurried down a passage, screaming at both when they stumbled in the darkness with sharp chatters of annoyance and yanking them to their feet again. With another push, Kenya stumbled into a small side pocket. Marcos came flying in next. All this time the creatures continued an excited prattle to each other in a squeaky language Kenya could not understand. One of the grey monsters shoved a firebrand into a bracket causing their silhouettes to dance in red, flickering on the walls. With a final glare the rat people filed out of the cave one by one until only five remained, and those in heated conversation, ignoring Marcos and Kenya. Once they weren't the center of scrutiny, Kenya wiggled toward Marcos pushing with the heels of her boots to scoot along the dirt.

"Do you think they'll let us go?"

Marcos squirmed closer to her. "I do not know. The Shadow People we know by rumor, but I have studied these carefully as they dragged us here. They are not the same as the ones we saw living in the city. I will swear to the fact." His frown deepened. "Perhaps they escaped before whatever magic trapping the rest rose into place. That we are not dead is a good sign, however, what the future may hold, I cannot say."

Kenya flashed the images of the creatures from Balaroon through her mind and compared what she remembered to the ones here. What Marcos said was true. These walked on the hind legs like men, only dropping to all fours when the occasion demanded they do so—and the eyes. The same evil intelligence lurked deep within but with greater awareness of self, as if they were humans in rat costumes.

Not too smart, thought. Her vision alighted on the belt strapped around Marcos's waist, and the hilt protruding from the scabbard. "They allowed you to keep your sword," Kenya gasped in disbelief.

Marcos stared down at his scabbard in surprise. "I did not even know my blade was there," he admitted. "I am so used to the weight on my hip." Marcos was silent for a time, eyes squinting in concentration. "I remember a tug on my waist after the fight. I thought they took my short sword." He surveyed the other side of his belt. A hilt protruded there also. "Why…Are they so stupid?"

Kenya was convinced there must be another reason for returning Marcos's weapons to him. "Did you see them with any weapons?" she said. "I don't remember seeing swords, knives or spears as they brought us in."

"You are right. Could it be they do not know what a weapon is? But I struck them. My sword flamed."

"Do rats know what a weapon is," Kenya countered. "Maybe they thought your sword was a part of you."

Marcos continued to stare at the blades on his hips. "Could it be they have no fear of weapons and report to a higher source who wants us intact?" He twisted his head to glance at the guards. "It matters not," he said woefully. "My weapons help me not. I am bound, and it is only a matter of time before our fate is sealed."

"Great." *How do we escape?* Kenya swallowed hard. In every book she'd ever read, every movie seen, the good guys always discovered a way, whether by some mistake of their captors or by their own wiles. *Maybe I'll wake up. This land can't be real.*

Kenya closed her eyes and waited to bolt upright in her bed, screaming. Delivered back into a world barely remembered. When she didn't, Kenya issued a noisy grunt of disgust. The glares the creatures cast at her and Marcos for the sudden loud noise prompted her to do something, anything, to try and escape. Kenya waited, feinting apathy, until the balance of the monsters drifted away and the two found themselves alone without watchers.

She wiggled as close to Marcos as possible, back to back until their flesh touched, and pressed her bound wrists next to his. "Hold still," Kenya whispered, "maybe I can work on these ropes and untie us."

With the tips of her fingers, she felt over Marcos's hands until she discovered the knots on the leather thongs binding him. After an indefinite time she located the ties and slowly picked away. It was slow work, her nails had never been long and the knots were tight. One loosened, and then another.

Light flooded their pocket. Another of the shadow people filled the opening holding a torch above his head, more crowded behind clutching firebrands. The leader in front was taller than the rest, his high-domed head bespeaking superior intelligence. He surveyed the two of them with red shining eyes and spoke in a deep, grunting voice so different from the high-pitched squeals of the rest.

"Yesss, you will make fine additions to the dark one's army." He looked at Kenya closely. "And a doe. He needs your kind for his breeding pits—he will be happy indeed." The leader thin lips broad out into a smile revealing his yellow pointed fangs, squealed a command to those behind him, and then said with a sneer, "Make no effort to escape, humans. You are well guarded and any attempt will mean your lives. You would cook up well over a roasting pit, and we will make an excuse to the dark lord why we have nothing for him." As if to punctuate his remark the leader kicked Marcos savagely in the ribs before he spun around and left. One of the shadow people assumed a position by the entrance and squatted, watching them with beady eyes in the flickering light of his torch.

Kenya glared back. Presently the creature looked away, yawned in boredom, and scratched himself on his belly.

That's right, you bozo—go to sleep. We're scared prisoners, our hands bound, we can't escape. Kenya kept her gaze steady on the shadow man, attempting by will alone to cause him to relax and doze off, even though knowing it was ridiculous to think she could make him do so. Instead, he stood, wandered to the entrance and peered up and down the outside corridor. He glared at Kenya and Marcos once again and hunkered down in the doorway, finally stretching his legs out to block the entrance from anyone entering or exiting without his knowledge.

Kenya kept repeating, *sleep—sleep—sleep.*

The creature's head bobbed, bounced up, and then by slow degrees sank lower onto his chest. The torch he held slipped from his claws onto the floor. Presently Kenya heard a soft, snoring rumble issuing from deep in his throat.

Yes. With renewed fury, Kenya's fingers flew back to the knots of Marcos's wrists while keeping her eyes fixed on the sleeping guard. She broke what was left of her nails in the fury, and felt the skin on the tips of her fingers start to shred away, but at last the thongs loosened enough for Marcos to twist his wrists loose. Cautiously he turned to attack hers.

When she was free, Marcos placed his fingers to his lips, and scooped up a jagged piece of rock pushed into the corner of the cave. With the stealth of a stalking tiger, he crept up to the sleeping guard. As he was about to strike, the shadow man's eyes flew open, and a shout issued from his mouth. One of Marcos' hands flashed down and throttled the cry as it sounded, while the other holding the rock crashed on the creature's skull.

An answering shout echoed from along the tunnel. Marcos seized Kenya's shoulder and scooped up the torch.

"Quick, they are coming!"

"You don't have to tell me twice." Kenya crowded on his heels as they hurried out of their prison and down the dark passageway, toward the mouth of the cave.

They burst out into starlight, gasping for breath, attempting to orientate themselves. *"Back to camp, this way!"* Marcos shouted as they broke into a run. "We must put as much distance between us and the creatures as we can."

Their fire had burned low to glowing embers, but the camp was undisturbed by the shadow people as of yet. Marcos sprinted to the horses whose eyes showed white at the foul smell of rat odor clinging to their clothes and in the breeze. The animals tugged at their halters, rearing with hooves pawing the air, in a vain attempt to escape. While Marcos struggled to get their mounts under control, Kenya hastily scooped up as much of their supplies as possible. She threw a satchel to him and vaulted to the back of her mount, digging her heels into its sides.

Her horse leaped away into the night. A squealing cry of anger rang out from behind her and a sharp stab of pain erupted in Kenya's left arm like the sting of a giant wasp. Kenya bit back a scream and glanced wildly to the rear, but couldn't see what attacked her or the shape of Marcos through the darkness. She tried to slow her mount, but the startled beast refused to respond in its fright to run from the flickering shapes of the shadow men and their menacing squeals of rage. She heard a pounding in the night to the left, but couldn't tell if it was Marcos, or the blood pumping in her temples. Kenya hunkered in her saddle, the horse's mane snapping in her face, riding until the horse slowed to a walk of its own accord out of exhaustion.

"Marcos!" she screamed into the night. Kenya heard no answer. She stood in her stirrups, positive if she yelled loud enough she'd hear a response no matter how faint. *"MARCOS!"* Her voice reverberated back from the cliffs in echoes slowly fading away into nothingness.

Kenya had no choice. She must keep forging on into the dark no matter where she might end up. To retrace her steps and hunt for Marcos in the night meant running into the shadow men who were bound to be sniffing out her trail somewhere behind. The pain in her arm was worse, a dull throbbing, but she kept riding until a red sun rose over the hills. When the sky brightened enough to see she stopped and examined her wound.

A sliver of wood protruded from her clothes at the bicep with feathers at the end, a circle of brown marking the heavy wool cloak at the entry point. Kenya tugged gently and the barb slipped out of her skin. She examined the splinter closely.

A dart? A drug? The shadow people did have weapons.

Kenya hastily pulled off the cloak and drew up the sleeve of her tunic. A faint dot with discoloration showed where the barb stuck in the arm. Fear twisted inside. *Have I been poisoned? Am I going to die?*

She flexed her arm. The muscle hurt, and a creeping numbness was beginning to spread up and down through the skin into the bone. A slight swelling bulged at the point where the dart entered her skin. Biting her lower lip, she rolled the sleeve of the tunic back down. The brown showing on the cloak also marked the heavy leather of garment she wore. Kenya hastily rubbed the wound as if the touch would make her feel better.

Maybe enough wiped off so I won't die. Maybe the pain will go away.

Uttering a shuddering sigh, she dismounted and climbed to the top of a high boulder, scanning the countryside slowly. Kenya saw no sign of pursuit. No sign of Marcos. He was gone. So were the shadow people. She was alone.

Chapter Six

Lost, dirty, hungry and thirsty, and where was Marcos? Dame his eyes. How could he leave me like this?

Kenya threw a fearful glance at the dark pockets of the cliffs as she rode under their brooding scrutiny, afraid at any moment a deadly monster would leap out and attack her. Rather than venture deeper into the hills and the stark mountains beyond and become more lost, she traveled parallel to the slopes in search of a road. Kenya was lucky, she supposed, at midday she crossed the tracks of the king's wagon train and followed their weaving way.

The pain in her arm had passed, replaced by a numbness encompassing shoulder to elbow. The swelling grown to a golf ball sized lump, dark maroon against the lighter brown skin.

By evening the ragged hills grew smaller behind her, more trees grew in a wide patch dividing hills from alps, before they marched up the slope of the high mountains beyond. Marcos said they would enter a forest. Milkwood, wasn't it the name he called the woods? She made camp and tried to collect her thoughts.

I must learn to adjust to these new circumstances. Marcos said two days through the forest. If I can reach Cliffward I can find help. I'll be safe.

She could do two more days. She once took a bus trip across country lasting for five, and survived living on the hard bench seat, eating out of vending machines, and using those nasty toilets. How much harder could this be? Must be water in the woods, trees didn't grow without water, right? She carried some food from the scant supplies scavenged before they fled the shadow men, a couple of apples, and some hard-as-a-rock bread. It wouldn't be so bad, she kept telling herself. She could make it.

WHERE WAS MARCOS?

Kenya never realized how much she'd come to rely on the man. How his laugh made her day, or when he smiled her heart raced faster. He was the one permanent fixture in this crazy world she found herself living in, and now he was gone, the loneliness was almost more than she could bear.

Kenya shook her head, as if trying to dislodge the thoughts from her mind.

I will survive this.

As soon as she entered the shelter of the trees the next day, the air transformed from hot and dry to cool and damp. A shiver ran through her body at the change of temperature as her parched skin absorbed the moisture of the air. The bright sunlight shaded to a filtered green, and she found water, a scum-covered pool half-hidden from view. Her horse discovered the pond among fallen trees and overhanging branches. They both drank their fill until they could hold no more and rode on.

A squirrel chittered at her from a low tree branch, strange bird calls echoed from the tops of pines. As the day wore on Kenya felt herself relax and enjoying the ride. By the time the sun faded from the red sky she was whistling, by force of will alone ignoring her throbbing left arm, which now hung useless at her side.

Kenya camped at night on the edge of a glade under an oak tree overhung with Spanish moss making the little area feel like her own private room. As the evening grew darker, a faint, white light emitted from the moss, painting the walls a pearly silver.

She survived the day, and was safe for the night, she hoped. The numbness of the poison appeared to confine itself to her arm and shoulder, at least not progressing into the chest and heart as Kenya feared in the beginning. She sighed and snuggled deeper into the moss and leaf bed she built for herself as protection from the chill of the night. She must still travel through the forest to find this Cliffward, but if she kept following the tracks…. Kenya repeated the phrase, "Follow the tracks. Never lose the tracks."

"It is here we dance for the night."

Kenya froze in the bed of leaves. The voice issued from beyond the moss, somewhere in the dark glade.

She rose cautiously, trying hard not to make a sound as the dry leaves surrounding her crinkled and the small twigs snapped. Kenya cringed, the noise sounding unusually loud in her ears.

A tramp of feet told her more people approached. Kenya slipped her feet along, hardly daring to breathe. Finally, she stood before the strands of hanging moss dangling from the tree limbs, pulled them aside an inch, and peeked out.

Dark shapes moved not forty feet from her. As Kenya watched, a fire sprang to life as if by its own accord and settled on a stacked pile of wood in the middle of the clearing. The flames spread quickly, leaping skyward in a shower of sparks. Kenya made out the shapes of five small, cloaked people, hoods drawn over their heads, standing around the blaze.

Midgets?

Every one of the five were no more than four foot tall. Kenya studied each in turn and realized they might be taller but all hunched over as if carrying a heavy weight on their backs. In the firelight, boney pale arms and withered hands protruded from the cloaks, and faint wisps of stringy white hair twisted in the breeze from beneath the hoods.

"This place will suit us well," one of the people remarked, bending low to warm withered hands at the fire.

"The moon is rising," another commented, shoving a gnarled finger toward the heaven. "We must hurry if we are to drawn upon its power this night."

Kenya shifted and drew her moss curtain wider, trying to have a better view of the speaker. Twigs underfoot snapped, and the five froze, faces pointing her way.

"Well, it appears we have a visitor, sisters," the speaker said. "Let us see if this night wanderer is animal or human." A long slim knife appeared from the beneath the cloak held in a scrawny hand. The figure crouched and took mincing steps closer to Kenya's hideaway and ordered in a sharp voice, "Whatever you are, show yourself. *Now.*"

The command ripped through Kenya like a knife. Before she realized what she was doing, her muscles locked as if her body were a puppet pulled on strings. She rose, stepped forward, parting the curtain of moss, and staggered forward into the circle of firelight.

"Human, I'd say." The voice was female. The woman threw the hood of her cloak back revealing an ancient face, lined with wrinkles, and white hair. Shrewd eyes scrutinized Kenya for a long minute. "I think we need not fear this one, sisters. Some scared maiden ready to faint away in fright at the sight of us." The rest cackled in agreement. The speaker waved a hand, and the paralysis clutching Kenya evaporated. "Speak, girl. Tell us your story. Why are you out here in the forest where you do not belong?"

More hoods flew off. The women crowded around Kenya in a semi-circle. Kenya looked from one seamed face to the next in trepidation.

"I....I'm lost." In a rush, the words spilled out of Kenya's mouth relating her plight for the last days. She ended saying, "...my shoulder is numb. I'm lost. Who— who are you? Won't you please help me?"

The women stared back, not speaking, and then at each other. A silent communication passed between the five Kenya was not privy to. Finally the leader spoke. "Call me Megoron. We," the crone waved a hand at the other women, "are the *ur-vins*. Name us witches if you will. Ours is the power of white or black magic, to heal or curse as is our whim." Megoron glanced at her fellows again and received nods. "Perhaps this night we will help. Take off your cloak and let us examine your arm."

Kenya did as told, revealing an arm swollen to twice its normal size. The women clustered around, not touching the inflamed member, and whispering to one and other in tones too low for Kenya to hear. Megoron said, "Shadow people you say? The ones who reside in the cliffs? We know their tricks of old." The witch held out a hand and snapped her fingers to one of the other *ur-vins*. A woman scurried away, returning with a poultice made of damp leaves. "Hold still, girl," Megoron commanded, applying the dressing to Kenya's arm.

The poultice clung hungrily to her flesh, shimmering with an internal crystal light. The *ur-vins* raised their hands to the moon and stars, chanting.

Light from the moon transformed into a beam centering on Kenya's arm. She immediately felt a tingling running from her wrist to her neck.

Pain.

Throbbing agony, worse than she'd ever felt before raced along her arm. It started as a dull stinging at first, and then drove into her muscles like a knife, a raging fire burning skin, flesh, and bone. Kenya clamped her eyes tightly shut, jaw muscles bunched attempting not to cry out at the torture within herself.

When Kenya thought she could stand the hurt no longer, the agony faded to a dull ache. The chanting of the *ur-vins* slowed to a whisper, and stopped completely, so did the pain.

Sweat covered Kenya, her body shook. *Have they burnt my arm to ash?* Still trembling she opened her eyes and looked down at her limb.

The swelling was gone. The limb was back to normal. Kenya raised the hand, flexed the muscles, and lifted the arm above her shoulder twisting to test the muscles.

"It's healed!"

"Indeed your infection is, girl, otherwise you would be dead in another two days." For the first time a hint of a smile passed over Megoron's lips. "For a moment I did not think our magic would work at all, so far gone was the wound, but your body helped to fight also. I am surprised. In time you may have the power within you to become an *ur-vin* like ourselves."

"Huh? I'm a witch?"

Megoron reached out with a finger and touched the tip to Kenya's forehead. A tiny spark exploded in her brain and the hazy doorways materialized again. "I see it. You have the power to open entrances to other worlds if you will. You have voyaged there before, I think. Use the potential in you wisely." The witch paused, thinking, and then said, "Some of our sisters use this ability for their own gain. This selfishness brings ruin on all of us. Be not one who draws evil for the sake of evil."

"Ah, yeah. Sure."

The group of *ur-vin* froze. Megoron spun and searched the darkness. "Come sisters, danger is afoot, drawn here by the goodness we have done." The witch turned to Kenya. "Beware of what you meet in these woods this night, for all is not as it appears even in daylight."

Before Kenya replied, the women scurried out of the glade and away into the darkness. She heard the noise of their retreat fading to a rustle in the bushes and in a second that disappeared also. Kenya was left with nothing more than the campfire to show the women were ever there.

Shocked by the rapid turn of events, Kenya stared into the night. A thought sprang up in her mind. *If I'm a witch I could sure use some of their power now. Wonder what they meant by dangers in the night? An animal attacking me?* She looked down at her arm to guarantee the limb was still sound and usable if necessary. It was.

Kenya surveyed the clearing once more for signs of danger, and then shaking her head, wandered back into the house of moss, her mind full of questions she did not attempt to answer.

Wetness trickled on her neck and Kenya looked up in alarm. Water dripped from the moss above her head. She moved over a fraction of an inch watching the ceiling for additional moisture falling and caught movement from the corner of her eye. The light from the hanging drapes was coalescing, drawing together into a radiant ball. The sphere detached itself from the rest of the mass and floated toward her.

"This can't end well," Kenya murmured aloud, eyes fixed on the light as she cautiously shifted away. The globe, however, made no attempt to harm her. The ball hovered, as if deciding what to do, and then passed through the curtain of moss and off into the glade.

Kenya stood and cautiously trailed behind, parting her brown curtain to peer outside into the clearing. Additional balls bobbed in the air, dancing with each other in an aerial display of light. She stepped out and they approached in a twirling mass, covering her body like shimmering diamonds.

A song sprang up inside her head, a tune without words, crystal wind chimes tinkling in her brain. Kenya raised her arms higher and the sound grew louder as more of the globes joined the group. In her mind, the tunnel of light seen in her dreams returned, more distinct than ever.

This time the doors open wide. Kenya strode forward without fear walking along the corridor, peering within. Strange objects rested on benches, or tucked away on shelves, which had no end. She stepped to the door she wished to open and entered.

One object drew her attention in particular. A silver lyre beckoned to her. Kenya's heart leaped. She reached to pick the instrument up....

A screech rang out, breaking the stillness of the air. The room dissolved and the light disappeared. Kenya stood in the darkness, the globes floating about fled in disarray. In Kenya's mind, a terrible sense of loss and a piercing scream knifed through her brain.

A feathered blur shot past her head, gaping talons and cruel beak open to strike. One globe, slower than the rest, jerked upward to escape as the phantom snatched the sphere out of the air.

Kenya tumbled backward, arms wind milling over her head to protect herself in case the phantom attacked her next. Dazed, she pushed herself into a sitting position and watched as the light rose in the sky, only to crash down to earth. The screeching started again.

"Ho, this way."

"Nay, from the right. I hear her speak."

Torchlight bobbed through the darkness Kenya's way, and two men pushed through the underbrush. They halted by the globe, which still pulsed with a faint yellow glow. They held their flaming brands high to see clearer what lay on the ground.

"She caught one. I told you she would. Good magic in these. The lord will be happy."

"Quick—Come here, we have snared more than a Quat, I think."

One of the torches moved Kenya's way and the light illuminated a short man who stood over Kenya dressed in a heavy leather tunic and tights. He frowned and surveyed her before extending his hand to help her stand. "And who are you, a night fairy out for a stroll in the woods?"

"Please," Kenya scrambled to her feet and brushed herself off, "I'm lost. I became separated from King Harold's party while traveling to Cliffward for a meeting."

"King Harold?" the other man said, strolling up. "You say you troop to Cliffward for the conclave?"

"Yes."

"You are in luck, then. We travel with our Lord Galvin to the summoning's also," he replied, staring at her in the dim light of the torch. "You may accompany us if you wish. I am sure my lord will extend his protection to you." In his left hand, he carried what appeared to be a deflated balloon pulsing with a faint inner glow. On his padded shoulder perched a brown hawk, which cocked its head and stared at Kenya with yellow eyes.

Kenya ran to collect her horse. When she returned, she noticed the light from the balloon was noticeably fainter. *I wonder? It can't be what was floating in the air. They were so beautiful.* She pointed a shaky finger at the object the man held. "Is that one of the globes dancing in the sky?"

The shorter of the two men said impatiently, "Yes, and a good one, too, fat and plump. You are ready, Lady? We must away before the Quat breathes its last. Once they die, they decay quickly and their magic is lost. Come. Let us proceed to our camp." He strode away rapidly through the trees holding his torch in the air to light the way.

The other man fell in beside Kenya. The hawk riding on his shoulder fluttered its wings and gave a soft cry. Kenya pointed to the balloon he clutched in his hand and asked, "What is that thing? You called it a Quat? It was so—pretty. Why did you hunt the poor creature? For food?"

"This?" He held up the animal he carried. On closer inspection, Kenya saw a hairless, translucent skin bag still pulsing with a faint amber iridescence. In the dim light Kenya could not see any face, tail, or wings to help it fly. "It is a Quat. They emerge at night at the rise of the moon to gain the power of the stars. Our Lord Galvin will use the magic of its essence in his incantations, but the beast must be fresh lest whatever power lies within drains away." He glanced upward to the sky as if speculating what the energy might be, but his stride never stopped.

Some sort of voodoo rite? How horrible to kill a beautiful animal like this. A scent of fear of these people caught her mind. Kenya cast a sideways look at the man and wondered if his lord practiced good or evil magic and would it be bent against her.

The hunter turned his head and, using two fingers, stroked the bird riding on his shoulder along the back and wings, ignoring the expression on Kenya's face. "We did a good job tonight, did we not, my pretty. Yes, you are a beautiful bird."

A campfire flickered in the distance and they entered another clearing with a cluster of low slung tents erected around a large fire. A dozen men sat, eating and talking, gruff laughter sounding through the trees long before the three emerged into the firelight. The laughter halted abruptly as Kenya and the two men tramped into view, and all eyes swung in their direction with curious questions.

A tall man rose from a cluster of his fellows and strolled toward them. Kenya noted grey tinged the temples of his short, curly black hair, and the expensive red cloak wrapped around his shoulders with a silver clasp of a bird holding the material closed. *Lord Galvin, no doubt. The leader of this band.* Her apprehension returned, multiplied by the eyes staring at her in astonishment.

The lord stopped in front of the man holding the Quat and surveyed all three with glee. "Alfred, I see your hunting has brought us more than a Quat this night. If I knew hawking would be this good, I would have sent thrice your number to scour the forest." He flashed a warm smile at Kenya, revealing white teeth. "And how are we honored with your presence, my lady?"

Kenya felt herself blushing. That smile. "I—I was lost, Lord," she stammered, surprised at her reaction as the feeling of this party melted by the warm greeting of its leader. "I traveled with King Harold's party and we were attacked, a wyvern, I believe the beast is called, and then—"

"A wyvern? And you survived?" He looked at her in surprise and a tinge of admiration clouded his eyes. "You are indeed lucky, My Lady…?"

"Kenya, my Lord. I am the wordsmith to King Harold."

"Wordsmith, is it?" Galvin nodded in thought and issued a light chuckle. "I have heard tell Harold is not the most eloquent of speakers. I can well believe he values you highly." His eyes rested on Alfred still holding the Quat. "We will talk on the morrow, Lady Kenya. For now I must attend to more immediate matters lest our hunting for the night go for naught." He turned to one of his men. "Set up a tent for this lady to rest in. Bring her food if she desires a meal, drink, and anything she may want." He bowed to Kenya. "Please excuse our rough camp. We trek with no women so you may not find the luxuries you are accustomed too, but you may journey with us to Cliffward, if you will, and be under my protection in safety." He made a short bow, snatched the Quat out of Alfred's fingers, which still gave off a faint glow, and hurried to his tent.

Alfred led Kenya to a place by the fire and a wooden bowl heaped to overflowing full of stew materialized in her hands while the men prepared a place for her to sleep. After she could eat no more Kenya thanked everyone gratefully and crawled into the small makeshift tent constructed for her.

Kenya relaxed for the first time in she didn't know how many days, delivering herself into the luxury of the fact she was finally safe and on her way to rejoin the king's party. *Why was I so apprehensive of these people? Galvin is treating me better than King Harold did.* Kenya rolled on her back and stared at the darkness above. *Probably my fear of meeting new people. I'm so timid at times.* Kenya closed her eyes and surrendered herself to the darkness.

***

True to his word, Galvin rode next to her the following day and kept her company as they traveled along the worn dirt trail to Cliffward. He was most interested in King Harold's preparations for war and quizzed her in endlessly detail on the castle's defenses. Repeatedly she found herself replying in bewilderment, "I don't know," or "I'm not sure," and was surprised at her lack of knowledge. She finally exclaimed in chagrin, "Lord Galvin, I am the king's wordsmith, not his Minster of War. I construct songs, poems, and tell stories, not weapons or gauge the thickness of battlements. On occasion, I help him with a letter he wishes to compose himself. You'd best ask King Harold what provisions he's made for attack and defense of Evertree."

"True," he murmured. "I worry about the other kingdoms of this land," he hurried to say, attempting to justify his unusual curiosity about another king's defenses. "If one falls, eventually all will fall. Evertree is a grand prize, and far removed from the rest. It is the key in any war of conquest, commanding both land and sea."

After Galvin finished with his examinations, Kenya asked, "What happened to the animal, Quat you called the poor thing, you caught last night? I saw many of the same creatures dancing in the sky. They looked so beautiful. It was a shame you must catch it. Why is it so important?"

Disbelief rose in Galvin's face as if he could not believe she didn't know the significance of the animal. "The Quat captures the light of the moon and the stars. The moon opens the pathways to dreams. The stars conduct you to realms beyond man's imagination. I strive to reach a place where all dreams come true, the other world surrounding us we never see without the inner sight."

The corridor. The door and room with the light and the lyre. *He's speaking of the same place I've seen in my visions and dreams. Maybe he knows why I keep picturing these objects in my mind, and why I keep seeing these things in the first place.* Kenya described what she saw in her dreams to Lord Galvin. He nodded eagerly in understanding as his eyes lit up in avarice. "I don't...I don't understand what is happening. Is this the place you're talking about? Is it real?"

"You have been there too, I see. Yes, the rooms are real. In ancient times, the lords of sorcery drew upon the power of this place easily. This is the place I wish to go, if only I could find the right means of unlocking the door." Unconsciously his fingers curled and uncurled grasping what he wanted inside. "Tell me, were you able to take what was within?" He eyed her narrowly. "If we knew how to do it, the ability would help all the kingdoms of the land in their battle against the evil plaguing the land now."

"No. In my vision I saw a lyre, I don't know what the sight meant, but before I could pick the instrument up the dream was lost." She studied him, puzzled. "Why a lyre, I wonder? How could a music instrument help the kingdoms, anyway?" Kenya tittered. "Maybe bore everyone with my singing?"

He scowled at the remark, and then shrugged, disappointment in his stance. "Songs are words. You are a wordsmith. In any case, the lyre is a symbol only of the magic you could bring out. The spirits governing this world work in strange ways and what you see is not always what is, or what it might be. What is important is the power it holds."

"What power?" *This is the second time I've been told not to be deceived by appearances and talks of magic. Damn these people and their hidden means. I wish they'd speak plainly in words I could understand.*

"The power of anything you wish." His voice fell to a hushed whisper. Galvin leaned forward, his eyes gleaming and said, "Tell me, what is it you want; what do you desire more than anything in the world?"

Kenya closed her eyes, thinking. What did she want? To return to the real world, of course, for this dream to end on a happy note. To make sure Marcos was safe.

Kenya chanced to look at Galvin's face. She saw something there, something unsavory, and the apprehension returned. He wore an expression like an avaricious man converting a bag of gold, which was not his, but hoped to steal. She replied in a cautious voice, "I guess I'd like to go home."

Galvin's next statement confirmed Kenya's feeling of uneasiness. "If we join together, perhaps we can achieve what we both desire most."

I hear deception in his voice. What does he want from me? The way he said join sounded…sexual.

Kenya's skin crawled and she glanced away, studying the road ahead. "I don't know. I'll have to think about your offer, and all this talk of magic," she answered.

***

In the afternoon, the forest thin to widely scattered clumps of trees with men and women working in plowed fields. The path they traveled broadened and small hamlets with thatched cottages appeared on the sides of the dirt trail. As the sun set a lone mountain rose into view against the skyline. Carved into the side of the peak was a city. Cliffward.

Surrounding the towering spires was an immense wall fully a hundred feet tall and fifty at the base. Beyond was another wall, smaller, but still stout enough to repeal anything but a determined attack. Before both walls, the builders diverted a river to create a wide deep moat twisting with swift flowing water. Towers studded the walls at thirty-yard intervals with archer's notches to create a crossfire. Massive iron gates guarded the drawbridge and no man's land lay in between the sole entrance to the fortress.

As the party rode over the stout wooden planks leading to the gate, Kenya gawked at the thick, towering walls and fortifications, trying to estimate how long and how much manpower the construction took to carve and erect each. "They take their defense serious, don't they," she remarked to Galvin after giving up. She spied a face peering from within a slit of the wall as they passed through. More slots showed at intervals both at shoulder and leg height.

The lord waved at the faces watching suspiciously, as they traveled through the tunnels in the wall, and poked a thumb at the cuts. "Try and walk this passageway if you are not expected and you will soon find an arrow or spear in your side."

"Sure is a shame to waste friendly visitors if you make a mistake," Kenya joked nervously as they passed another cut.

Lord Galvin issued a gruff chuckle but was more sanguine. "During the great battles of the ancients, this castle was never taken, although many tried with both magic and men. You cannot see the sorcery in the rocks, but if you have the knack you can sense the enchantments buried within. Nevertheless, it is possible. Yes, given the right strategy this fortress could fall." They rode silently through the gap between walls and he eyed the inner wall on the outside and as the passed through the passageway, and then the inside construction. Pursing his lips Galvin swung in his saddle with a hand signal to his men and shouted in a loud voice, "Ho, we sleep in beds tonight."

A few cheers rose from his troop. He commented to Kenya, "Once we are inside the fortress I will locate King Harold's chambers and return you to your household." Galvin leveled one of his charming smiles at Kenya. "Then my duty as guardian to you is done, Lady. I hope this will not be the last I see of you, though."

In spite of her distrust of the man, Kenya felt a thrill shoot through her body at his smile. She blushed and said, "I am sure we will meet again. The fortress is not *that* big."

The problem of locating Harold's chambers solved itself with the arrival of Jessica. As they entered the courtyard of the castle, the princess was out strolling with a group of her friends. Her eyes narrowed in recognition as they lit on Kenya and remarked in surprise, "Well, our misplaced wordsmith. We thought you were lost." Kenya heard the disappointment in the princess's voice and cringed inside. Jessica's eyes shifted to Lord Galvin and his men. "At least you have fetched some new guests along with you to entertain us. This is better than you have done so far this trip, I must say." She showed a brazen smile to Lord Galvin. "And such a handsome man."

Jessica's friends giggled and hid their mouths, making whispered remarks to each other, keeping one eye on the princess to follow her lead as their vision shifted between Kenya and the lord.

Yeah, I'm glad you're safe, too. Kenya bit back the remark and said, "Lady Jessica, can you direct me to where the king resides? I feel I must report to him what has happened to the rest of his party, and I have imposed enough to these kind men."

The princess smirked and motioned to one of the other girls and snapped her fingers. "Take the wordsmith to my father. We will dally here with her brave savior until he finds he must leave." Jessica sauntered over to Galvin, and stared up at him with batting eyes and laid a hand on his saddle.

Galvin's winning smile, which he leveled at Kenya all this time, shifted quickly to the princess. "We have traveled for many days, my lady. A wait of a few more minutes in your presence and the other ladies will be a welcome diversion before we find quarters."

Kenya clamped her lips tightly shut and murmured a thanks to Galvin for his help, snatched her gear from her horse, and hurried after the other girl who was already disappearing at a fast walk into the fortress entrance.

Kenya thought the castle at Evertree was vast, but the whole keep could have fit into one corner of this fortress with room for three more. Kenya could not understand why they made it so *big*. As she trailed behind Jessica's friend striding hard to catch up through the wide stone corridors, Kenya did not see more than a score of people in the half deserted hallways.

"Here." The girl stopped and waved a finger to a heavy oaken door. "King Harold has taken up residence within." She turned to leave.

The usual sentries who stood before the king's residence, temporary or otherwise were absent. Kenya halted, bewildered, afraid to walk in. "Isn't there anyone to announce me?" she asked.

The girl glared at Kenya and glanced up and down the corridor. "Do I look like a sentry to announce the presences of others to the king? No doubt, the guard had to use the jakes or set off on an errand. He will return shortly. Besides, even if I were the guard, I have better things to do than to announce a wordsmith," she replied with faint scorn. "Wait until he returns or you may announce yourself." With a faint snort reminding Kenya pointedly of Jessica's, the girl swung on the balls of her feet and stalked away.

Kenya averted the further humiliation of knocking on the door and peeking inside, when the entrance open wide and King Harold himself stepped out with two attendants trailing behind him. He halted and stared at her for a moment in amazement as if not realizing who Kenya was, or what she was doing standing outside his door.

His eyes opened wide and lips curled up at the corners. "Well, if it is not my wayward wordsmith. We thought you lost in the attack of the wyvern," he exclaimed peering over the top of Kenya's head down the hallway. "What of the rest of the party? Have they finally arrived also?"

Kenya's stomach twisted into a knot with a sinking feeling in her chest. Her eyes dropped to the king's feet and she said in a low voice, "All dead, Sire. Marcos and I survived, but I don't know where he is now. We became separated on the way here."

The king nodded thoughtfully, studying the stone blocks of the floor, digesting the news of his people. He looked up and asked, "I felt in my heart this was true, but you say Marcos still lives?"

"After the attack we traveled this way, but were captured by a group of the shadow people," Kenya explained. "We managed to escape in the dark, but during our flight we became separated afterward. I haven't seen him since. I was fortunate a party of Lord Galvin's men found me. I travelled here with them."

Harold nodded as if this explained her presence at Cliffward. "When Marcos and the rest of my people did not catch up to us after the wyvern's attack, I felt he failed me, but then we were attacked in turn again and barely escaped with our lives. I realized no amount of men could stop the beast. Well, you are here and I am glad at least one of my people survived. You must be made of stronger steel than I gave you credit for, and who knows, if you have returned, Marcos may yet find his way back here." His eyes took on a faraway look. He nodded to the guards behind him and said to Kenya, "Come along, the council meets now and I may have need of you, and your advice." The king stepped around her and proceeded down the hallway.

"Me?" Kenya squeaked. "Of course, if you wish, My Lord, but I don't understand...."

Harold stopped and turned back to her, waving a hand in dismissal. He rubbed his forehead in weariness, his lips moving wordless and said, "When the wyvern caught up to our party the beast took a terrible toll on our numbers. In the battle my most trusted advisors who accompanied me died. You are the only one of rank left." He stalked off down the corridor with Kenya hurrying to catch up.

They arrived at another, smaller door with two grim-faced sentries standing with pikes at the ready. They surveyed King Harold, his guards, and Kenya. With a nod, they swung the door open and the king swept inside.

Kenya was surprised. The council chamber of Cliffward was much smaller in comparison to the rest of the rooms she'd observed in the castle of Evertree. Dominating the middle was an oaken table, at the head of which sat King Goron, Lord of Cliffward. Five other lords clustered around in deep-seated chairs, attendants standing behind them ready to advise their lords at a moment's notice. Kenya noted Galvin already found a seat next to Goron on the right side as if he advised the ruler of Cliffward directly.

I wonder how he shook off Jessica so easily? I figure she'd keep her claws in him for the rest of the day.

King Harold took this scene in with a sweep of his eye and sat at the remaining seat while Kenya waited behind him with his two guards.

King Goron bowed politely to the lords sitting around the table and stood, took a deep gulp from a wine goblet, and cleared his voice. "Now we are all assembled, let us discuss the attacks on our kingdoms." He took in each of the other lords by eye and slammed his right fist in his left hand. "Evil stalks our lands. Evil I say. Do you hear me? How do we propose to fight this menace laying like a black blanket upon our lands?" He dropped back into his chair in a huff, glaring about as if daring for any of the lords to deny his statement.

King Harold half rose from his chair, shouting, "I was attacked on my way here, my people killed by a demon not seen in this world for a thousand years. Why—why...?" He shot a questioning looked to Kenya as if to supply an answer he knew but couldn't express in his own words. She bent and whispered urgently in his ear. He nodded sharply. "We should band together, pool knowledge," the king exclaimed to the council as he banged one fist on the table. He glanced back to Kenya and she whispered something else. Harold's eyes flashed with acknowledgment and he nodded his head in agreement. "Yes, set up lines of communication between our kingdoms so we can combine our resources and exchange information about this menace. This is why we have gathered here today, to stand united as one."

A few murmurs of approval rose from the lords sitting around the table. King Goron pounded the bottom of his pewter goblet on the wooden surface of the table in agreement and declared, "Wise council, Harold. We shall discuss more of the details tomorrow."

King Harold smirked, leaned back in his chair with arms folded across his belly and nodded, pleased his words were acknowledged and with himself.

Galvin spoke up. "I was not attacked traveling here, and saw nothing of the menace plaguing the land." He leveled his gaze at Harold and said in a half mocking tone,

"I did not, however, trek with my women, in a slow caravan, which would be a tempting morsel for demon or monster to pounce on if they so wished."

Harold glanced sharply at Galvin in surprise and a gurgle of confusment erupted from his throat as he leaned forward and started to say something. Kenya placed her hand on his shoulder and whispered urgently in a low voice, "We should not argue in this council, sire. It is better to wait."

I hear deceit in his words and arrogance. Is he trying to provoke Harold for some reason? Or is he a conceited fool who speaks without thinking first?

Galvin observed Harold's reaction and continued in a more conciliatory tone, "My kingdom is well defended and because of the rough terrain we have never been bothered by the evil stalking the land. I will offer warriors to any lord who may need men for scouts or messengers." He made a short bow to King Goron. "If need be, I can also supply a limited number of soldiers for the protection of their kingdoms if this is necessary."

"Bravo," exclaimed Goron, standing. He nodded to each of the lords. "We will discuss more on this on the morrow, for today we are finished, I think."

The rest of the lords rose also, King Harold appeared undecided if he should corner Goron before he left the room and begin private discussions for the defense of their kingdoms, or leave himself and wait for the great lords to meet again tomorrow. A few of the rulers who possessed smaller holdings gathered around Galvin fawning on the lord with sickly grins. Harold glanced from one to the other, shrugged, and said to Kenya, "Come. There is much here I find disturbing, and more I am unsure of. Why would Galvin offer men to us he would surely need in case of attack, and why would Goron be so happy he did?"

Kenya didn't know, either. She knew so little of these kingdoms or the manpower each possessed, but received the impression King Harold did. Something was happening which neither Harold nor she understood, something they had no knowledge of, something strange indeed.

Chapter Seven

The council met once a day after the lunch meal, hammering out details of mutual defense, speculating on the rise of ancient evil and its origin, or where, or whom the malevolent spirits stalking the land would strike next. Kenya attended King Harold at these meetings, at times providing advice, but more often than was the case, helping him express his own thoughts.

Galvin continued to ingrain himself in the good graces of the other lords by promises of men, supplies, and aid to any who desired his help. Kenya noticed he also embedded himself with the ladies of Cliffward, and the rest of the women who attended the conclave from the other kingdoms, notably, Jessica. He became a frequent visitor to King Harold's section of the castle, and could be seen walking with Jessica late at night holding her hand as they joked and whispered to each other in the moonlight.

Kenya found herself increasingly isolated. The women from Evertree did not talk to her, and the people of Cliffward refused to acknowledge her also with no more than a nod of recognition. She wondered if Jessica spread rumors about her, or if the inhabitants of the castle were naturally uncivil. During this time, Kenya missed Marcos more and more. She never realized how much she'd come to rely on his friendship, smiling face, and the mere presence of him being there for her when no one else was.

With nothing to do other than wait on the king, and no one to talk to, Kenya found herself watching Jessica, surreptitiously of course, but nevertheless observing a subtle change come over the princess, and not one of friendship for Galvin, something different, evil.

King Harold did not notice, but the rest of the attendants at the summit did with knowing wags of their heads. The wrangling of the conference took up most of his time, and he paid little notice to the events surrounding him. Increasingly, he sought Kenya for advice; although he still possessed a few of his senior captains with him whom Kenya felt were more qualified than she to give military counsel.

After an hour-long session listing the monsters already seen invading the plains in increasing numbers, and those from legend that might still exist in another realm and how to kill these beasts, Kenya felt she must speak up.

"King Harold," Kenya said in a low voice when she heard the lords talking about *ikkitousens*, dog-like demons; *azemans* females dressed like animals who drank one's blood, and ogres called *yurupair*, "I have no knowledge of these creatures or how to defeat them." Kenya laughed and shook her head. "I can hardly pronounce their names."

For the first time since the conference started Kenya saw Harold's lips curl upward into a smile of agreement. "Go," he said. "For this I do not need you. Fighting and killing of beasts both myth and real I know well, equally by study of the ancient tales and practice while hunting."

Kenya left the council chamber and hurried along the corridor to her own room. As she scurried down the hall, a dirty, bloodstained figure stalked toward her.

"Marcos."

Before Kenya knew what was happening, she ran to him, and threw her arms around his neck in a tight embrace.

The weight of her body bent him over until her toes brushed the stone.

"Ho, Kenya, I am glad to see you too, but..." Marcos gently disengaged the young woman's arms from about his neck and stood upright with a groan. "You are achieving the destruction the shadow people failed to do."

"Oh," Kenya surveyed the man in bloody tattered clothes. "What happened? I lost you in the night. I searched, I swear I did, but..." Kenya shrugged and took his hand. "A party of Lord Galvin's men found me and brought me here."

She tugged Marcos forward. "Your uncle is in the council chamber with the other lords. He will want to see you."

"I enticed the shadow people to chase me," Marcos explained as they walked. "I did not know where you were, but I took them along our back-trail assuming you would continue the way we rode." He issued a gruff laugh. "A merry chase indeed. After the second day, I attempted to turn back, however I discovered my way blocked by the *tengus*—"

"Tengus? What the heck are they?"

"Dog-like demons who take on the form of raptors," explained Marcos. They paused before the door of the council chamber. "They foretell the arrival of other demons, war, and death." He shuddered. "Much evil is stalking the land if *tengus* are about."

"Are they the ones who attacked you?" Kenya waved a finger at his torn clothes. "You're a mess."

Marcos glanced ruefully at himself as if realizing for the first time what a sorry jumble he was. "No, I rode far to the north, where the land becomes cracked, broken, with deep crevices and buttes. There, at night, I met *nar-riders* and..."

"Nar-riders? What are *they*?"

Marcos gave a small shiver and his face went blank. Kenya felt a sensation of bugs running up and down her spine. "At the end of the last great war when the dark lords were destroyed or departing from this world into other realms, a company of cavalry men were captured who had sworn allegiance to the evil," Marcos began. "In retribution, the victors cut off the heads of the men and horses—"

"What? How could they?" Kenya was shocked.

"You must remember hatred was felt on both sides. Fathers, mothers, and children lost," Marcos explained. "The bodies of the men were buried along with their horses, the heads of both burnt, so in the next world, they were deaf, dumb and blind."

So cruel. This must have been a horrible war.

"One of the departing dark lords took pity on these men, or perhaps wished to leave a taste of evil to stalk the land, no one knows, but he brought their spirits back from the dead. They roam the land now, headless on their headless horses, only able to see at night by the light of a dim moon. Bright sunlight blinds them and will cause their bodies to change into dust."

The bugs running up Kenya's spine lodged into the back of her neck. "Is this true?"

Marcos raised his shoulders and dropped them again. "This is the tale, whether the story is true or not I do not know. All I know is one found me and followed at night. I saw him in the light of the moon on my trail and he scared me to death." He glanced down at himself again. "This is how I come by my appearance. I scouted a ravine on foot in the dark, searching for the best trail down. I slipped and fell."

"Oh, no." Kenya paused, considering what Marcos said. "What happens if they catch you?"

Marcos cast a sideways glance at her, his lips bending downward. "They feed on the life-force of a person, their soul. Once you have been caught, the *nar-riders* leave you as a mindless husk, as devoid of love and humanity as they are."

Two sentries stood guard outside the council room door. They dropped their pikes in an X, baring the entrance as Kenya and Marcos attempted to step inside.

"No one may enter. The lords are still in session and may not be disturbed," one grim-faced guard stated firmly.

"I just left," Kenya protested indignantly glaring at the man in disbelief. She knew they'd seen her walk out the door minutes before. "We have news for King Harold. His nephew," Kenya inclined her head toward Marcos, "has returned after a long and dangerous journey."

"Nevertheless," the guard replied sternly, refusing to remove his pike. "We have our orders not to allow entrance to anyone until the lords have concluded their business or we have been told otherwise."

"Of all the...." Kenya fumed, muttering under her breath about the stupidity of some people. She looked to Marcos helplessly and raised her palms upward in defeat. "We'll have to wait."

Issuing a deep sigh, Marcos slumped to the floor and braced his back against the wall in resignation. "We wait," he agreed with a lop-sided grin. "At least here I am safe for the moment with no fighting to worry about," he scowled at the guards who glowered back, "I think."

Kenya dropped next to him with a glare at the sentries. "When I was in the chamber the lords discussed how to fight the approaching battles," she commented. "From what you have told me, the war may be happening soon. When we rode here I never realized so many demons roamed the countryside."

Marcos bobbed his head in understanding. "Nor did any of us. The plain will soon be a battleground again. I am glad the lords think ahead at a time like this. It is wise to plan beforehand strategy rather than wait until the heat of battle and you stare your enemy in the face," he remarked. "You said you were rescued by Lord Galvin and his men?" He bent his head toward the door. "He is in there now?"

"Yes." Kenya debated in her mind if she should tell Marcos of her misgivings about the lord. As if prodded by some unseen forces she blurted out in a low voice, "I don't trust the man. He's—creepy."

"Galvin?" Marcos raised one eyebrow and studied Kenya. "I do not know much about him. He rules a kingdom in the high mountains, but what I have heard, he has always been of the light, not darkness."

"Maybe I'm mistaken," Kenya admitted, "but on the night his men found me he had them out searching for quats? You call the creatures? Such pretty animals. He said he needed them to open up the dream place where all desires come true. He wanted me to help him. I was there once."

"You were? You remember your dream now?" Marcos regarded her with deep respect.

"Ye-Yes. I am sure of it. A place of shining lights and doors."

"This is high magic beyond me. None I know of has ever ventured into the other world. Did you help the lord in his quest?"

"No, and he has not asked again, thank goodness." Kenya relived the episode in her mind. She continued in an even lower tone. "He's associating with Jessica, too. A great deal from what I've seen and heard."

Marcos guffawed and slapped his knee. "He must be evil, indeed, then."

"Go ahead and laugh," Kenya retorted, grinning in spite of herself, "but it's not funny. You told me yourself Jessica was a wielder of magic. I wonder if he is trying to acquire from her what he could not get from me."

Marcos sobered instantly and pursed his lips. "Possible," he admitted. "However I do not think my cousin would help him in any evil. To do so would be—"

"When you have a chance, talk to her," Kenya said. "You'll see. Jessica is not the same person you knew. It is if a strange possession is being thrown over her, a little at the time."

The opening of the council door interrupted their conversation. Lords and advisors piled out, many talking eagerly to each other in loud voices.

Marcos and Kenya leaped to their feet. The last to exit were King Harold and Galvin still deep in discussion.

"...if you wish I will lend you twenty men and as many supplies as you need," Galvin said to Harold.

"I do not wish to strip you bare," retorted the king shoving one brawny hand up with palm out. "I know you are sending men and arms to the other lords also, and I still cannot understand how you can afford to do so. I have sufficient..."

"Nonsense. You would be doing me a favor," said Galvin with a pleasant smirk on his face and a clasp to Harold's back. "Too many men on the battlements is no blessing as you quite know. They hamper each other. I told you of those rings of fire my master smith invented. They work fine, but you need room to light and fling the loops over the walls. My men can also show yours the construction of these devices if you wish."

"Well...a tempting offer." Harold rubbed the rough stubble on his chin as he gazed down thinking. He looked up, realizing others stood before him, and then his vision rested on Marcos standing, patiently waiting to be recognized. Harold's mouth dropped open in amazement and then broadened into a wide smile. "We thought you dead," the king exclaimed as he strode forward. He smacked the younger man on the shoulder and pounded his back.

"Almost, Sire," Marcos replied. He filled the king in on his adventures since being separated from the rest of the party, what he'd done, and the demons he'd seen and fought.

"*Tengus*, huh, and *nar-riders* also?" Harold shot Galvin a sideways look of concern. "This is no small evil we fight, then. Matters are worse than we feared, and have grown even in the short time we've been here."

"All the more reason to take the help I am offering you," Galvin said quickly.

Marcos studied the stone blocks on the floor and said, "Forgive me, my liege. I failed you. I swore I would vanquish the wyvern, and instead lost the men who stood by me, and killed the monster not." He waited for Harold to give him a sound rebuking.

Harold saw the remorse in Marcos's face, the slump of his shoulders. "This was my fault," the king said at last. "I should have realized all my men could not stand against the beast and ordered you to flee with me. Standing against the beast was a brave thing you did, and I cannot fault you for the loss of the men. I am still surprised you and Lady Kenya survived at all."

Marcos stiffened as if stung by a hornet. "Thank you, Sire," he murmured, gazing at his uncle, stone-faced. "Still, I sorrow for the loss of my men. I will do better in the future, for you and Evertree."

"Hmmm…" The king's eyes swept over Marcos and landed on Kenya as he arrived at a decision. "In this case I have a mission for both of you. Accompany Lord Galvin tomorrow when he leaves and assess if he can truly spare the men and supplies he offers to Evertree. Lady Kenya, Jessica has requested to ride with Lord Galvin to his fortress. At first, I was unwilling, since I cannot spare the men or the women to ride with her, but I trust Marcos will defend his cousin to the death. Both of you have shown courage on this venture, and luck, too. I will not need your assistance after this conclave, but you have shown a shrewd understanding of the hazards facing Evertree, so I will grant her request and on this trip you will act as her lady-in-waiting also."

A wave of homesickness overwhelmed Kenya and she instinctively reached out and touched Marcos's arm to reassure herself a friend was near to stand by her. *Oh, God no. I'd rather kill myself. I want to go back to* Evertree, *home, anywhere except with these two people.* "Your Majesty," Kenya began tactfully, "I will be glad to go, but do you think it is wise for the Lady Jessica to accompany Lord Galvin's party? There might well be great danger stalking the land as Marcos has already explained, and even with Lord Galvin and his men as protection, what possible purpose could her presence serve—"

"The princess was invited by Lord Galvin," The king replied, dismissing Kenya's objections with a flick of his wrist. "I dare not risk any of the other women of the court who accompanied us here. Far too dangerous, and, at least you have endured hardships on this journey and know what to expect in case there is danger." He said to Marcos, "After your ordeal, are you fit to travel, or should I dispatch someone else? If you refuse, I assure you no dishonor will be placed on you."

Marcos bowed low and touched the hilt of his sword. "As you command, My Liege."

Lord Galvin watched Kenya avidly during this exchange, his eyes flicking from her face to Marcos and back again, as if speculating what their relationship might be and how he could profit from the connection.

"So be it." Harold said to Galvin, "I will leave these two to determine what aid is proper for you to bestow on me, with your thanks." He made a short bow to Galvin. "Now I am off. We leave on the morrow also to return to Evertree. Let us pray our passage is a safer and swifter one than traveling here."

As Harold strolled off to his chambers, Galvin watched him go with a tight smile on his face and said to Marcos and Kenya, "You need not worry about bringing supplies with you for the trip, or staying at my fortress. We are well protected and your every need shall be provided for, have no fear." He smirked at Marcos. "I understand all your gear was lost?"

Marcos nodded sheepishly. "Yes." He waved to his ripped clothing. "What I arrived with here on my back and in my saddlebag is all I have at the moment."

"I shall send one of my men to King Harold's section of the castle with warm clothes, and sleeping blankets for you." He winked at Marcos. "We brought extra, and the mountains of my home grow cold at night and the wind blows strong." He bowed to each. "Now I must be off also to see my men are prepared for the trip tomorrow. If you will excuse me?" He spun on the balls of his feet and strode off.

As Galvin left Marcos remarked to Kenya, "You still do not trust him? He seems like a very affable host to me."

Kenya bite back a reply, her misgivings unaltered.

A blood red sun greeted Lord Galvin's party the next morning as they mounted their horses and set out from Cliffward. Kenya rode beside Marcos, now outfitted in a sturdy leather tunic, pants, and a warm cloak wrapped around his shoulders. Jessica shot glares at Kenya, who trailed behind her and Lord Galvin, and refused to look at the princess, instead she kept her eyes fixed straight ahead on the bleak landscape, only turning to Marcos when he said something or wished to talk to him.

Jessica swung to Galvin and remarked with contempt, "Why did you agree to allow *her* to accompany us? Really, a wretched, smelly creature this woman is. My father could not locate anyone better? After all, I did bring my own ladies-in-waiting with me."

"Your father's wish," Galvin replied smoothly. "Apparently he has faith the Lady Kenya can keep herself alive and you with it in case of danger." He glanced over his shoulder at Kenya. "She does not appear to be so wretched at all, though, and I doubt there will be much danger, but have no concern. When we reach my castle, I have servants aplenty to cater to your every whim. You needn't bother at all with her if this is your wish."

"Thank goodness," Jessica replied loud enough for Kenya to hear. The princess threw Galvin a quick smile. "You are too good to me. I will enjoy this outing, I think, with you."

Kenya stared at the back of the princess's head. *You are too good to me, too. The farther away from that bitch, the better I'll like it.* All through the morning, and well into the afternoon, Jessica left no opportunity untouched to discover some way of belittling Kenya, whether it was by some snide remark, or completely ignoring her to the point she whined to Galvin her father supplied no one to wait on her during the ride. Kenya kept her temper—barely, but her jaw muscles ached from clamping her mouth shut, and her teeth hurt.

As she and Marcos sat by their own little campfire that night, Kenya asked Marcos, "Why is Jessica so mean to me? Since the first time we met I..." She shook her head in disgust and snuck a glance at the princess, who laughed at a remark made by Galvin and laid one small hand on his shoulder while gazing up into his face.

"Jessica treats all with contempt," remarked Marcos. He took a bite of the concentrated travel rations they carried on the road, swallowed, and added, "Since birth everyone has fawned on our princess, jumped at her slightest word. In this case, I believe Jessica feels her father has placed you as a watchdog over her. Someone who will carry tales back to him about what she has done when out of his sight. My cousin resents your presence, especially since you show no fear of her or her wrath and not directly subject to her as her own ladies are."

"I heard stories of her from the other women when we were on the road," admitted Kenya thoughtfully, "not nice stories." She watched Princess Jessica and Lord

Galvin. "What do they see in each other? Playthings? Lovers?"

"Playthings, yes. A royal husband for Jessica if she thinks she can control him. My cousin knows one day she will rule over Evertree, but it is always wiser to have a man by her side. For Galvin?" Marcos pursed his lips in thought. "His holding is poor, the land mountainous and rocky. Their only exports are trees and furs, and not much of those since winter sets in early in the high wastes. A union with Evertree whose land is rich and in need of lumber for shipbuilding would be a good one for him."

"A match made in the stars," remarked Kenya, wryly. "I wonder if either will survive the union."

It took four days of hard riding to reach the fortress of Lord Galvin. Along the way, they wove deeper into the stark mountains, tall snow-covered alps covered in dense forest rising all around, or deep valleys shrouded in shadows.

In places, Kenya noticed trees cut down and asked Marcos, "How do they transport the lumber to market? Carry the wood by wagon?" She surveyed their back-trail, a rocky track with ruts from melting snow, hardly wide enough for a cart to travel. "It must be a terribly hard trip."

He laughed. "Of course not. Anything traveling this road carrying weight would break an axle at the first runnel, or sink deep in mud during spring and autumn rains." He swept his hand across the earth. "After the ground freezes in early winter the logs slide easily enough pulled by mules to the rivers and cast in to float downstream until the water freezes. After which, the lumber is stored in great piles until the rivers flow again during the summer. A short season, to be sure, but between the trees and trapping for furs the people survive."

Kenya nodded and swung in her saddle to survey the mountains and hollows. "If Galvin rules all this, why is he named lord and not king? At the council he was treated as an equal by the other rulers."

"A technicality," Marcos replied, scanning the bleak landscape surrounding their party also. "In this region each clan deems themselves independent of each other, and so acknowledge no one man as ruler over them, but," he issued a hearty laugh, "when Galvin blows his pipe, you can be sure they all dance to his tune and come running to his summons."

Galvin's castle rested on a high pinnacle of granite, devoid of trees with three sheer drop-offs on the flanks and back. The fourth side was a rugged slope, in places the rock worked by man so to allow horses or a single wagon to creep up the rough trail in single file. The lord hung back, waiting for Kenya and Marcos to ride abreast of him as their party rode up the path.

"So, Sir Marcos, Lady Kenya, what do you think of my place of residence?" Galvin waved a hand at the stout rock walls rising high in the near distance and the crevices surrounding his fortress. "Protection enough I would say against any attack, large or small. One reason I have soldiers to spare. I have no triple walls to defend such as Cliffward does. The terrain does it for me. You may tell Harold the same thing."

Marcos scanned the walls and sloping grounds. "A formidable keep indeed, Lord Galvin. I do not think I could breach your battlements with a thousand men."

This invoked a chuckle from Galvin. He traced a line with his finger along the trail to the portcullis rising to admit the party's entrance. "And if you had a thousand men to your back, where would you place them? A scant hundred or so can attack at any time."

"True," Marcos murmured as he surveyed the limited amount of space.

Galvin gestured to the ground. "And if an enemy decided to tunnel under my walls, he must dig through solid rock. Not a nice task winter or summer."

"What happens in case of a siege?" Kenya asked suddenly. "True, this place is impregnable, but an army wouldn't have to attack your walls. All they'd do is squat here on the trail and starve you out. You have no way of bringing in food or escape if escape need be."

Galvin studied her with new respect and stroked his chin. "I can see why King Harold asked you to ride along, Lady Kenya. A good question, indeed. I keep five years of stores in case the enemy wishes to play that game, and I guarantee you, no one would stay outside my walls in the dead of winter for one season, let alone five."

Kenya started to say something else, and then held her peace. *I wonder how he would fare against these dark forces I hear so much about, or a flock of those wyverns that attacked us on the trail?*

They rode through the massive entrance, the sound of the horse's hoof-beats creating muted echoes off the stone walls, and entered a bleak inner-courtyard.

A troll of a man with wisps of thin grey hair sticking out of a woolen cap in all directions rushed forward. "Lord Galvin, we are happy of your return," he exclaimed bobbing his head, a sickly smirk on his face. His eyes roved over the rest of the party, marking Jessica, Kenya, and Marcos. "I see you have brought guests as well. What a pleasant surprise." His tone left doubt whether the visitor's presence was pleasant or not.

Galvin dismounted. Servants and stable-hands appeared out of nowhere, unloading packs and luggage from horses and leading the animals away. Sarth," the lord said, "these are the Lady Jessica, King Harold's daughter, and Lady Kenya and Sir Marcos from his court. They are staying with us to observe our defenses," he flashed a smile at Jessica, "and to be entertained by our poor hospitality."

He waved Sarth forward and said to Marcos and Kenya, "Sarth is my steward." He chuckled and rubbed the side of his nose. "Knows more about the castle than I do, I would say. Good man." Sarth's mouth opened in a toothless grin. "He will conduct you to suitable rooms, and provide whatever you desire. I will show Princess Jessica personally to her chambers." He bowed low to Jessica and extended one hand. "If you will, my lady."

The princess took his fingers with a quick curtsy and the two disappeared into the castle. Sarth said, "Sir? Lady? If you will follow me, please, I will take you to your chambers," and swung about, trailing his lord at a good distance.

"Wait." Kenya hurried after him. "I have been charged as Lady-in-Waiting to the Princess Jessica," she explained to the steward, trying to sound as reasonable as possible, although Kenya wished she didn't have to put herself in the position. "My...our chambers," she shot a quick look at Marcos, "should be close to hers."

Sarth's shrewd eyes flicked from Kenya to the retreating figures of Galvin and Jessica as they marched up a winding staircase to the upper reaches of the keep. "I will try my best, Lady," he hedged carefully, "however...." The steward shrugged as if the matter was not entirely up to him.

Kenya quickly replied issuing an internal sigh of relief, "I quite understand. Whatever you arrange will be fine. I am sure you'll do your best. Inform the princess where I'm located and explain the circumstances to her if you will in case Jessica has any complaints."

The man nodded silently and plodded up the stone steps into the upper portion of the castle. Along the way, four servants fell in behind them, two men and two women, at a respectful distance behind the party. Sarth stopped before a stout oaken door and said to Marcos, "Your sleeping chamber. You should find this adequate sir." His eyes flicked to the two male servants. "These shall serve you." He said to Kenya, "Yours is the next chamber. They are connected by a common sitting room if you wish to converse. The princess, no doubt, is housed in the rooms above these next to Lord Galvin's. I will inform the princess of your location in case she needs you, or you her." He nodded to the two female servants who stood patiently waiting. "These will attend you, Lady, during your stay here. If there is anything you desire, inform them and it shall be speedily brought." The steward bowed and swung about to the staircase, first giving the servants a stern look, before he disappeared.

The two women rushed to the door and threw the portal wide open for Kenya to enter. She shot a quick look at Marcos who nodded silently back and disappeared into his chamber accompanied by the attendants.

The room was dark, well furnished with heavy drapes covering windows to keep out cold drafts, with another door leading out onto a balcony overlooking the mountains. The women set about lighting oil lamps, and turning down the four-poster bed complete with curtain. Kenya scanned the room curiously. Crossed axes, swords, and spears covered the walls along with shields painted with boars and stags. Tapestries of hunting scenes hung between the weapons, while a large painting of Lord Galvin himself clung to the wall directly opposite the bed. The eyes appeared to follow her every movement as she wandered about the room. Kenya sat on the edge of the mattress and bounced lightly. *Feather mattress, linen sheets and down pillows. Not bad.*

"Your packs are being brought now," the shorter of the two servants said after they'd completed opening the room. "Is there anything else we can fetch for you?"

Kenya wasn't use to having people wait on her, especially when she didn't know their names. "Who are you girl?"

The woman curtsied quickly and took a step forward. "My name is Aila, Lady." She waved a finger at the other girl. "This is Cadha, my sister." Her nose wrinkled and she stepped back quickly. "We are yours to command while you are here. Is there anything we can do for you?"

Kenya noted the quick step backward, and rubbed her forehead, felt grit from the long ride, and realized how filthy she was. "Is there some place I can wash?" Kenya held out her grimy hands, turning them over to show her palms. "I'm wearing four days' worth of dirt piled on, and," she cocked her head, sniffing at her armpit, "I must smell like a dead rat."

Cadha broke out into a tight smile and nodded knowingly. "I can well image, Lady, after such a long trip. Traveling here is a long dusty ride. It shall be taken care of." The girl sauntered out the door. After a short wait, returned accompanied by four husky men toting a large wooden washtub, which Cadna directed them to place carefully on the floor. The men hurried away only to return carrying bucket after bucket of steaming water and filled the tub, placing a tray of soap, linen washcloths and towels on the bed before they left. After the door closed, Kenya stripped and eased herself into the warm water with a sigh of relief. The tub was large enough to stretch out full length and Kenya submerged her head, resurfacing and blowing long black hair out of her face. She laid back and relaxed with a moan of pleasure letting the warm water ease away the aches.

While Kenya was bathing, a polite knock echoed on the door. Aila rushed to answer and whispered to whoever was outside. A hand reached in and Kenya's packs discreetly appeared. Aila issued a 'Thank you,' and took them.

Cadha handed over a cake of yellow soap and one of the washcloths. Kenya started at the top of her forehead, scrubbing herself raw downward, and digging out ingrained dirt from hands and feet she'd acquired from the dusty days on the trail. When satisfied with her appearance, Kenya rose and the attendants brought in buckets of lukewarm water, drowning her as they dumped pail after pail over her head to rinse off the soap.

"For you, Lady, if you will." Aila offered a masonry jar with a questioning expression on her face.

Kenya sniffed cautiously. "Not bad." She dipped a finger in and held the tip to her nose for a better smell. "What is it?"

"Rhubarb elixir and molasses water," the woman explained. "The mixture will keep your skin soft and smelling nice." Aila smiled mischievously. "The men like the smell too."

Kenya shrugged. She wasn't worried about men approaching and sniffing her. Well, maybe Marcos, but.... "Sure, why not." She rubbed her body with the lotion. "This stuff does smell nice," she commented feeling the smoothness of her skin.

After applying the elixir, Kenya donned fresh clothing from her pack, feeling more relaxed and comfortable than she had for many days. A knock on the connecting door between chambers sounded. Cadha rushed to open it and Marcos strolled in. "I see you thought the same idea I did," he said, eyeing the tub. He sniffed the air and then drew close and took a whiff of Kenya's neck. "But you smell better."

Kenya broke out into a giggle and felt an electric shock run through her body. "Why thank you sir," she exclaimed.

Marcos continued, "I have been told a banquet is being prepared for the arrival of Lord Galvin. Hungry?"

"Famished." Kenya said to her attendants, "Can someone show us the way, please?"

They marched down the staircase led by Aila into another part of the castle to the main hall. Workmen busily laid boards onto wooden supports for tables, and set benches for the guests to sit on. To amuse the waiting diners minstrels strolled about playing their instruments and singing ballads, mostly about the greatness of Lord Galvin and his mighty deeds of old or yet to come. Servants hurried about with tankards, filling goblets of wine or handing out containers to the guests who were without. Two cups found their way into Kenya and Marcos's hands.

An old man with a stiff grey beard and eye-patch ambled over to them. He nodded politely. "I am Baron Abos of the Ru clan. You two must be the new arrivals from Evertree. How fares the coastal people?" His one good eye studied them with interest.

"Well," Marcos began guardedly. He took a sip of wine and added, "We hear trouble stalks the western plains, and ran across much as we traveled here, but it is yet to move in our direction in any great number. How is the danger with you here in the mountains?"

The old man bobbed his head. "We have been lucky, also. Whatever ancient evil has arisen has not troubled our doorstep yet although we hear of murderous beasts every day." He lowered his voice and said, "I fear it is only a matter of time, though, before conflict spreads across the whole region as war did in ancient times."

"Let us hope such an event doesn't happen," Kenya said with sincerity taking a gulp of wine from her goblet.

"We are graced here to have Lord Galvin," the baron confided in a low tone. He waved a hand vaguely toward the stairs to the upper chambers. "Now if only the clans will unite fully behind him for once and acknowledge his kingship my worries will be laid to rest."

The hearty odor of roasted meats accompanied by wood smoke filled the chamber as cooks carried platters of beef, pork and chickens into the room and buglers summoned the guests to the tables. Pies, both savory and sweet followed as the guests eagerly took seats and waited for Lord Galvin to make his appearance on his raised platform at the front of the chamber.

The baron dropped down heavily next to Kenya on the bench, inhaling the aroma of the foods and fingering a platter of beef. He remarked, "Galvin sets a fine table, doesn't he."

Marcos leaned forward and said across Kenya, "Indeed he does, Baron. King Harold himself does not do better."

Directly opposite Kenya was a small staircase leading up to one of the highest towers in the castle. A grey haired crone of a woman sat on the stone steps watching the feasters with interest, but not attempting to join. Her quick bird eyes flicked from face to face, finally locking onto Kenya's with interest, and for a moment, she received an impression of amusement and something else—disdain?

"Who is the woman on the steps," Kenya asked the baron in a whisper. "A servant? A Lady? Why does the old biddy sit and watch everyone? Why doesn't she join us?"

The baron looked up quickly and as fast away again. "Feg," he muttered keeping his gaze fixed on the tabletop before him. "Servant, yes, but she has no duties and will not join us. Feg is different…."

"A pensioner?"

The baron issued a low snort. "One might say so. The woman arrived at this castle the day Lord Galvin was born." His eyes shifted to the woman and quickly to Kenya. "No one knows from where, and immediately took charge of the infant. Again, no one knows why the old lord and lady allowed her to do so. They possessed nursemaids aplenty."

"Odd; and she never left?"

"No," replied the baron, "and after Galvin was weaned, never attended him again for his upbringing. Feg took up residence in the highest room of the fortress and lives there until this day."

"I'm surprised Lord Galvin's father didn't kick her out," said Marcos, who'd listened to the story with interest. He studied the old woman and added, "Sounds as if the woman was very presumptuous."

The baron lowered his voice even further, hardly above a whisper. "Some say she is a witch and laid a spell on the old lord and Galvin." He shuddered. "I would not try to toss her out. Only Lord Galvin visits her. The servants fear her."

Witch? I wonder.... Kenya studied the woman closely while trying not to appear to do so. She couldn't be certain, but this Feg resembled the *ur-vins* in size, shape and the questioning sarcastic gaze.

The arrival of lord Galvin and Princess Jessica at the feast interrupted the conversation. Galvin raised his hands. "This is the Princess Jessica from Evertree, my honored guest. You will treat her as if she were me," he exclaimed in a loud voice. Jessica blushed, and curtsied to the crowd. "Now let the feast begin."

People rose, cheered, and sat to begin to eat.

"I can see how much we rate," Kenya muttered. "Not even an honorable mention."

Marcos shrugged, cut off a hunk of black bread with his belt knife, and buttered it. "I am the second son of a second son. We get used to being ignored." He jabbed a boiled tuber and laid the vegetable on his trencher with a wink to Kenya. "But as long as the food is good, who cares?" He took a bite of the bread and smiled.

He's right. Who am I to complain? Soft bed, good food, and we'll be leaving in a couple of days. I'll be shut of Jessica when we arrive at Evertree, and my life will be back to normal.

The aroma of the food on the table finally broke into Kenya's conscience. She realized how hungry she was and filled her trencher with vegetables, reaching out with a long arm, nabbing a roasted chicken quarter from a platter before they all disappeared. A hollow cackling rang across the hall. Kenya looked up, startled from her meal and glanced around for the noise. The old crone on the steps was gone as if she never was.

Chapter Eight

"Good night, Lady Kenya." Marcos issued Kenya a warm smile and short bow as he exited the common room and swung the door open to his bedchamber. "Sleep well. I am sure tomorrow will be a busy day. Galvin has promised us a tour of his battlements and all the defenses."

Kenya entered her bedchamber. Aila had lite lamps and stood waiting by the poster bed. The girl drew back the curtain. "Sleep now, Lady?" she asked.

A yawn broke past Kenya's lips. The feather bed looked so inviting. "Yes. You needn't stay." She didn't know if the woman and Cadha planned to wait on her all night, or not, but didn't want to be a bother. There was really no reason for them to remain anyway.

"I will be setting up a cot in the next room, Aila explained. "Either I or Cadha will be here all night. If you need us, call." With that, the girl disappeared through the door, leaving Kenya alone to prepare for sleep.

Kenya stripped off her clothes and fell onto the mattress, sliding her legs between the fine linen sheets, drawing it up to her neck, and dragging a heavy woolen blanket over her body. She snuggled deep into the mattress, stretched, and fell asleep at once.

The room was cold. Colder still were the stones on her bare feet. Kenya briefly wondered what she was doing standing in the chamber, in the dark, yet she could see plainly, and herself sleeping in the bed. Kenya dismissed the thought with a narrow heightened awareness. She had urgent business to attend to. She was summoned.

Kenya stepped cautiously into the common room, careful to remain silent. She needn't bothered. Her footfalls made no sound on the stone. Aila snored gently on a cot, face turned away from Kenya's door. Kenya crept out of the chamber, wandered silent hallways, and located a single staircase leading upward to the top of the fortress.

I know these steps. The steps the woman Feg sat on at supper.

Kenya felt light as if her body was a feather drifting in the wind. Amazed, she still saw perfectly well in the semi-darkness with only the occasional flickering oil lamp attached to brackets on the wall to light the way. She climbed, a silent wraith, until she could go no farther.

A heavy oaken door stood in her path, blackened with age. Kenya placed a palm against the surface and pushed. The portal swung noiselessly open.

A room filled with sweet smelling smoke confronted her, emitted from an iron brazier set low on the stone floor.

Parchment scrolls lined the walls in wooden cubicles while shelves containing leather bound books stood against the walls. Above, more pictures of hunting scenes covered the open spots as in her chamber, along with brightly colored tapestries depicting swirling lines disappearing into dots in the center.

The wall hangings, books, and scrolls kept slipping out of focus, however, as if another room superimposed on top of this one, shifting when she concentrated on any part too long.

In front of one tapestry, a black, wavering mist awaited her. The summons issued from within. Kenya hurried, knowing she was expected.

The cold of nothingness, the absence of being, overwhelmed her as she entered the chilled fog. Pain swept into her body, a keen wailing echoed in her ears. Kenya took another step and the sensation ceased. She found herself in the room she'd vacated a moment before, this one occupied by Lord Galvin and the crone Feg. They stood, hungrily watching her approach.

"See, I told you the girl would come to our summons," whispered the woman to Galvin. "Do as I have told you. Link your mind to hers. The other one we have ensnared already, but this is the key to what we desire."

Kenya tried to speak, cry out. The muscles in her jaws bunched and she quivered in the attempt, but discovered she could not. Lord Galvin's hand reached out and grasped her firmly by the wrist. She felt a tugging, a flash of light, and together they stood before a door in a misty, silvery chamber.

Sing for me wordsmith. Galvin's words echoed in her mind and ears. *Make your song open the door for us.*

Song? Kenya didn't know any songs to open doors. Where was this place, anyway? Kenya glanced left and right. She stood on nothing—the total absence of everything. No sky above, no floor below. The sole object the portal before her waiting for words to fling the entrance open wide.

When Kenya hesitated, Galvin's voice rang out all about her, *Do it now, woman. As I command.*

Some unseen force goaded her into action. Kenya rebelled, her eyes narrowed, flashes of anger bubbled up inside her mind at Galvin's order. *Arrogant bastard. Thinks he can order me around as if I were a maid, and I'll jump like a trained monkey, huh?* Kenya opened her lips and chanted,

> *"Dreams unfocused sought my mind,*
> *Draw me close and open wide.*
> *I sing for you a song of grace,*
> *Let us enter, souls to test."*

The words weren't a tune, certainly not the type she would compose and try to sing, anyway. Kenya couldn't see what good they would do floating in a void.

The words flew around her mouth like silver birds, changing into fierce white darts of light igniting the air with their glow at the passing. The bolts struck the surface of the portal and disappeared within. To Kenya's amazement, the door silently swung open with a brilliance of shimmering color blazing out and bathing her body.

Mesmerized, drawn by the secret charm of the place, Kenya took a step forward over the threshold.

Invisible fingers jerked her back roughly.

You stay here, woman. This is for me. Galvin's voice echoed with an arrogance Kenya couldn't believe possible. He strode past eagerly and took her place before the portal.

The door slammed shut in his face.

A bellow of rage escaped the man's lips. A thunderclap accompanied by a flash of light exploded around them. Kenya tumbled through the void, spinning in a kaleidoscope of colored emptiness from which she found no escape.

Kenya bolted upright, her body covered in a thin layer of sweat. She lay in bed, the last flickering of the empty oil lamp casting dancing shapes on the walls and tapestries. Was it all a dream? Lord Galvin? The old witch? The room of desires?

How did I...?

Still trembling, Kenya slipped out of bed, quietly tiptoed to the door of the common room and gently swung it open. Peering out, the servant still slept soundly on her cot. Kenya wandered back to her bed and lay down, thinking.

It must be a dream. Some horrible nightmare from the long trip and excitement of the day.

Suppressing a yawn with the back of her hand, Kenya drifted off to sleep.

***

"Did you have troubling dreams last night?"

Kenya woke at daybreak, dressed, and discovered Marcos already waiting for her in the common room. His brown hair wet and tousled, hastily combed back with his fingers. They shared a cup of sage tea from a pewter service on the table and strolled downstairs for breakfast. The events of the night still confused in Kenya's mind.

Marcos looked at her curiously. "Nothing out of the ordinary," he replied. The warrior rubbed the stubble on his cheek. "In fact I slept rather well. Must be this cold mountain air and the long trip. Why?"

"It's probably nothing." Kenya took a seat on a bench next to him. The odor of fresh baked breads and frying ham filled the air. "Last night I dreamt I was in a place. Galvin and the woman Feg were there also this time. Then the lord and I were in the dream place and he wanted me to open a door...."

"Did you?" Marcos swung his complete attention on her.

"Yes," Kenya replied slowly, thinking hard, "but when he tried to enter, the door slammed in his face."

"What happened then," Marcos asked eagerly. "Did you enter too?"

Kenya chuckled and shook her head. "No. I found myself waking up in bed."

Marcos fell silent, thinking. Platters of food arrived and set on the table. The rest of the guests fell on the bounty and piled their trenchers high, beginning to eat.

"Sometimes dreams are dreams," Marcos remarked slowly as he chewed and swallowed. "Brought on by past events or worries about events yet to be," He selected a warm roll, split it open and spread on jam, "and sometimes they are more. I remember you telling me Galvin one time asked you to open the door you saw in a vision."

"Yes, but...." Was Marcos accusing Galvin of her nightmare? How could he.... "I never left my bed."

Marcos lowered his voice to a whisper, peeking sideways at the people sitting beside them eating. All were engrossed in their food or private conversations of their own. "He is a lord, and so commands great magic. The witch Feg may also traffic in the dark arts, who knows? From what we heard last night, it sounds as if it may be so. If a person has no conscience, there are ways of separating a person's soul from their bodies for a time, uh, discorporating that which makes them human, without killing the person, and use the portion with no flesh for their own ends."

Appalled by the thought, Kenya's expressive eyes opened wide. What Marcos talked about sounded close to rape or murder. She whispered back, "Do you really think that's what happened to me? Galvin and Feg stole my soul to open a door to another world without my knowledge?"

Marcos raised his hands, dropped them, and started to fill his trencher from a platter of fish without looking at her. "I know not. Nevertheless, I have a small knowledge of potions," he said in a low voice. "Tonight, if I can locate the ingredients without Galvin's knowing, I will concoct a brew that should stop any such trafficking. Tell me if this happens again during the day."

Kenya mulled over these strange revelations while eating, hardly tasting the food in her mouth. Had Galvin possessed her somehow? To what end? To gain entrance to the room where all things were possible, of course. She scanned the chamber, searching for Galvin. He wasn't there, nor was Jessica, or the woman called Feg.

A servant sauntered by carrying a platter of baked bread. "Excuse me," Kenya said, "has Lord Galvin come down yet to eat? I haven't seen him this morning."

"Lord Galvin breakfasts in his room, m'lady," the woman replied, "as is his usual custom." She waited patiently to see if Kenya had any other questions or requests.

"The Princess Jessica," Kenya persisted with an air of pretended concern, "she breakfasts in her room, also?" When the woman hesitated, Kenya added, "I am Princess Jessica's Lady-in-Waiting. I should really know if she wants me, or her location if I need attend to her."

Relief shone on the servant's face. "Oh, no, Lady. The Princess Jessica is with Lord Galvin. All her wants are taken care of for now."

I'm sure they are. "Thank you."

As Marcos and Kenya finished eating, Sarth appeared at Marcos's elbow. "When you have concluded breakfasting, Sir, Lady, Lord Galvin requests your presence on the battlements. I will wait for you to don warm clothing and show you the way."

"I am done now," Marcos said, standing. "Lady Kenya?"

Kenya popped a last bit of sausage into her mouth, chewed, and swallowed. "All through here," she replied sucking on her fingers, rising also.

"The lord has called out his whole guard," The steward informed Kenya and Marcos as they trudged upward after stopping at their rooms to wrap themselves in heavy cloaks, and then continued up along the long winding staircase toward the parapets of the castle. "Quite impressive, I must say."

They passed one landing and Sarth paused long enough to cast a thumb at a stone alcove where narrow slits built into the wall lead to the outside. "Archer's notches, if need be," he explained, holding an imaginary bow and drawing back the string. "They surround the wall. Even those sides abutting the cliffs, where no one is able to approach." Marcos nodded as if this was to be expected, but made no comment. Kenya said nothing. She followed

Marcos's lead and bobbed her head up and down in agreement.

They reached the top of the staircase and Sarth swung a door open for them leading to the outside. "After you," he murmured in deference with a bow of his head.

Kenya stepped out onto the walkway and a cold, bitter wind smacked her face and twisted the long hair into tight coils. Vertigo swept Kenya as she gazed passed the battlements at a vista of peaks with no apparent bottom. She clutched at Marcos's bicep for support.

He wrapped a protective arm around her. "Are you okay?"

"Yes," Kenya gulped, regaining her composure and releasing him. "I don't do well with heights, and I didn't realize we'd climbed so high."

"Not so high, m'lady," Sarth piped in with a wave of his hand. "Remember, we sit on top of a mountain."

"*Ho.*" Galvin strode toward Kenya and Marcos, bundled in heavy furs, a broad smile on his face. He jabbed a finger left and right along the walk. Men crowded every few feet standing at the ready. "Do you think I have enough warriors to hold my keep under any attack?"

"More than enough, I would say," replied Marcos as he scanned the soldiers facing them.

"Of course not all would be up here at the same time," said Galvin smoothly, "too many. Did Sarth show you the notches for the archers below?"

Kenya said, "Indeed he did, Lord."

Galvin nodded as if he expected this. "Some would be manning the notches, others waiting on the staircases to replace fallen comrades as they are needed." He waved Marcos and Kenya forward. "Follow me and I shall show you the new weapon my master smith has invented for our defense." He spun and strolled along the battlement with Marcos and Kenya trailing until they arrived at a group of men standing beside three thick, straw covered hoops. A smoking bucket full of coals with torches poking out stood well away from the soldiers.

"These are weapons?" Kenya asked incredulous.

Marcos approached the hoops, prodded one with his foot, and then bent close to sniff. He straightened, nodding, while he stroked his jaw. "I think I see already what your master smith has in mind, if it works. Clever."

"Indeed. He is a most clever man," said Galvin, smirking. "First he took a coil of wire and wrapped the metal in linen soaked with brandy and pig's fat. Next he covered the cloth in pitch mixed with brimstone, cotton, and added straw. Watch what happens when the circle is lit."

Galvin nodded to the soldiers standing by. Two of the men picked up the heavy loop on either side while a third ran to grab a torch from the bucket. Kenya noticed the two holding the hoop wore long, thick leather gauntlets up to their elbows. Scorch marks covered fingers and hands.

"Stand well back," cautioned Galvin throwing out an arm in glee as he took a step backward himself from the loop, "by the parapet of the battlement. Watch what happens when the circle is thrown over the edge."

Marcos and Kenya backpedaled and swung to the edge of the wall. Galvin nodded and the soldier holding the torch ran forward, igniting the hoop in several places. The burning loop flared and the two clutching the coil tossed the flaming cloth over the side of the keep.

Kenya peeked over the edge and watched as the fabric bounced against the stone walls, causing no damage, but flaming higher as the wind whipped around, sending a shower of burning sparks in every direction. The cloth, starting to unravel, struck the ground at the base of the fortress scattering flames in a wide circle.

"See," shouted Galvin, obviously pleased by the demonstration, "imagine yourself an assaulting army standing there as my fire hoops rained down on you, burning clothes, flesh, and weapons. How long would they hold their ground and fight before they bolted and ran?"

"Not long," admitted Marcos. He stroked his chin, gazing at the fire below in speculation, imagining the damage the hoops would cause whether a soldier was covered in armor or not. The cloth still flamed, showing no signs of dying out, while burning the short, dry grass at the bottom of the wall and creating a wide black spot around the circle.

Kenya asked a question, which was on her mind since they first arrived. "Lord Galvin, we see you are well prepared for any assault by man, but traveling from Evertree our party was attacked by flying beasts, wyverns, I believe they are called. They soared through the air and breathed a poisonous gas exploding into flame at the touch of fire. What," she gestured to the base of the wall, "will fire hoops, or for this matter, archers do to stop an attack from above."

"You leap straight to the throat of the matter, Lady Kenya," Galvin replied with a knowing bob of his head. "I like the way you think." He spun on his toes. "Accompany me," he shouted over his shoulder, striding along the walkway, "and I shall show you how we would deal with such a monster."

The milling soldiers jumped out of their lord's way as he hurried along the battlements, Kenya and Marcos trying hard to keep pace with him. He strode around a curve in the walkway and stopped. "This is what we have in store for wyverns, or fire drakes as we call the devils in these mountains and their kin, if they decide to attack this fortress."

Twenty largish machines on wooden carriages lined up along the walk. Three-man crews stood at the ready by each device. To Kenya's eyes, they appeared to be gigantic crossbows pointing to the sky with cranks to pull the string back. Galvin stepped forward and withdrew a five-foot bolt from a wooden case tipped with a sharp iron barb. He held the miniature javelin out to Kenya with a shake. "My wasps have a large sting, do they not, lady, and one machine can throw a shaft six hundred feet to the mark. I moved the bolt throwers here to make more room for my troops, but if battle calls they are spaced every one hundred feet along the wall." He swung his attention to Marcos "Do you wish to see a demonstration?"

"A display of their operation is not necessary," Marcos replied easily with a wave of his hand. "We have machines similar to these at Evertree, however instead of firing bolts, they throw red hot cannonballs, which set the sails of approaching ships on fire, or burn through their hulls."

Galvin nodded shrewdly. "I thought as much. Lady Kenya, what is your opinion? Am I protected from above as well as below?"

Kenya could think of no other objections to the defense of the fortress. "I think you are will fortified against any attack, Lord Galvin."

"You will tell King Harold this?" Galvin said earnestly, "both of you, so he will have no qualms against accepting my men to help him? During this time of trouble in the land, we must all strive to assist each other. My greatest fear is if one falls, we all fall. I wish to do my part to stop this menace before it has a foothold in our land. I have offered Harold twenty of my men, but I can as easily send him fifty, for Evertree is the lifeblood of this land, our conduit to the rest of the world."

"I can see no reason he would not accept your people," Marcos replied slowly, thinking, "especially in the construction of the fire loops you showed us. Your wasps are easy enough to duplicate. They are similar to our catapults and may even be modified to fire arrows."

The lord slapped his hands together in glee. "Good. Now I must be gone. Duty calls, and although my personal supervision is slight, still," he shrugged, "when my people are in need I must respond."

The three strolled back where the steward waited. "Feel free to walk around my keep, the grounds, anywhere you wish," Galvin said expansively. "Talk to the people if you will. In fact," he paused, considering, "I wish you would. Perhaps a notion will come to your mind, some fact, which I have not thought of. Any you think of, report to me before you leave."

"If we notice anything worth reporting we will, Lord," Marcos assured Galvin.

Kenya asked, "Lord Galvin? I haven't seen Princess Jessica this morning. Is the lady to make an appearance?" Kenya cringed inwardly, but felt it was her duty to add, "Is she feeling all right? Should I attend to her?" *Please say no.*

Galvin guffawed and slapped his thigh. "What a girl. Stayed up over-late last night, jabbering like a bird to me. I am afraid this morning the lady sleeps late. I am sure Jessica will be up and around, when, I cannot say, though. Your presence is not required. The princess has servants of mine aplenty to wait on her."

Sarth stepped forward. "I will assign one of the staff to accompany you on your tour of the fortress," he offered.

And give us a very guided tour, I bet. "It won't be necessary," Kenya replied. "I'm sure we won't become lost, and I wouldn't want to take someone away from their household duties."

The steward backed off with a quick glance at Galvin, who raised his shoulders slightly and let them drop. "As you prefer. Now I must be gone. I will see you tonight when we sup." He spun back to the stairway with Sarth in step whispering in his ear.

Once the two were out of hearing, Kenya remarked, "Galvin seems eager for us to take his men back to Evertree with him, don't you think? Odd."

Marcos scratched his cheek. "Now you mention it, he did try hard to convince us, didn't he? And he keeps pressing the issue. The secret of his fire hoops is well worth having, but fifty men? Unless they are well versed in the use of magic, they would make little difference in a battle or a siege."

"And again, his men can be kept below on the staircases for reserves as he said," added Kenya. "They needn't crowd each other up here on the battlements at all."

"True." Marcos surveyed the walkway of the battlement. His eyes rested on the fire loops lying in a pile. "These I would examine further," he said as he strolled over to the men standing by. He bent over to pick one up.

"Be careful, sir," one of the soldiers advised. "The pitch will rub off and the tar is impossible to remove from your arms and fingers." He pulled off the long leather gauntlets he wore. "Put these on."

Marcos accept the gloves gingerly. "Thank you."

He drew the gloves over his hands, and lifted one side of the loop with a grunt. "Heavy," he muttered. "I see why you need two men to throw the ring."

The soldier who'd given Marcos the gauntlets replied, "One man can fling the loop, but it takes strength." He added with a gruff chuckle, "Of course, when you toss the loop by yourself you must be quick enough not to set yourself ablaze, either. This is why when we practice two men are used. The teams must learn to coordinate their efforts and toss in unison."

The warriors gave Marcos and Kenya a slow motion demonstration of lighting and throwing the hoops without using the fire. When they'd finished Kenya said to Marcos, "Galvin said we could wander about his keep and grounds as we will, right?"

Marcos was in the middle of picking up a fire hoop to see if he could fling the loop by himself. He dropped the ring, and nodded, perplexed. "Indeed he did. Why? Did you want to take a tour?"

Kenya seized his hand. "C'mon. I know exactly what I want to see." She dragged Marcos away from the soldiers and back to the steps leading down to the main hall.

Confused, Marcos asked, "Where are you taking us? We have been here before. I do not…."

Kenya dropped Marcos's hand and ran eagerly to the staircase they'd seen Feg sitting on the night before. She took two hesitant steps upward and said to Marcos over her shoulder, "These are the stairs I saw in my dream. I wonder if they lead to the same room." Cautiously she trudged upward, straining her ears for any sound, Marcos close on her heels. After what seemed an eternity, they halted before the exact blackened door as in her vision. Kenya tried the latch. It would not open.

"This is the door," Kenya exclaimed in frustration, rattling the latch again. "I know I have the right door."

"At least we know this part of your dream was true," agreed Marcos as he turned to leave.

Kenya issued a deep sigh and followed. Behind, the creaking of the door opening brought her to a halt. Both spun around as one.

The old woman Feg stood watching the two, a malicious gleam in her eye, and wisps of hair like dirty snow around her face. A thin woolen shawl draped about the thin shoulders for warmth. "You dare to disturb my rest?" the crone hissed. Her mouth worked as if ready to spit in their faces.

"We, uh…" Kenya sputtered, taking an involuntary step backward, courage evaporating, and bumping into Marcos who steadied her with hands on her back. "I…."

Feg swung the door open wide. "Well, if you are so curious about me, enter. Your man friend, too, if he will."

The old woman watched Kenya, studying her face and waiting for a reply.

Kenya endured the scrutiny for as long as possible then glanced over her shoulder at Marcos who shrugged.

Legs weak, Kenya summoned up her courage. "Yes, I think we will." Showing more bravery than she felt Kenya strode forward through the doorway.

Chapter Nine

The room was exactly as Kenya remembered the chamber to be, with the bookshelves and scrolls lining every space.

Except the chamber was not the same.

The shifting of images was gone. Even the strange tapestry hanging on the wall stretched before her, but this time with no shimmering mist before it. No scented smoke drifted from the brazier. The room was cold. A typical chamber for an old, but respected pensioner, who wished her privacy.

The same place, I'm positive. Was I having a dream within a dream? I know this land isn't real—Impossible. As unbelievable as my words manifesting before my eyes. It doesn't happen this way.

Feg hobbled before Kenya and Marcos, settled into a rocking chair, drew the shawl tighter around her scrawny body with a groan of relief. "What brings you to my door, Lady?" she asked, eyes seeking Kenya, ignoring Marcos. Kenya swore she heard a silent chuckle in the old woman's voice as if she knew the answer already and found Kenya's presence here in the room humorous and expected.

"Lord Galvin granted us permission to walk around his keep and grounds, investigating his ability to ward off attack by any army of demons who attempted to breach his walls," Marcos answered at once, taking a step forward in an attempt to protect Kenya from Feg's glare with his body. "We saw the stairs leading up and we decided to climb them here to see where they led."

"I see." The crone murmured. She nodded, her attitude indicating she knew this information, but Marcos's answer making little impression on the arrogance displayed in her glare. Feg kept her vision steady of Kenya, waiting for a reply.

"I—I...was here last night," Kenya finally blurted out, realizing how ridiculous the statement sounded. A chilled wind blew through her bones, not knowing, dreading a reply of yes or no with a sense of foreboding flooding her soul no matter what the response would be.

A dry cackle like the snapping of brittle twigs answered her. "I think I would have noticed, Lady if you graced my apartment during the night," said Feg, glancing around the small chamber, her eyes lighting up in mock surprise as she studied the corners. "I have not left this room since yesterday evening. In fact I fell asleep in this very chair."

"But I saw you," Kenya explained, waving a hand toward the tapestry. "Beyond, in the next room. Both you and Lord Galvin waited for me to arrive."

The cackle rose again into high-pitched humor.

Either this woman is crazy or I am. She is playing with me as a cat plays with a catnip toy or a ball of string.

As if to confirm Kenya's thoughts, the old woman said, "There is no room beyond my hanging. Only the wall and the outside beyond. What you see here is all there is." Feg added in a sly voice, taunting, Kenya, "You think I am a witch who can float in the air and walk through walls?" The crone ran a hand over the shawl covering her. "These old bones can barely rise from this chair, but to satisfy your curiosity I will show you what lies beyond my poor wall decorations." To prove her point Feg rose with a groan and drew back the hanging, revealing grey stone blocks held together with mortar.

The mocking expression on the woman's face as she held the fabric aside and her own mounting frustration made Kenya shout, *"I don't know what to believe anymore."*

As Kenya shouted, Marcos focused on her face, alarmed by her outburst. He said, "We had best be leaving Lady Kenya. We have seen all there is to be seen in this part of the castle and we still have much to view if we are to give a good report to Harold after we leave."

Feg bobbed her head up and down. "The delay is my fault. I should not have kept you here so long talking. I am a poor old woman and sometimes forget those about me have work to do." The woman teetered to the door on her thin legs and opened it, nodding to herself in agreement. "No doubt we will meet again, Lady, before you depart. I hope while you are awake and not dreaming, as you seemed to have done. I assumed you have satisfied yourself as to my poor living chamber and your stay here is a pleasant one."

Kenya twisted around, darted out the door and leaped down the steps, taking two at a time in terror, her mind shaken to the core, the old woman's words still ringing in the air. *She knows. Feg knows I remember last night and is teasing me.*

Kenya stumbled into the main hall gasping for breath, halted her blind rush, and bend over panting hard, holding her side. A few startled heads swung in her direction from the inhabitants and a low mutter circulated around the room at her frightened appearance. Marcos wrapped his arm around her. "Are you all right? I thought you would kill yourself leaping down the staircase as you did."

Kenya managed a weak smile. "I'm okay now. The old biddy spooked the heck out of me, that's all. I swear she knew what I was talking about and baited me on purpose. What is going on here?" Kenya swallowed hard, and willed her heart to slow.

"Odd old lady, isn't she," Marcos agreed as he eyed the staircase. "Handed you a scare, huh? I do not blame you. Feg hardly noticed me, but still I felt the terror of her stare and laugh." Marcos pressed his face close to Kenya's ear. "Perhaps we should sneak back up to her room and tie the old woman up until we leave."

Kenya recognized the tone in his voice. "Don't try to make light of this. Feg is hiding something. I just don't know what it is, or why her plotting involves me."

Marcos still wasn't satisfied about Kenya's meaningless talk of Feg. "Well the old lady seemed harmless enough. Odd bird and I would not wish to associated with her every day, but maybe the woman is going senile in her old age."

"Feg is not senile. She is evil. I don't want to ever see that old crone again," Kenya exclaimed, standing with a shudder and wrapping her arms around her chest. "Witch she named herself and witch she is. I am sure of it."

Marcos released her. "I doubt we will ever see Feg again, Lady. Day after tomorrow we leave, and if what we have heard is true, the woman keeps to her room most of the time. From the looks of her I would say Feg can barely make the trip down the steps by herself."

"None too soon for me," Kenya snapped back. She took a deep breath, attempting to slow the shudders still racking her body, and straighten her shoulders. "C'mon, let's inspect the rest of this pile of rocks before it becomes too dark to see."

They strolled around the interior of the stone fortress poking their heads into storerooms and estimating provisions in case of a siege. Marcos pointed out to Kenya how the lower entrances and windows of the castle were easily sealed off in case of attack.

"Food they have, yes," Kenya wondered aloud to Marcos as they walked to the main exit, "but where do they find their water to drink and cook?" They stepped into the courtyard and strolled outside the walls of the fortress. Abruptly, a chilled wind whipped at Kenya's face, twisting her black hair into a coil. She hastily drew the fur-lined hood of her cloak over her head, and scanned the landscape about the fortress. "I see no streams, or rivers nearby, and they sit on top of this mountain. I doubt if there are any underground springs bubbling up out of the earth. Possible, I guess, but still, we have discovered none."

Marcos allowed a slight smile to cross his lips and jabbed one index finger at the surrounding alps and the far vista beyond. "Snow and ice collected in the winter, stored in the lowest reaches of the castle below the permafrost line and melted as needed. Remember the huge piles of wood we saw stacked at every corner. No doubt this is where they keep their meat also." A few flakes of snow drifted down from the sky as if agreeing with him. "Although it is only fall, and still feels like summer on the plains, in the highest portions of these hills the snow collects already. I would no doubt even during the warmest summer there is snow or pockets of ice still laying on the ground Galvin would draw on during an emergency."

"Never thought of that," Kenya said, as another gust of blustery wind tugged at her clothes. She pulled her cloak tight around her body to keep the chill from seeping any farther between the cloth and her skin.

Marcos followed her example. "After all, this is where the water for streams and rivers comes from, right?"

Kenya nodded silently. "Let's hurry," she urged, "before we freeze into ice."

Outside in the chilled mountain air, they strolled along the granite walls along a dirt path just wide enough for repair crews to transverse the drop-off between the keep and the cliff it rested on. Vertigo swept over Kenya every time she glanced over the edge, which was a scant five feet away. She found herself hugging the granite walls when the strong wind blew, pushing her toward the empty expanse and the craggy hollows far below covered in snow and fog.

The hour was late when they returned to the main hall, feet wet and freezing from the snow, and shivering from the cold. Servants busily prepared the dining room for the evening meal. Kenya rushed to the huge stone fireplace and ripped off her gloves, warming her hands in the heat of the blaze. "My fingers are icicles," Kenya commented as Marcos joined her.

"Now we know what Galvin meant by an army not wanting to spend the winter here on his doorstep during a siege. You would lose your troops to frost bite by the spring."

As Kenya took her seat on a bench, Marcos excused himself and hurried away to the kitchen. He returned a few minutes later holding a crude woven sack.

"What's this? A snack for later on?" Kenya quipped. She cocked her head to one side, studying the bag. "Can't be a cake. Too small."

"For tonight," Marcos whispered. He glanced around and stuffed the bag into his purse. "You claimed you experienced bad dreams last night, and I have been thinking of our meeting with Feg today. These," he patted his purse, "are herbs for a sleeping draught for you. I begged them from one of the cooks, claiming I couldn't sleep during the night and my head ached. What I could not find in the kitchen I stepped into their stillroom and located. I will prepare a drink for you tonight before you go to bed."

"After last night and today I could use a good sleep," Kenya agreed. *I wonder if a sleep potion will help. I wasn't awake last night, but still, somehow, Marcos says my soul was taken. Will it happen again?*

Kenya picked at her food, keeping one eye on the staircase, wondering if Feg would make an appearance. She continued to fret about falling asleep, desiring the rest, but dreading the night.

By the end of the meal, the crone did not show her face, and the warm room, and food in her belly won out. When Kenya finished eating, she stifled a yawn with the palm of one hand and said to Marcos, "I think I shall retire. Today has been long and tedious, my feet hurt from wandering around the castle all day. Tomorrow is more of the same I suspect, and we must prepare for the journey back to Evertree the day after."

Marcos placed his hands on his knees and pushed himself erect. "We can both use a good rest after today. I will prepare the tea for you now so you may have pleasant dreams tonight."

In their small common sitting room, Marcos called for hot water. Steaming bowls appeared, and after he dismissed the servant, he withdrew the sack and shook out small packages of dried herbs on the table. Kenya watched curiously, as he dropped pinches of each in the water and stirred the steaming liquid with his belt knife. The aroma of honeysuckle, wild roses, and linden flowers wafted up her nose.

"This is magic potion?" Kenya asked incredulously. She bent forward, inhaling a deep whiff of the potion and flicking one of the pouches with her forefinger. "Smells good, but junk from the kitchen? I don't see how…?"

"Individually they are used to flavor or enhance food," replied Marcos, giving the brew a final stir with his knife and waiting for the ingredients to steep, "but the right herbs, in the right combinations, have all types of medical or magical uses." He held up a bag. "Sage. We make tea from the leaves in the morning, but the herb also has uses to keep evil spirits away. Usually burnt, but the plant works as well in a drink."

The water slowly transformed from clear to a brownish-green. Marcos blew on the liquid and handed the bowl to Kenya. "Drink the potion all down, even the dregs will not harm you, and then climb into bed. A dreamless, peaceful slumber awaits you tonight."

Kenya accepted the bowl, savoring the warmth of the wood in her fingers and sipped the contents cautiously.

The taste wasn't unpleasant and an undercurrent of sweetness made her drink more. She kept gulping the potion down, unsure of the effects, but enjoying the taste.

A golden heat immediately flowed through her body, radiating from her stomach into thighs and chest. Before Kenya realized what happened, she'd drank the entire contents and handed the empty container back to Marcos wondering if an additional bowl was possible. "That was good," she admitted. "Do you think…? More?"

Marcos pulled the container from her hands. "No. No more. Too much and you might not wake in the morning. We cannot have you sleeping the day away, now can we?"

The warmth entered Kenya's head and legs. She released a huge yawn and her eyelids fluttered. "Maybe you're right," she muttered as a soft cotton blanket closed over her mind.

"Now, quick to bed, before I must carry you," urged Marcos, rising with a chuckle.

"Uh, yeah. I think you're right." Kenya repeated dreamily as she stood, swaying, a feeling of light-headiness drifting over her as the blanket of white covered her head in slumber. Kenya released a huge sigh, tottered, and held onto the back of the chair for support as her eyes flickered shut. Marcos wrapped his arm around Kenya's shoulder and helped her walk to the bedchamber. With another yawn, a languid smile, she dropped on the mattress. Marcos pulled the covers over her and Kenya curled into a tight ball, falling asleep at one.

Invisible fingers played tug-of-war with her arm attempting to lift her up out of the bed. Kenya grunted in her sleep and refused to remove herself from the soft mattress holding her so snugly in place. She rolled over onto her other side and gripped the sheets.

Arguments erupted in the air, a woman's voice quarreling with a man. In her minds-eye two phantom silhouettes floated over the bed and debated fiery what to do.

Will you two stop fighting and let me go to sleep please.

Still asleep, Kenya drew one of the pillows over her head to drown out the noise of the arguing.

The voices drifted away. Dreamless slumber engulfed Kenya.

***

"Hunting? What could possibly be worth hunting in these mountains?" Kenya tugged her fur hood closer around her head as wind whipped around her. Their small party gathered outside the gates of Galvin's keep shivered in the dawn cold. He, Marcos, Kenya, two shield men, and four beaters in the freezing cold weather sat on their mounts waiting for Galvin to lead the party on an early morning chase.

"On the slopes we will locate mountain sheep," cried Galvin attempting to make himself heard above the shriek of the wind. He gestured with one gloved hand at the rocky tree covered inclines of the mountains surrounding their party. "Below, stag and boar roam in the forest, fattening themselves on leaves, grass, and nuts against the coming of winter. We shall find something to hunt, never fear, Lady Kenya."

An orange sun peeked over the mountaintops, changing the pre-dawn gloom of the sky into amber. One of the servants woke Kenya and Marcos early in the morning, insisting they dress warm, hurry and eat, and meet Lord Galvin in the courtyard. Still half-asleep Kenya found herself eating hot porridge in the empty main hall with an equally sleepily Marcos sitting next to her and staggering outside.

As Kenya hugged herself and waited for the riders to move out, a soldier standing nearby thrust both bow accompanied by a quiver of arrows and long spear into her hands, neither of which she knew how to use or wanted. The night before Galvin insisted before they leave on their journey back to the coast, a hunt on his domain was an excellent way to seal the friendship between Evertree and his kingdom. Kenya hadn't realized the hunt would start before the sun rose in the sky.

Their party progressed along the rocky trail leading to the vales below. The beaters ran ahead, searching the slopes for signs of game, the lord in the lead with Marcos and Kenya behind.

Galvin slowed and rode abreast of Kenya watching her fumble with the bow with a puzzled expression on her face as she tried to hold both weapon and reins at the same time. "Lady, you need not shoot if you are not so inclined. Stay close to me, ride in pursuit, and enjoy the excitement of the chase and kill. We will have both, I assure you."

Yeah, I love watching animals slaughtered. Fun. "If it is all the same to you, Lord Galvin," Kenya replied tactfully, "I'll watch you dash away after anything your beaters flush." She issued a small laugh and glanced down at her saddle. "I am not use to riding at full tilt, and am afraid I might fall off. I wouldn't want to slow you down to assist me off the ground and spoil your fun." Kenya pretended to glance around in surprise and asked innocently, "Princess Jessica is not joining us? I'm sure you invited her. Where is she?"

The lord sat in his saddle, studying the rocky trail. "The princess Jessica said the chilled morning air was no good for her complexion, and begged off the hunt this morning," he replied drily. "I am sure you realize a delicate flower such as she cannot stand the cold."

"Hmmm." *In other words, Jessica didn't want to wake up in the middle of the night and freeze her bottom off.* Kenya touched her cold, dark skin. "I should remember the advice. I wouldn't want to become old and wrinkled before my time."

Galvin frowned in annoyance at her obvious reluctance to join in the chase but chuckled knowingly. "As you wish, Lady. It is true, I would not wish to see anyone injured on our little jaunt this morning, and I certainly would not want you to grow old and wrinkled." He bowed his head to her in a quick nod. "Enjoy the hunt as best you can." The lord dug spurs into his horse's ribs and sped up to the head of the party.

Marcos ran a hand under his hood and pushed back a stray lock of hair as he watched Galvin. "If you do not wish to participate in the chase, Kenya, you do not have too. Enjoy the day out in the fresh air with no worries." He inhaled deeply of the crisp mountain air with the forest about them, leaves changing to red, orange, and bronze. "The landscape is amazing."

The party rode until the fortress passed from sight among the pines, and then halted on a flat piece of the trail. The beaters fanned out along the rocky slope searching for signs of mountain sheep. After a few minutes, they returned shaking their heads and raising their hands in frustration. With a shrug, Lord Galvin waved the party forward and the group proceeded into the lower elevations of the dark forest below.

They rode past the tree line until a logging road rose into view. The beaters continued down the trail while the rest of the party swung into the road. After a quarter of a mile, Galvin called a halt. "We'll spread out here," he announced. "My men will cut along the slope and drive whatever game is afoot back up to us." He swung in his saddle and shouted to Kenya, "Even if you do not wish to hunt, Lady, 'twould be best to notch an arrow for your own safety. If boar are about, they may well charge you, and wolves run in packs seeking the same prey we do." He did a survey of the landscape. "Snow leopards also prowl these heights, but I doubt we will flush one. They hunt at night."

Kenya looked nervously about.

Boars? Oh, my...! These people are bound to get me into this one way or the other.

Marcos sat on his horse thirty yards away and shot her a reassuring grin and a thumb's up sign. Kenya smiled back and then laid the spear across the saddle while fumbling with the bow, and then drew a shaft from the quiver. She'd shot arrows before, twice, at camp when she was twelve. Both bolts flew wildly away, missing the large red, white, and blue target, the rest of the girls laughed, and Kenya vowed never to attempt such a ridiculous sport again.

Kenya tried to fit the notch of the shaft into the bowstring and draw the cord back.

The arrow swung madly to one side and dropped from her fingers onto the ground.

"Damn."

Kenya's face burnt with embarrassment and she glanced around quickly hoping no one was watching, and drew a second arrow from the quiver before Galvin or one of the shield men made a comment. She bit her lower lip, concentrating, and placed the notch in the cord, cautiously tugging the string to assure herself she wouldn't lose this bolt. Kenya rested the bow on the saddle and attempted what she thought was an expression of confidence. *Well, I don't look like a total fool. I hope nothing charges my way. I'll probably shoot myself in the foot.*

Off in the distance the noise of men yelling and the beating of sticks upon sticks filtered through the trees, growing louder as Kenya listened.

The crashing of underbrush and weird snorts echoed in the air.

Oh, no. It's happening.

Directly in front of her a stag burst through the brush, shaking off loops of vines from the massive antlers with a toss of the head. In her sight, the beast appeared larger than an elephant, mucus dripping down from the black snout. The animal froze, gaze fixed on Kenya and her horse straight ahead of it. The beast snorted and pawed the earth.

Kenya glared back, petrified.

Their eyes locked.

The animal's head twisted, searching behind as the noise of the beaters drew closer, and then in two great bounds leaped over Kenya and disappeared across the trail, up the slope, and into the woods behind her.

The whole scene took less than a heartbeat. Cries of *"After him,"* rang out around Kenya. Men and horses spun and jumped, horns blew, and the hunters set off hot on the trail of the beast before the animal dropped out of sight among the trees.

As the stag cleared Kenya, the rear hooves pounded on the rump of Kenya's mount. The horse reared. Screaming, the mare pawed the air in terror, bucking as Kenya tried to get the animal under control. The spear on the saddle bounced to the ground, and Kenya dropped her bow as she fought with the reins, while the arrows from her quiver flew in all directions to disappear under the brush. The horse bolted straight down the slope, away from the stag, the noisy hunting horns, and the shouting men who rode uphill into the woods.

Branches whipped in Kenya's face, ripping at clothes and tangling in her hair. She clung to the horse's neck, eyes squeezed tightly shut, and pressing her face into the mane; the smell of the animal's coat in her nose, as the mare's frantic charge bounced her up and down.

"Slow down, stupid, SLOW DOWN," Kenya shouted into the horse's ear, as the mount dodged past trees, weaving deeper into the forest.

Later, Kenya was unable to recall how long the wild ride lasted. All she remembered were leaves striking her face and thorns gouging hands. White froth from the horse's mouth flew back into her face matting her hair.

They hit the flat of the slope. The horse slowed, sides heaving from exhaustion, but with single-minded purpose kept forging ahead at a brisk walk. When an obstacle presented itself too dense to push through, the animal dodged left and right, refusing to slow no matter how much Kenya implored the mare with curses or pleas. Kenya sat up, scrubbing dust from her eyes and attempted to comb twigs and leaves from her hair with fingers. Hastily she studied the earth passing beneath the horses' belly. *I never realized how high off the ground I am when I'm on the back of a horse. I could jump off but....Darn it all. If I did, I lose the horse, then where would I be.*

"Will you stop, *please?*" Kenya jerked on the mare's reins. She swung her head to glance at Kenya in annoyance and slowed, finally completing a wide circle before stopping at a stunted tree. She commenced to browse on the foliage, swishing her tail, as if nothing out of the ordinary occurred.

Taking a deep breath of relief, Kenya slipped out of the saddle, rubbing her back and bottom, still shaking from the ride. "Stupid horse," she muttered swinging in a wide arc searching for the back trail. The dark green of the shady forest stretched in every direction with no break in sight. Tall trunks of trees blocked a clear view except for a few yards ahead. Kenya didn't have the faintest idea which direction the horse ran from and the terrain indicated no clue.

The horse ran downhill. She stopped in the flat section of the slope. Kenya was sure the animal hadn't turned around in its panic and run back uphill. The ground was level. Issuing a deep sigh, she grabbed the reins, resigned to a long trek uphill back to the trail where Marcos and Lord Galvin probably waited. "C'mon, stupid," Kenya said, beginning to walk, "Let's find our way back to the fortress." If she continued in a straight line, the ground would either fall or rise. If she hit a downward incline again, she was walking the wrong way, and then it was a matter of turning around, retracing her steps and hit the slope back to the road and safety.

The ground rose. Kenya breathed a sigh of relief and hurried, tugging on the horse's reins to make her walk faster. Sharp pains stitched her side. Kenya's legs grew leaden and thighs quivered. The rocky earth and trees continued to loom upward with no end in sight. Finally she stopped, squatting on her haunches, panting as if she were a dog.

How far did this dumb horse run?

Gulping air into her lungs, Kenya rose, wincing in pain and marched on, determined to reach the summit and Marcos before dark, who she knew would be frantic with worry, if not already searching the forest. In fact, it dawned on Kenya no one shouted her name. No one scoured the countryside for her.

The summit of the hill appeared. Breathing deeply, Kenya tugged the horse forward, eagerly scrambling the last few feet and bursting out into the open searching for the trail.

She stood on a tree bare ridge with no path anywhere about. Behind, a forested depression with sides sloping upward filled the view. Before her was another valley, dense with vegetation. Kenya inched in a circle, attempting to force all emotions under control as wetness formed in the corners of her eyes.

She was lost.

Chapter Ten

Kenya waited on the ridge the rest of the day searching the valleys for sign of men walking or riding on horseback. Even the signs of smoke curling into the air would allow a point in which to find the hunting party. She was sure Lord Galvin send out multiple search bands in every part of the wilderness when he saw she hadn't returned, or Marcos would charge up the hill and rescue her from danger. A red sun dropped below the mountains and disappeared leaving pink ribbons across the clouds and changing the forest from dark green to black. The wind already chilled, blew colder plucking at her cloak and attempting to slide under the tunic. A pale moon rose with grey clouds floating across its face, and a few stray flakes of snow drifted down out of the sky. The horse seemingly not at all affected by the blasts of fridge air, calmly faced the other way, swishing her tail, and continued to crop leaves and the scant grass.

Kenya glared at her mount, eyes blazing. "In the movies you're supposed to lay down and keep me warm," she muttered, scraping deep into the rocky earth with her fingers and scooping leaves, pine needles, and twigs from a wide circle around her new nest into a mound. "Don't you dare eat these," Kenya warned the animal as she took a step closer and sniffed at the pile. "This is all your fault, anyway." She tied the horse's reins securely to a bush to guarantee she wouldn't wander off during the night and continued to scooping leaves off the ground. She took one last look around the slope in a forlorn hope a campfire would appear in the distance. Nothing. With a sigh, Kenya returned to gathering pine needles and leaves. Once she'd gathered a large enough pile, she burrowed into the center until only her face showed and snuggled down trying to stay warm and hidden from any large predators during the night.

I feel like a stupid bird. Hope nothing comes close to investigate me. Oh, lord, what do I do if one of those leopards or wolves Galvin talked about finds me?

Eerie cries rang through the night, the same wolves or cats hunting prey Kenya was afraid would discover her. Kenya's nerves stretched taut, eyes darting every time a twig snapped or the blustery wind rustled a bush nearby. Her imagination ran wild and the black trees overhead morphed into lurking beasts ready to pounce on her hiding place. To calm herself Kenya started singing, making up words as she went along.

It's lonely here.
The sun's gone away.
Night closes in.
I will not fear.
Take my hand,
We'll walk away
My bravest dear.
Your light shines on,
And holds me close,
My terror vanished,
Disappeared.

In the darkness, her thoughts darted to Marcos. Sometimes when he said, "My Lady," and gazed into her eyes, little shivers ran up and down her spine and made her heart beat faster, breath deepen. Kenya was never someone's lady before, never expected she would be. The expression made her feel special, wanted, loved. For some reason Kenya pictured Marcos spreading a warm, yellow glow around her, protecting her from the terrors of the night, standing over her with his blazing sword drawn. In her mind, Kenya hear him saying, "I will find you, my

Lady," over and again. She huddled down deeper into the nest of leaves, eyes closed, recalling each line of his face as she'd seen him last.

"Well, what do we have here?" A leather-clad foot kicked the pine needles away from Kenya's body exposing her head, chest, and arms. The sun was high up in the sky. Two men stood over her, leers on their rough faces as they raked Kenya with their vision curled up on the ground. "Looks like we've found ourselves a tasty morsel," the taller of the two remarked to his companion. He ran his tongue over his lips. "Never know what you might find under a pile of leaves, huh?"

Kenya bolted upright, tousled haired, eyes still bleary from sleep while clutching her cloak tightly around her. "Wh—Who are you?" Kenya shuddered as a sudden chill ran through her body not caused by the early morning weather. She stared from one face to the other. Terror gripped her throat.

"More to the question, lass, who are *you*?" The shorter of the two said. He looked her over shrewdly and remarked to the other, "I'd say a runaway servant of some highborn's household staff would be my guess. Too pretty to be a logger's wife or a trapper's."

Events of the previous day rushed back to Kenya. *What do these men think I am? A piece of meat?* Her terror turned into fury and she snapped angrily, "I am a guest of Lord Galvin's." Kenya struggled to stand up, brushing at her clothes with as much arrogance and displeasure as possible to muster under the circumstances. "I was separated from his hunting party and became lost in this forest yesterday. No doubt, he sent searchers out for me all night. In fact, I am surprised they haven't located me yet. I thought you were they in fact. Take me to his castle and I will see you are well rewarded for your time and effort."

"You're one of Galvin's, are you?" The tall man scratched the black stubble on his chin, thinking. "He don't cut wood in this part of the forest, lass, but maybe we could use you for ransom. I'd wager he'd pay dearly to have you returned to him if what you say is true."

"I don't—I don't understand." What was "cut wood"?

This invoked chuckles from both men. "You will understand soon enough, lass." The tall man gave Kenya an evil grin. He reached out, grasped her roughly by one sleeve, and spun her around until her back faced him.

Kenya fought to free herself. "Hey, let go of me." She tried kicking backward, met empty space and received a cuff on the back of the head in return.

"None of your sass." He seized the other arm in a vice-like grip and twisted both painfully behind her waist. The next thing Kenya realized he tightly bound leather throngs around her wrists.

"Luke, fetch her horse."

"Wha…Where are you taking me," Kenya whimpered as she squirmed in his grasp. Her anger melted away and the fear laying dominate in her stomach blossomed into full terror.

Before she knew what was happening, callous hands grasp her waist, lifted Kenya bodily off the ground and dumped her onto her saddle. She swayed precariously, attempting to keep her balance with no way to grasp the saddle horn before jamming her feet into the stirrups to keep from tumbling off the horse and onto her head.

"Semus, we taking the girl back to the lodge?" Luke called to the taller man as he jumped into his saddle and snatched the reins of Kenya's horse, waiting for a reply.

"Aye." Semus scrambled onto his mount and started a slow amble down the opposite side of the ridge following a faint path. Luke tugged on Kenya's reins and the two trailed a few paces behind.

Thoughts of escape raced through Kenya's mind. *Kidnapped? Taken hostage?* These men talked of ransom and she was sure they rode away from the safety of Galvin's keep, not toward the fortress. She could only hope the lord paid the ransom quickly and rescued her from this mess. Otherwise god only knew what these people intended.

The men tied her hands, though. What to do? Kenya flexed her wrists to see how tightly they tied her. The throngs refused to loosen no matter how hard she twisted her hands. After a minute's struggle, Kenya gave up and attempted desperately to think up another scheme of escape.

Kenya glanced left and right along the route they traveled, frantically trying to devise a way of leaping off the horse, tied or not, without killing herself in the process, before it was too late and they arrived at wherever this Semus was leading them. They rode into the lower elevations of the forest. Tall trees and brush sprang up again, creating a canape over her head and obscuring vision for more than a few feet on either side. If she could convince these men to untie her, she'd run as fast as a rabbit in the opposite direction. Maybe hide in the dense underbrush, lose herself in the woods until nightfall and make her way back to the fortress before the men captured her again.

Kenya made a decision and called out suddenly to Luke, "Hey, I gotta go—bad. Let me down for a minute off this saddle, will you?" She looked at him imploringly, trying to appear as embarrassed as possible. It was worth the chance.

Luke stopped and glanced back at her, a speculative cock to his head. Semus ignored the plea and kept riding, although Kenya was sure he'd heard her. Luke saw his master refusing to stop and shrugged. "Pee in your pants," he grunted and tugged on her reins while digging heels into his mount's sides to catch up to his leader.

Kenya slumped in the saddle. *Oh, well. It was a thought.*

To make matters worse, she really did have to go. Kenya spent an eternity of hours in misery squirming and biting her lower lip until they reached another valley. This one contained a half-timbered longhouse set in the middle of the forest with a thatched roof and four outbuildings. Three chimneys ran down the middle of the top of the main structure filling the air with the acid odor of wood smoke. A dug out trench surrounded on the outside by sharpened stakes ringed the complex. Inside the trench was a tightly woven wicker fence with four entrances, one on each side. Three stood tightly bared, the fourth open. Kenya and her captors rode over a crude plank gangway through an open gate scattering chickens and pigs into wild confusion who seemed to roam everywhere of their own free will. Semus dismounted in front of the longhouse while Luke snatched up his reins and guided all three horses around to the back where a barn stood.

"Okay, Missy," he declared, hauling Kenya out of her saddle and setting her on the dirt, "If yah have to go…" he walked her over to a small wooden shack and untied her arms, opening the door, "…go." With one sweep of his arm, he pushed her inside.

The fetid stench of urine and feces struck Kenya in the face like a mallet. The low drone of flies buzzed in her ears while a swarm of gnats investigated her eyes and lips. Through the faint light filtering through cracks in the wall, Kenya made out a low bench against the far wall with crude holes cut into the middle. Trying hard not to breathe in bugs or odor, she hurried forward, sat quickly, and relieved herself.

Luke watched from the open door, a lewd smirk on his face. When Kenya stood, he said, "Finished? Let's take yah back inside and see what the laird going to do with yah."

This time he did not retie her wrists, but kept one hand firmly on her shoulder in a tight grip as he marched Kenya roughly to a side entrance. His fingers tightened into bone crushing force as he yanked the door open, pushing her inside into a large common room filled with people and a pale of smoke covering the ceiling. Semus sat by himself at a table raised on a platform, eating. Other diners rested lower down at a long bench, trenchers set before them. All eyes swung to her and Luke as they entered. The two waited for Semus to look up and acknowledge their presence.

"About time," Semus finally mumbled around a goose leg. He gestured with the drumstick toward an empty space at the end of the long table. "Might as well feed the woman. I think I'll be keeping her for a while to see what happens."

"Yah heard the laird." Luke pushed her forward toward the bench. "Sit." He snatched out a food-encrusted trencher from a cupboard and thrust the dish into Kenya's hands.

"Now then," Semus continued after Kenya took a seat, "I have already dispatched a rider to Lord Galvin's fortress to see what kind, if any, ransom he's willing to pay for you. In the meantime you can earn your keep around here by cleaning and cooking." He ripped off another mouthful of goose, swallowed noisily, and shook the bone at her. "And don't think of trying to escape, yah hear me? My men and I know every inch of this forest. There's no place for you to hide. You'll never make it." He tossed the bone to a dog squatting on its haunches at his feet wagging its tail in anticipation.

Kenya huddled in upon herself, not daring to look to either side. A bowl of boiled tubers sat in front of her along with a plate of ill smelling meat. She snatched up both and scooped some into a dish. The odor of the food made her sick to the stomach but Kenya determined to eat it all. She chewed and swallowed, trying hard not to taste what she ate.

***

The next three days dragged by indeterminately. Every miserable task the cooks or scullery maids found distasteful to do found its way thrust onto Kenya's back. Her clothes, already dirty and torn from being lost in the woods, grew filthy. Bathing was out of the question. As far as she saw, no one in the compound washed, not even their hands, and she stank, her hair a stringy tangle of greasy knots. Whether she was feeding the pigs or cleaning out the horse's stalls, someone always stood guard, watching over her. Kenya saw no way to escape. The only time not under constant scrutiny was at night while sleeping, but even then, her thin pallet of dirty straw was in the kitchen huddled next to the other kitchen drudges who slept as close to the ovens as possible for warmth. A sentry stood by the door guarding the exit against intruders. If she were lucky enough not to wake anyone and sneak past the guard in the middle of the night, someone was sure to notice she was missing at first daybreak when the workday began.

By listening closely to comments made by the inhabitants of the longhouse, Kenya learned Semus ruled over three valleys, but he was more brigand than chief. His main source of income was preying on the trappers who roamed the woodlands, stealing their furs, or waylaying lone prospectors for what scant riches they dug out of the rocky mountains. The longhouse contained four families, some sixty people in total, all related to Semus in some fashion—Luke was his nephew.

The other kitchen drudges were slaves, captured during raids on small homesteads unable to protect themselves. One old woman told Kenya a tale of her son, and daughter-in-law deaths, when they refused to hand over their merger collection of furs to Semus. The old woman hid in the back of their hut under a pile of straw, but Semus's men found her before they burnt the home and she was taken away to serve his table and clean.

By the morning of the fourth day, Semus commented to Kenya as she carried plates to the breakfast table, "Appears Lord Galvin isn't much interested in you, lass, or some mishap has occurred with my messenger." He tore savagely at a chunk of black bread, plainly perplexed by the lack of news.

Kenya kept her head bowed, and laid platters on the table, but was thinking the same thing. It shouldn't take this long for a messenger to ride to the fortress and return with ransom, or at least some note setting up a meeting between the lord and Semus. Had Galvin killed the messenger in a fit of rage and at this very minute planning an attack to rescue her? Maybe another clan, taking revenge on Semus for his raiding, waylaid the messenger?

Kenya studied Semus's face seeing the same thoughts crossing his features. She muttered under her breath so no one would hear, "You're a dumb bastard. Send out someone else."

After a long day of cleaning and serving was finished, ovens emptied of ash, and animals fed, Kenya lay down on her pallet, hands behind her head, staring at the ceiling beams. She wondering what Semus would do, attempting to relax her aching body and think. Keep her as a servant? Kill her? He certainly wouldn't release her again. Kenya kept running scenarios over in her mind until they mixed together in a cloud of confusion and jumbled images.

A haze developed before her eyes, the shimmering door seen before. Was this a dream within a dream? Kenya cooed softly at the portal, not knowing why she did so, but certain the entry awaited some signal. An eternity passed without results, and then the door creaked open emitting the pearly light, bathing her in radiance.

This is a dream. I know it's a dream.

Kenya rose, stepped forward into the room with the dazzling glow all about. Again, strange objects lay on tables stretching out in endless rows to disappear into the white fog. Some she recognized, most she possessed no knowledge of their use. One table nearest drew Kenya's attention, filled with musical instruments both ancient and new. On the top rested the lyre. The glow of the polished wood drew her eyes. Without thinking, she reached out and drew it to her, cradled the object, on impulse strummed on the strings.

Sleep, wordless sleep.
Spreading throughout,
And falling deep.
A rest, cast into the night.
Slumber keep
Me safe in flight.

As the last strands of the song faded from her mind the lyre glowed, dissolved from her hand into oblivion. Kenya hurl backward out of the room with the door slamming shut in her face. She blinked, finding herself standing in the dark kitchen with an arm outreached holding nothing. Startled, not sure if she were awake or asleep.

The room was still, the drudges huddled on their pallets slumbering peacefully by the stoves. Even the guard at the door slumped on the floor, dozing quietly. "Must be a dream," Kenya muttered swallowing hard. She touched her ears, realizing for the first time, she could not hear the noises of the kitchen help or guard snoring although from their open mouths they plainly were. It was if a soft blanket spread over the room in the air deadening all sound. Kenya walked to the kitchen door and pushed it open. The unoiled hinges failed to make their usual creaks and groans.

Can't be real. A dream within a dream world.

Nor did she hear the night insects or birds while stealing across the bare earth past the barn. Darkness surrounded her, the stars overhead but a faint flicker of light. The side gate of the wicker fence swung open at a touch, unlatched by some mistake and Kenya kept walking, unsure of where she headed, but an inner urging drew her forward over the gangplank into the line of trees barely discernible through the dimness of the gloom.

Blackness engulfed her. The heavy branches hanging above her head shut off even the faint glow of the moon. Her footsteps muffled in the night as she tread over pine needles, but no noise of the snapping of twigs underfoot or the crackling of dried leaves marked her passage as she wove her way deeper into the woods.

Strangest dream I've ever had. I wonder how this vision will end.

Kenya continued to wander through the silent world until false dawn broke, slowly surrendering to the red dawn of the morning with a blood sun rising ahead in the sky. Kenya stopped, panting heavily, and gazed around in wonder.

The world returned to her in a rush of noise, light and sensation. Birds chirped; cool mountain air blew against her cheeks and fluttered her hair, the odor of the pine trees flooded into her nose.

This wasn't a dream, but how...? Did the lyre have something to do with this? Some magic from the outside like the limerick I made up the first day I arrived here.

Kenya struggled up a granite uprising facing the rising sun. The endless series of valleys and dales had passed, replaced by a flat landscape of rolling yellow grass she recognized. The plains traveled through so long ago from Evertree in the disastrous trek to Cliffward.

"I've made it this far," Kenya whispered stumbling downhill amidst dancing rocks and dust, almost falling on her face in her haste to make a headlong rush down the slope. She pushed her way through the underbrush and boulders at the base of the hill, sped around copses of trees blocking the way, until she stood at the beginning of the grass and could survey the distant horizon with nothing obscuring her vision.

So far to travel. Demons and monsters stalking the savannah waiting to attack at a moment's notice. The lord only know what else—hungry cats and wolves, I guess. Only a fool would try to walk all the way back to Evertree by herself. Never make the trip, what am I thinking of?

Kenya glanced back at the towering alps she'd emerged from capped with snow at the peaks. *Go back and try to find Lord Galvin's fortress? Marcos? What if I run into Semus and his men. He swore he'd follow me. I don't know how I walked out of there in the first place. Could I make my way back through the forest not knowing where to go?* Kenya turned to the rising sun again, tension twisting her neck, her heart hammering in her chest as she tried to make up her mind.

She fixed her vision on the tall grass and the rising sun. *Long way,* she mused, striding forward. *No food, no water, no weapons.*

Kenya threw her head back, squared her shoulders, and gazed at the sapphire sky.

I will survive.

Chapter Eleven

Kenya shook her head attempting to clear her vision.

"I am Kenya—Queen of the jungle."

The days mingled into one after the other. Kenya tripped over an unseen rock, teetered, and righted herself.

"Like my African ancestors I trek across the savannah hunting elephants and giraffes. I am Nyabinghi, warrior goddess."

Kenya stopped, stuck her arms out, and swung in a circle, staggering and fell into a crouch.

"Pretty soon I'll be chewing on my own leg."

Kenya giggled. *Better stop playing. This is stupid. I'm talking to myself. In a minute I'll start believing what I say.* She stood abruptly, shook her head to clear her mind.

The hot, merciless sun beat down on her body. How long had she wandered across this savannah of endless waving grass? Lack of food made her faint. The absence of water cracked her lips and skin. Her memory slipped. She must get a grip on herself. Five days? That was it. Five days wandering in the wilderness.

She rested by a small stream. Water was not hard to find. Brooks and shallow rivers wound their crooked way across the earth, crisscrossed the terrain Kenya traveled, but she possessed no way of carrying the precious liquid, and hadn't discovered a stream in the last two days. After an hour, trudging over the brown earth with the burning sun pounding on her head, Kenya was parched dry with sweat drying on her skin as fast as she perspired.

Locating food, however, was a different matter. Kenya survived on berries located along the way, and to her disgust, small grasshopper like insects living in the tall grass. The first time she tried eating one, she almost gagged, then gritting her teeth, telling herself people ate them covered in chocolate. She chewed grimly and swallowed.

The nights were the worse. With no way of building a fire Kenya huddled in the darkness, hoping whatever hunted these plains didn't discover her. As the stars appeared, she heard wild screams as prey fell to hungry predators. On the eve of the second day's march, she was lucky enough to stumble across a crude shelter built of sticks and grass ripped out of the ground. A hunter's shack meant for a two-night stay while he stalked the plains for game. Kenya crawled in breathing a small prayer of thanks and slept well during the night. Since then, however, she was not so fortunate and the terror felt night after night kept her awake and exhausted during the day.

Twilight turned into night. Rustling noises circled Kenya. Along the way, she'd discovered a stout wooden stick she used for walking up hills and probing streams to assure herself no deep pockets lurked in the murky water to step in. Kenya clutched the club, fingers tightening around the wood until her knuckles paled at the effort.

Kenya parted the clump of tall prairie grass she hid in and peered out onto the plain. On a rise perhaps a quarter of a mile away, she made out a figure of a horseman in the dim moonlight. The rider swung as if searching for something and then ambled down the hill in her direction.

Is this a searcher from Evertree out looking for me? Should I rise, and hope he sees me? Yell?

She decided to stand and call for help. After all, if not from Evertree, this rider was probably a hunter out on the plains, or with any luck, a wayfarer traveling to the coast. In any case, he could confirm the direction of the castle and perhaps supply her with food, or even a weapon. Kenya started to rise.

A stray beam of moonlight fell on the rider and illuminated the figure completely.

The rider had no head.

Neither did his horse.

Kenya ducked back down quickly. *Oh, gosh. What did Marcos call those things? Nar-riders? Yeah. He's going to suck out my soul and eat it.* She swallowed hard and waited, pinpricks of fear running up her back and shoulders tensed, waiting for the rider to discover her. Kenya clasped the stick in two hands determined to go down with a fight, although knowing it was useless to try to kill a spirit with a club.

The "clop-clop-clop" of the horse's hooves drew closer and stopped.

The noise of moving bodies surrounded her. Faint grunts and hoots issued from all sides, drawing closer. The horse reared, screaming and the figure of the nar-rider blocked out the moonlight as he towered over her. More hoots started, turning into a blare of roars, shaking the night.

The silhouette of the rider and the horse slipped away. The wild screams died into silence. Kenya waited tensely for whatever drove the demon off to attack her.

Nothing happened. Quiet stretched across the savannah. Kenya stood cautiously, revolving in a slow circle, waiting for the attack of wild beasts she was sure would occur at any moment. Her nerves grew taut as the seconds dragged into minutes, and still nothing happened. Finally, she could take the suspense no longer.

"If you're going to kill me—*kill me!*" Kenya screamed at the top of her lungs. The tension within her stretched to the breaking point. She hoped to scare whatever stalked her away or bring on an attack and get the waiting over and done with. Instead, a small hairy man appeared in front of her, and then ten more. Both men and women materialized from all sides.

The people were short and covered in long, soft, brown hair reminding Kenya of a Persian cat. Kenya guess the tallest no more than two foot. None wore garments, the women only slightly less furry than the males.

"Wh—Who are you? Are you the ones who chased the nar-rider away?" It did not seem possible. With one swipe of the club, she could crush half of these little creatures to death.

The tallest, a man, stepped forward and said softly, "We are *Bohpoli*." He raised his hands. "Spirit and horse—gone. You…What do you do here by yourself? No safe place for stranger."

In the waiting silence, Kenya backed away, only to halt when she realized the creatures surrounded her. She decided these little people wouldn't hurt her otherwise they would have attacked already. "I mean no harm," Kenya replied, not lowering her club. "I am traveling to the castle Evertree." When the little man made no reply, Kenya added, "The ocean? Can you help me? Or, at least, not stop me?"

The people broke out into high-pitched squeaks, reminding Kenya of the chirping of birds. Finally, the spokesman waved her forward. "You—Come." Without waiting to see if she understood, the Bohpoli disappeared back into the grass.

"Wait."

Kenya plunged into the dark vegetation trailing the sound of rustling stalks, three-toed feet creating no sound on the dry earth, until she caught up to the end of the line of marching creatures.

The Bohpoli took a weaving route through the savannah and Kenya was sure they re-crossed their path at least once. She began to wonder if these people knew where they were going, or were as lost as she was, when they arrived at a low slung mound, barely higher than the grass surrounding it. Leafy materials growing on the ground covered the entire hillock. The little people filed down a dug out cut, swung a moss-covered door open, and trooped inside with Kenya stumbling after, at the last second falling to her hands and knees, dropping her club, and crawling through the low-slung entrance.

Kenya straightened up in a brightly lit room dug beneath the earth, a smokeless fire in an open stone hearth, greenish-blue, burning in the middle. An iron cauldron hung by a hook over the flames, steaming with an appetizing aroma. More of the little people squatted around the strange blaze. Blacker openings shone around the walls. Doorways leading into other rooms, Keya supposed gazing about.

"You—Sit." The spokesman waved to the fire and motioned to one of the other Bohpoli who rose, fetched a crude, wooden bowl, and filled the container to the brim with the contents of the pot. Kenya received the vessel along with a wooden spoon and sniffed cautiously.

Don't care if I turn green and die. This smells great.

She tasted the broth and then a large bite of what she assumed was meat and an orange vegetable. Her chewing and swallowing didn't stop until the bowl was empty and the stew nestled comfortably in her belly. Kenya looked up, hesitating, wondering if it was polite to ask for seconds. The same little person who served her the first time snatched the bowl from her fingers, refilled it, and handed the dish back with her not having to say a word.

"Thank you." Kenya ate slower, relishing the taste this time, attempting to decide if she was a prisoner, a curiosity, guest, and if these creatures meant to help her. "Uh, you live here on the prairie?" she asked. "You know the way to Evertree, or the sea? How far I have to walk?"

Puzzlement cross the face of the head Bohpoli, and then he said hesitantly, "We live here," he waved his hand at the interior of the hut, "and there." This time he pointed straight up in the air. "Two worlds."

Kenya wasn't sure if he meant the savannah outside the hut, or what, but asked, "Can you take me to Evertree, or at least give me supplies? Anything? Some help?" She waited, expecting a refusal from these strange little people, but hoping they'd have pity. After all, they had fed her and saved her from the grasp of the nar-rider. "At least tell me if I'm heading in the right direction?"

Again, bemusement crossed the face of the Bohpoli. He made his chirping noise and one of the men sitting at the fire rose and hurried to a closed doorway, disappearing within.

Kenya blinked. She was sure the door had not opened, but one moment the Bohpoli was there, and the next, dropped out of sight without the door opening or shutting.

She swung to ask the headman, but before she spoke, two of the creatures appeared out of the doorway and walked to the fire. The one who'd left, accompanied by another, from appearances an old female with sagging breasts down to her knees and covered in silver-grey hair.

The old woman squatted opposite Kenya and said in a soft voice, "You wish our help?"

Finally. Someone who knows what I'm asking. "Yes, can you?" Kenya replied eagerly leaning forward. At least she was getting somewhere. "Anything, please. I'm lost and I've been walking for five days trying to return to Evertree."

The Bohpoli appeared thoughtful and squinted her eyes, first at Kenya, and then at the ceiling as if asking a question of a higher authority. "Only you may help yourself," the creature answered, jabbing a four-fingered hand toward the roof of the hut, "in the other world you must seek if you wish to find the aid you need."

The elation Kenya felt evaporated. This woman was speaking nonsense. The savannah was where she needed the help, and if the woman were referring to praying, she'd prayed since first starting this trek. In desperation Kenya asked, "Can you take me? I must return to Evertree."

The ancient nodded and stood. "Come with me."

Kenya sprang up and hurried to the woman who walked away with amazing speed back toward the door where she'd appeared from, falling in step with the woman.

This is more like it. Finally got through to these people.

They reached the portal. Kenya stepped ahead to push the door open. As her fingers touched the wood, nothingness surrounded her. She gasped, yelling in silent fright and clamped her eyes shut.

"Why do you scream?"

Kenya unclenched her eyes. She knew where this was. *That place.* Laid out before her on tables, the shimmering objects seen before, including the silver lyre, awaited an owner to approach and make their selection.

"Why do you scream," the question was repeated by the woman. "You have been here before. I sense the recognition in your mind. Choose. One will be your salvation." The ancient stood next to Kenya, head cocked, watching with intense interest.

Without hesitation, Kenya scooped up the musical instrument and hugged the lyre tightly to her chest. A warm, soft radiance of heat pulsed from the metal. It felt somehow—right. Kenya snatched the carrying strap and slung the thong over her back while tucking the lyre under one arm.

"You have picked well, what your talents are best suited for," the Bohpoli murmured in approval. She clapped her hands and the room disappeared. Kenya was back in the thatched mound. The woman was gone.

Joyful chirps echoed around Kenya. The headsman gazed at the lyre in admiration. "You go now. Safe." He pushed her toward the door they'd entered from.

Unsure of what was happening Kenya took a hesitant step in the direction of the door.

"Wait."

Kenya halted. The Bohpoli reached into the fire pit and withdrew a flaming brand. The fire curled around his fingers and crept up his wrist, but the soft fur on his hand and arm remaining unsinged. He held out the wood to her. "Take," he said haltingly. "Darkness. Warmth. Cooking."

He is crazy.

The little man waited patiently with flame curling around his hand for her to accept his gift.

Against her better judgement, Kenya reached out, ready to snatch her arm away at the first sign of pain. With a last convulsive effort, she squinted her eyes and wrapped her fingers around the wood tightly.

Nothing.

Not really nothing. A sensation of crawling caterpillars flickered in her palm. The wood felt cool. Even the little tongues of flame dancing over her knuckles to her wrist did not burn. Kenya gaped at the headman in amazement.

He broke out into a grin and jabbed a gnarled finger at the exit. "Go."

In a state of shock, Kenya nodded silently. The lyre she strung over her back by the carrying strap, and crept forward through the opening holding her burning brand before her to light the way.

Dawn was breaking outside on the plain. She must have been inside the mound for hours, but it felt like no more than a few minutes. Kenya pulled the lyre off her back and held it at arms-length, the flaming torch clutched in the other hand. *I never said thank you.*

Back down we go. Kenya dropped to hands and knees again and inched through the doorway, meaning to thank the headsman and old woman if she could find the two of them.

The room was dark and empty. The Bohpoli gone. Even the green fire was missing from the pit.

***

Kenya gazed around the vacant chamber. A thick layer of sand covered the floor, dusty cobwebs hung from the ceiling. She held her brand high in the air and scrubbed at her eyes, positive her imagination was playing tricks on her, or the dim illumination from the torch failed to reveal the inhabitants of the room. She'd fallen down the rabbit's hole; she muttered, "Curious and curiouser," swinging around and creeping back into the bright sunshine. Kenya held the lyre and brand out in front of her face, assuming they would vanish before her eyes as surely as the little people did.

When they didn't disappear as expected Kenya shrugged and started walking East again. Her stomach was full, and for the first time since becoming lost, she didn't worry about hunger or thirst.

The sun reached its zenith and she halted by a small brook, a few trees growing along the bank. Sighing Kenya located a rock half-submerged in the water, covered in shade, and slipped off her boots, splashing and letting the cool liquid soothe her tired feet as she sloshed to the boulder. Kenya cradled the lyre in one arm, attempting to pick out a simple cord. The instrument was strange to her, but after a few attempts, found notes flowed together. She hummed to the rhythm, eyes closed, attempting to visualize words to go along with the tune.

A furry animal appeared with long ears and strong hind-legs. The creature sniffed the air and another appeared from behind a bush, and then a third out of the tall grass. With curious eyes, they stood motionless, lining the bank within touching distance of Kenya, watching her.

She giggled and made a cooing noise matching the melody. The animals slowly hopped closer up to their chests in the stream until they rested at her feet in a circle.

How cute. If I wanted, I could bend over, pick one up and sit it on my lap. Must be music lovers. My new fans.

A twinge of hunger rumbled in her belly and Kenya remembered her last meal was many hours ago. She surveyed the animals in a different way.

Capturing one would be easy.

Her stomach twisted at the thought of butchering one of the animals, and bile rose into her throat. She coughed, gagged. The startled creatures splashed away in fright.

Kenya sighed and watched the animals disappear into the brush. She would stick to bugs and berries. Perhaps a fish caught in one of the streams, eaten raw, even though they looked disgusting like flatworms with feelers, would keep her going until she arrived at Evertree. She'd made the journey this far. One more hole in her belt wouldn't matter anyway.

A stubborn streak of defiance against the terrain kept her going throughout the day. Toward evening, Kenya stopped on a mound and made camp for the night.

During the march, the flaming brand rested in a pouch of her tunic. The wood still burnt, but not her or her clothing. She couldn't understand what the little man meant by the stick would help with cooking if the fire didn't burn anything, nor did the flame give off heat. The torch did emit a feeble light, however, and she rested the wood between her knees keeping the growing darkness at bay.

As Kenya nested into a pile of grass torn up and heaped into what she hoped was a soft bed for her, the faint noise of "Clop-Clop-Clop" echoed across the prairie. Kenya sat up and peered into the darkness over the vegetation.

The nar-rider had returned.

Not again. Please tell me this isn't true.

Desperately Kenya tried to devise a plan of escape. Run? No, if she stood up the rider would see her. There were no Bohpoli to help either this time. She was alone and afraid.

Kenya took deep breaths attempting to dispel the rising terror. Her heart still hammered, but she tried to think rationally, and with an explosion of clarity knew she had only one choice. Stand and fight.

The muffled pounding of the spirit horse's hooves on the dirt drew closer, the sound coming straight for her hiding spot. With one last gulp and a silent prayer, Kenya clutched her club in one hand, her torch in the other and stood.

No head, but scarlet orbs hovered above the skull-less shoulders where a face should be. The horse and rider turned to confront Kenya squarely and kept walking toward her.

"Get out of here. OHHH—GET OUT OF HERE, I SAY." Kenya screamed at the phantom, jabbing the tip of her stick at the demon like the point of a sword. The nar-rider halted, and although the red orbs showed no expression, the body poised as if she'd said something humorous.

Faintness swept over her, loss of well-being and self. Kenya staggered forward, the stick dropping from fingers. She staggered toward the waiting rider.

NO.

With one last effort, Kenya drew herself upright. The stick was gone, but she still clutched the flaming torch in her left hand. Kenya lunged out in a crooked run, meaning to jab the nar-rider through his chest.

The demon reined in his horse. At the same time the torch Kenya held flamed bright, casting it's glow over both her, rider, and horse. A keening wail erupted from the nar-rider. His horse reared, pawed the air, screaming. In reflex Kenya dropped the torch to the ground, stumbled backward, and landed on her butt with a grunt.

Instantly the dry grass caught on fire, spreading in a circle to engulf the phantom. The horse frozen, a statue on two legs with forelegs raised, the noise of terror from rider, mount, ringing in Kenya's ears as the two turned translucent, and faded.

The two spirits didn't disappear at once, but as the flames of the grass burnt closer, they shimmered, the light from their bodies running up the spectrum until, with a burst of sparks, exploded into shimmering purple motes dissipating as the wind swept the glimmers away.

The light from the fire destroyed the nar-rider. Marcos said they can't abide light. How did the torch...?

The fire smoked and burnt itself out. Kenya scrambled back to her feet, trembles shaking her body. The torch rested on the earth flickered with the same blaze the wood showed before. Kenya carefully picked up the brand and studied the branch. No burn marks showed, nor did the flame scorch her fingers.

Why did the torch set the grass on fire?

More clumps of grass grew all around. Kenya touched the brand to one and immediately the leaves caught on blaze. Kenya put her hand to the flame, and snatched it back as quickly. The fire was hot and burnt her fingers. She ran her hand through the flame of the torch and only felt the caterpillars wiggling over her fingers.

Of course. The torch won't burn me, but anything else the wood sets on fire.

Shaking her head, Kenya returned to the nest she'd built. This time gathering a pile of dead branches and grass. *Well, here goes nothing.* She touched the torch to the pile and the heap flared into life. The warmth and light giving a sense of security. Kenya wrapped her arms around herself, and closed her eyes, the soft whispering of night insects lulling her to sleep.

She groaned and rolled over.

Marcos said there was more than one nar-rider. Better check in case another demon is out there somewhere.

Shaking herself awake, Kenya rose to her feet, the possibility of other threats flashing through her head now she was up and thought about the risk.

Kenya surveyed the plain one last time for danger before settling down for the night. She gasped and caught her breath. A campfire blazed in the East, and, oh, yes, to the North too. She was sure they were small fires set by men. The twinkling on the ground could be nothing else but people camping out for the night.

Kenya tried to stay objective while hope rose in her throat. Of course, those who camped couldn't be out searching for her, probably not even from Evertree, but still....

They are people. They will help. I know they will.

Without thinking of the darkness, or the possibility of more nar-riders about, Kenya threw her lyre over her shoulder and snatched up the firebrand, stumbling off into the night, positive if she didn't reach the people now, they'd be gone at dawn break.

Strange night flyers swooped over her head. One dive-bombed her and she swatted angrily at the pest with the torch before the beast tangled in her hair. Kenya tripped over unseen rocks in the tall grass, once tumbling into a dry streambed, hidden in the dark, before realizing the fires were farther than thought and slowed to a fast walk.

Kenya angled toward the nearest blaze, keeping the faint glow in sight and breathed a sigh of relief when the fire grew steady brighter. She waved the torch over her head in hopes the campers would see the light.

After an eternity of struggling, the campfires were within hailing distance. Three figures huddled around the blaze, four horses picketed close by. Sobbing in relief, she put on a burst of final speed and staggered forward.

"Help me."

The men looked up, staring into the darkness at the vicinity of Kenya's voice. One pointed a finger at the glowing torch and shouted to the others, standing, and drawing his sword.

"Please help me." Lungs on fire, Kenya lunged within the circle of fire. The three men glared at her, first in distrust, and then wonder.

Three swords jabbed in the direction of her belly. "Who are you?" one of the men demanded, "What are you doing out here on the plains? Are you friend or demon?"

What the heck is he talking about? "Friend, of course," Kenya gasped, attempting to catch her breath and regain composure. "Do I look like a demon?" Kenya stepped deeper into the firelight, glancing down at herself. Her riding clothes were shreds. She was bare to the knees. Mud, grass and twigs clung to her. Kenya hated to think what her face and hair must appear like to these men. *Maybe I do look like a demon.* Summoning up as much courage as possible, she stood erect and said with the last of her strength, "I am Lady Kenya from Evertree, Songsmith to King Harold himself." Her voice tapered off to a whisper. "Can you help me?"

The men glanced at each other and then hurried forward. The spokesman exclaimed, "Lady Kenya, we thought.... Your party returned days ago and said you were lost."

The last of Kenya's strength fled and she slumped. The warrior flung an arm around her waist before she collapsed to the ground. "Here, to the fire. You must be exhausted."

He led her back to the campsite and settled her by the blaze. The remains of their dinner still rested by the fire, the odor of roasted meat wafted to her nose. Kenya was hungry, and the smell made her hungrier than ever remembering before. She reached out toward the food. "May I?"

"Of course, Lady." Food and a crude wooden plate found their way into her hands along with a skin of sour red wine. "I am Randall," the warrior said as he held the wine skin for her. "You probably don't remember me, but I am one of Marcos's rangers. These are George and Jeffery. We are the king's men, scouts."

They're from Evertree. I'm safe.

Kenya breathed a sigh of relief and related her adventures since becoming lost, along with the run in with the nar-rider, taking breaks to gulp down more food and sips of the wine. The scout's expression showed signs of doubts about the strange tale until Kenya held out the lyre and torch to verify her story.

When she ended, Randall nodded. "We saw the glow of a fire but thought the blaze created by heat lightening striking the ground. When Lord Marcos and his band returned, he reported search parties set out from Lord Galvin's fortress in all directions seeking you. The brigand who kidnapped you was located and attacked, his holding destroyed. None left alive knew what became of you, or your whereabouts, and your body never found."

He gazed at the lyre and brand. "You say you met Bohpoli also? You were fortunate. They bring good or bad luck according to their mood. Be glad they decided to bestow good luck upon you. The power was theirs that rescued you from the nar-riders."

"Yes, I guess you can say they saved me. Odd people. One moment they were there, the next-*poof*-They disappeared."

"Odd, indeed. They are the little people. Few see them, and," Randall reached out a tentative finger to touch the lyre and drew his hand quickly back, "even fewer receive gifts from their kind. Do you know how to use this power?"

"I...." Kenya was about to say no, and then remembered the warriors asleep and the animals gathering around her. "I'm not sure," she said at last, casting a look into the campfire to conceal her confusion. "I didn't know how to use this torch either," Kenya held the brand up, "but now I do." To change the subject, she asked, "You are scouts for the king? What are you doing so far out here on the plain? What are you scouting for, is there added trouble since I've been absent?"

Murmurs of agreement arose between the three men. "Aye, and more's a brewing I fear," Randall replied bitterly. "The ancient evil stirs, stalks the earth once more as it did in the old days. Demons of legend and some no one has heard of before. After your party left, nameless creatures of the dark attacked undefended villages far and wide. On their return, King Harold himself and his troop were assaulted on these very plains again by a host of demons and many of his men killed."

A pang of anxiety ran through Kenya. "And Sir Marcos? The Princess Jessica? What of them? Do they still reside at Lord Galvin's fortress?"

"Princess Jessica remained at Lord Galvin's fortress for her own safety once word reached his castle of the evil stalking the savannah. Sir Marcos and a party of Lord Galvin's troops managed a crossing in a running battle and won to Evertree," came the swift reply from Randall. "They reside now at the keep." Randall chuckled to himself, but said soberly, "Sir Marcos has risen high in the council of King Harold since then. The king has lost many of his top captains and advisors, and Marcos shows great bravery in these times. Harold takes him into his confidence more every day, and increasingly passes responsibility onto his shoulders."

Kenya breathed a sigh of relief. Marcos was safe, and what's more, he was finally receiving the recognition he so richly deserved.

"I will escort you to Evertree," Randall said, checking with his companions by eye for agreement, "in the morning. Even though we put you on horseback, travel across this region is not safe. The ways are dangerous.

Even more so since now we know nar-riders are afoot. I am surprised you made the journey across the plains this far by yourself."

"Almost didn't," Kenya replied. She released a huge yawn. The world spun slowly around as her chin touched her chest. She raised her head up with a jerk. "Sorry, tired," Kenya mumbled, trying to keep her attention focused. You can understand…."

Randall leaped to his feet. "Of course, Lady Kenya." He strode to one of the horses, withdrew a spare sleeping blanket from a pack, and spread the wrap out by the fire. "Rest while you can. We have a long and dangerous journey tomorrow if we are to arrive at Evertree."

Kenya smiled wanly, and stretched out, releasing herself to sleep. She could forget the dangers still approaching, for the time being she was safe.

Chapter Twelve

The warriors distributed the saddlebags and bundles from their packhorse onto the other two mounts. Randall announced to Kenya, "We break camp. These two to continue their watch, you and I to ride swiftly to Evertree. I hope you rested well last night."

Kenya mounted. Relief and excitement racing in her heart, lightness in her step. The ordeal was over, soon to be secure behind strong stone walls, a soft bed, and warm food in her belly again.

As much as Kenya wanted to hurry to the fortress, Randall did not push their mounts to the limits. Nevertheless, they made good time. A combination of galloping, trot and rest for the riders and mounts by walking the horses through the knee-high grass ate up the distance as much as a harder pace would have and left them relaxed and fresh.

When the sun hung high in the sky, they'd traveled more than half the length to Evertree. Randall didn't stop for lunch. Instead, he fished around in his pouch and handed Kenya a parchment wrapped hard brick of travel rations. "Eat if you would, Lady, and drink from your water skin. For now we venture into the most dangerous part of our journey and will not have time to tarry for food."

Kenya broke the bar in the middle, stuffing half into her saddlebag for later and sucked on the other half, a pounded bar of nuts, berries, and dried meat held together with honey and cast a frightened glance around her. The plain spreading out in all directions was empty except for a hawk making lazy circles in the sky as the raptor glided over the air currents seeking prey on the earth below.

"I don't see anything to harm us," Kenya commented scanning the waving grass. "Why are you so worried? We're making good time, I would judge. The castle can't be so far away, is it?"

"This is where you are wrong, Lady." The warrior rose in his stirrups, surveying in all directions. "Anything which has skulked past the scouts lurks here. We cannot stop them all. They are too few in numbers to attack Evertree, and not yet bold enough to do so. Small holding and travelers such as ourselves are their meat. No doubt this is where your nar-rider was heading until he met you."

As if to prove him correct a ragged vee swayed the tall grass to their right, moving their way at tremendous speed. "See what I mean Lady?" Randall swung a hand in the direction of the wavering vegetation. "Danger stalks us already and quickly." He booted his mount in the sides and snapped the reins, shouting at the same time to Kenya, "Let us ride, and pray our horses are fast enough."

Fearing the worse, Kenya clutched the burning brand in her hand, the warmth somehow reassuring to the touch. A potential weapon also if needed.

The two rode knee to knee, angling to the left as they attempted to avoid whatever chased them, but still pressing forward in hopes of outdistance the new menace. Kenya threw glances all around her, watching for the approach of more danger. In spite of the swiftness of the horses, the disturbance in the grass drew closer, changing direction to cut off the avenue of safety.

The horses burst into a section of bare, blackened ground, burnt off by a lightning strike and prairie fire, the horse's hooves sending grey ash floating into the air in their wake.

Randall searched the area in desperation for a new route of escape. "We make our stand here," he announced. "They run too swiftly and will exhaust the horses. In the tall grass, they would hide until it is too late to detect them.

We would be easy prey." He jerked his sword from its scabbard and drew out his short sword, handing the blade hilt first to Kenya. "Prepare to defend yourself."

Kenya fumbled with the large grip of the unfamiliar weapon, feeling the steel blade heavy in her hand. Dread laced up her belly, lodging in her chest. For an unknown reason, instinct maybe, she withdrew the lyre from her saddle horn, clasping the instrument hard while transferring the sword to the hand holding the torch.

Howls rang out, incessant baying of hungry beasts on the hunt. The grass parted and man-like creatures stalked into the clearing on all fours.

Their legs were crooked as a dog's hindquarter, each sporting a long black tail, but their fronts were those of a man. Sharp yellow canines protruded from the upper jaws and the eyes shone scarlet with madness.

"Ikkitousen." Randall spat out the name in disgust. "Perverted abominations breed from women and wolves in the foul pits of the dark lords. There is no escaping their attack. We must fight or die."

The monstrosities circled. The ring around Kenya and Randall slowly growing tighter with each pass. The leader of the pack made a sudden lunge, darting in with snarls and slobbering jaws, not at Randall but at his horse's legs. The beast reared, screaming in fright and defiance, and lashed out with sharp front hooves. The *ikkitousen* leaped nimbly out of the way with a howl of rage, and the circling began anew with increased speed.

This time an attack came to the rear of Kenya's mount. Her horse bucked, kicking as Kenya twisted in the saddle, short sword held ready. A second buck sent her over her mount's head to sprawl on the ground in a heap.

She scrambled to her feet, clutching sword and brand in one hand, lyre in the other. Two of the beasts slunk toward her, bellies scrapping the earth, lips curled in snarls.

Kenya back peddled hastily until her shoulders brushed the sweaty sides of her mount.

"Beware."

One of the two demon dogs bunched. With a roar, the beast launched itself through the air straight at Kenya's throat. Without thinking, she whipped her blade around, the tip pointed at the monster's chest.

Fire from the brand crackled up the metal, erupting into a piercing sword of flame.

Randall's horse pivoted, kicked out with iron hooves. The warrior slashed at any beast within his range with deadly accuracy. Screaming howls of pain rang out through the air, the blackened earth red with splattered blood.

The flame from Kenya's sword engulfed the demon, setting the hairy body aflame, searing skin and blowing ash on the ground. Kenya's mount shrieked in panic as the charred body slammed into the earth at Kenya's feet, bowling her over.

Randall vaulted from his saddle, swinging with his sword, battling in Kenya's direction as the rest of the demons leaped in for the kill.

Kenya landed, and flung out her arm, dropping both sword and torch. In a panic, she grabbed the lyre in both hands and held the instrument out, a slim shield of defense. Her fingers ripped across the strings.

Kenya did not strike a chord, rather a random set of notes—a discord.

The second ikkitousen confronting her rose on its crooked doglegs, clasped dirty hands over its ears, and howled in pain. In desperation Kenya hit the strings again, harder, louder, not caring what notes played or in what order. Shrieks surrounded her. The ikkitousen ready to attack backed off, dazzled and whimpering as they rolled on the ground.

Dumbfounded, Kenya glance quickly about. The rest of the demons backed off also, some staggering away on their legs, others crawling on their bellies. A shadow passed over her.

"What did you do, Lady?" Randall stood above Kenya, bloody sword in hand, dazed by the rapid turn of events.

"I-I-I don't know." Kenya held the instrument up. "I hit the strings by mistake, nothing musical, random notes, and the monsters went crazy."

Randall's mouth opened and closed wordlessly. "I see," he said at last. He swung in a wide circle, scanning the area. "Do it again, louder."

Hesitantly, almost fearful, Kenya plucked a few strings haphazardly as hard as she could. The notes sailed out through the air. From afar, howls of anguish arose. Kenya cringed at the cries of torment.

Is it the lyre or me?

Randall cocked his ear, listening carefully. "I feel naught," he admitted, rising on his toes, hunting for the direction the howls originated from, "but it appears the ikkitousen think otherwise." He scratched the black stubble on his chin, and swung sharply to Kenya, searching her face. "I wonder if your lyre works as well on other demons."

Kenya took a deep breath and issued a hollow laugh. "I hope you do not plan on seeking more out." She gazed at the burnt body and the rest slaughtered by Randall's sword. "What we have found is more than enough for me."

"And more than plenty for me, also," the scout agreed. His smile dropped from his lips and he held a palm up. "Nay, Lady, you are right, but this is a potent weapon, indeed, as is your firebrand." He bent to pick up the flaming wood from the earth, thought better of his act, and instead, offered his hand to Kenya, drawing her up off the ground.

Kenya saw his hesitation and scooped up both sword and torch. "We'd best be riding," she mumbled looping the lyre over her back.

Randall nodded and strode off to collect the horses. "You are right, Lady. The quicker we are off this plain and returned to Evertree, the safer we will both be."

They rode. Within the hour, the odor of the ocean blew in Kenya's nose and sea birds mewed overhead. After another hour, they crossed a stone paved lane and swung onto the highway, the faint pounding of surf and waves whispering in their ears, a wet breeze in their faces.

They sped around a curve. Randall slowed his horse to a walk as they approached an ox cart. Strung along the highway more wagons ambled in the direction of the castle, all loaded with people and household furnishings piled to overflowing.

"Why are so many people on the road," Kenya asked as the horses passed a wagon stuffed with pigs, chickens, and children.

"They abandon their homes and flee the plains from the farther holdings," Randall replied grimly. "They fear attack and escape to Evertree to huddle in the safety of the fortress walls. Too many farms have been destroyed already. The people abandon all they have worked to create. For them it's stay and die."

The castle loomed into view. Since Kenya's departure weeks ago, the small village surrounding the keep blossomed into a shantytown, a collection of makeshift shacks, patched tents, and wagons. The nearby ocean teemed with people fishing or bathing in the salty water. The wind shifted in Kenya's direction and she received the fetid odor of too many people crammed into a too small place.

They rode to the drawbridge with the imploring cries of *"Food—Food—Food,"* from the children and old women who hurried to line the road at their approach. One, a young mother in ragged tunic, holding a baby to her breast said nothing, but watched Kenya steadily with bleak eyes.

Kenya fumbled at her saddlebags, drawing out whatever travel rations remained from her lunch, and flung the bits into the crowd, making sure the largest chunk landed at the mother's feet. The woman scooped up the morsel with a silent "Thank you" on her lips.

"Can't King Harold do something for those poor people?" Kenya asked Randall as their horses tromped over the wooden drawbridge into the courtyard. "These folks are starving."

Randall dismounted and pursed his lips, obviously disturbed also. "The king can do naught, for to feed all he need empty his storehouses, and he fears a siege if the castle is attacked. If this be the case, all these you see here," he waved a hand outside, "will be dead or fled anyway. It is a hard choice, but one the king has made for better or worse."

Kenya compressed her lips and said nothing. She understood the king's viewpoint, but didn't have to like the conclusion he'd reached. The inhumanity sent a cold shiver along her spine.

"Announce me to the king," Randall commanded to one of the guards at the entrance to the castle. "I have found Lady Kenya and brought her from the plains."

The sentry hurried away and Randall, followed closely by Kenya, strode after him into the fortress.

Harold's great hall hadn't changed since Kenya's last visit. People milled about with the king keeping watch on the crowd, but Kenya noted many of the familiar faces who once advised Harold no longer graced the closest places to the king. The guard marched up to Harold, whispered urgently and waved a hand in the direction of Kenya and Randall standing anxiously at the entrance to the hall. The king glanced up sharply and motioned for them to approach. The crowd grew quiet as they weaved their way forward through the throng, with a low babble of amazement trailing in their wake.

Harold addressed his first words to Kenya. "We thought you lost, Wordsmith." His eyes roved over her sorry appearance. "You must tell us later of your journey. I am sure the story you have to relate is a tale worth hearing." To Randall he asked, "What news of the plains? Does the evil still mount?"

The warrior raised his shoulders and dropped them. "Yes, Sire. The evil keeps massing, never striking in great numbers at any one spot, but in small, quick raids like a hen pecking at grains of corn in the dust. Each day they grow bolder, a hangman's noose tightening about our necks waiting for the trap to be released under our feet."

The king nodded sadly, knowing the truth before Randall told to him. "It is much as I feared, and the other reports I received are much like yours." He issued a troubled sigh. "Go, eat, and fill your bellies and rest. You must be sorely tired from your trip."

"Lady Kenya."

Kenya turned at her name. Marcos stood behind her, relief etched on his features, his eyes fixed on her face.

"Marcos." Her first impulse was to leap on him, wrap her arms around his shoulders in a tight hug. Kenya restrained herself and instead, approached him slowly and offered him a hand. "I thought I would never see you again." She gazed back at him, their vision locking as they stared into each other's eyes.

"Nor I you," he replied with a smile, intertwining his fingers with hers with a squeeze and tugging Kenya back through the crowd. "Your old chamber is still vacant, I would not allow the steward to disturb your belongings even though the castle thought you would never return," Marcos said eagerly. "I will have food and drink brought. You must be exhausted." He gave Kenya a questioning glance at the burning torch and lyre slung around her back, but since she did not mention where she acquired her new possessions he refrained from asking.

Marcos left her in the chamber with a promise he'd be right back and disappeared out the door, returning with a try laden with roast chicken, boiled tubers and small cubes of red and orange fruits. "Eat," he urged, setting the tray on an end table next to the bed.

Kenya stuffed her mouth, savoring each bite never remembering eating so good a meal. In between chewing and swallowing, she related the adventures since last leaving Galvin's castle.

Marcos finally asked, "And those?" He pointed to the torch and lyre she left sitting on the bed, "Where did you find these?" He watched the flame of the torch creep around Kenya's fingers without harming her. "True magic, which I have never seen before."

"These saved us," Kenya said, holding up the lyre and torch, "from the ikkitousen, and when I was captured I played the lyre in my dreams, and," she raised her hands, "it was as if I were sleep walking. When I woke up I was free."

"Most powerful magic indeed," Marcos said. "We searched for you, every inch of the forest. I sought you, until I was frantic and could not sleep from the worry, but it was as if you departed from the face of the Earth. When we discovered the lair of the brigand Semus, Galvin and I questioned every man, even to the point of torture, until the men screamed in pain. He even summoned," Marcos shuddered, "something dark from beyond, but to no avail."

Kenya's awareness of the potential danger of Lord Galvin leaped to the front of her mind. *If he goes over to the dark side so easily, he must have done so before. Each time the doing becomes easier so soon there is not distinction between the two.*

"Do you then know how to use this magic? Summon it's power to your will? You would be a great aid to the kingdom if you could."

"I'm not sure. Yes—No. Maybe," Kenya admitted, forgetting the worry about Lord Galvin in the face of this new question. She purposely wiped her fingers on a linen and selecting a cube of fruit while debating an answer. The problem mulled over in her mind since discovering the supernatural properties of her new possessions. Kenya nibbled, savoring the juice and sweetness and said with certainty, "I will learn."

"You will, my lady," Marcos replied. He reached out and gently squeezed her shoulder. "I wish your wisdom extended to my cousin."

"Jessica? What is the matter with her? I thought the princess stayed at Galvin's fortress for safety."

"My cousin did, but Jessica made it clear in no uncertain terms she possessed no desire to return to Evertree. Nothing I can lay a finger on, but at our last meeting before we rode for home the princess acted— different, as if Galvin was her lord and she acted on his whim."

"How so? Modest? As a lady should?" Kenya quipped.

Marcos chuckled feebly. "No," he denied. "Her eyes were unfocused, as if her body was there, but her being was discorporated from the flesh. I felt as though I spoke to a golem of clay. You said this happened to you at the fortress. I am afraid the same thing has happened to her but worse."

More of Galvin' trafficking with dark forces? I knew it. "Could Galvin or the witch have laid a spell on her? You said in the questioning of Semus and his men he conjured up—evil." Kenya recalled the strange experiences with Feg. *Maybe the witch controls both Galvin and Jessica.*

She heard no answer from Marcos, but the worried look on his face told Kenya how disturbed he was.

The next morning, Kenya, accompanied by Marcos, again related her story, this time to the king in detail and not leaving out any of her thoughts or impressions. In the middle of the tale as she explained the torch and lyre, shouts and screams rang through the air from outside the castle walls.

A guard bust into the great hall, out of breath. "Sire, the village—the refugees are under attack."

Harold bolted upright. *"What?"*

Marcos already hurried to the door, drawing his sword.

"Wait for me here," he ordered Kenya as he bolted to the corridor.

She hurried after him, slinging the lyre over her shoulder.

Outside the screams rang louder, more terrifying, mingled with the roars of a beast. Marcos sprang ahead as the portcullis lowered and drawbridge drew up, leaping outside to land rolling in the dirt as they closed behind. Kenya faced a locked barrier.

She glared up at the sentries on top of the wall. "Oh, let me out," Kenya yelled in frustration and shook the iron bars. The guards stared at her and then turned their attention to the events outside the walls.

Cursing under her breath, Kenya located staircases leading upward to the battlements and ran up, taking two at a time in her haste. Archers stormed behind her, pushing Kenya forward in their haste to man the walls. Kenya scrambled to an empty archer's notch and gazed out onto the village below.

Terrified women and children scrambled in panic running in all directions. A thin line of desperate men brandishing rusty swords and shovels stood between them and a monster from the beginning of time. Greenish-grey armor plates covered the creature, the stubby tail ended in a spiked ball. Sharp claws ripped at the dry earth as the beast lowered its horned head and charged the men.

A few of the bravest defenders held their ground, battering away at the armored skull with their makeshift weapons only to be brushed aside, or trampled underfoot at the monster's charge. Most others fled, joining the women and children as they ran for cover.

Steel-tipped arrows peppered the beast's flanks and back, fired by the archers from the battlements. The bolts bounced off without effect. The monster snorted a foul, yellowish gas emitting from its nostrils and one of the hovels flared into blaze. The creature rumbled forward toward the castle leaving a line of destruction as it crushed over the tents while the armored tail whipped back and forth, smashing through shacks as if constructed from parchment.

A flicker of light caught the monster in the snout, shortly halting the advance. A warrior dodged in and out of the fleeing people, advancing toward the beast with a wild yell of combat, sword erupting in fire.

Marcos.

Kenya put her fist to her mouth as the monster swiped at its nose and glanced around for the source of this unexpected nuisance. *He's going to get himself killed. What can I...?* She remembered the lyre on her back, snatched the instrument out of the carrying sling, and hit the string, producing a racket of noise.

The sound had no effect on the demon.

In desperation, Kenya hit different notes as the creature spotted Marcos and his sword. The demon bellowed and rumbled headfirst at the warrior.

Marcos stood his ground, jaws clenched, and flicked his blade into the face of the behemoth charging him. Fire engulfed the head, crackling along the spine, but to no effect. Issuing cries of rage, the beast continued to advance, stomping its feet until the earth shook with horn lowered.

At the last second, Marcos leaped sideways as the demon sprayed its putrid yellow breath over the spot he'd stood on a moment before. The monster whirled, unbelievably fleet of foot for so large an animal, and charged after the man. Marcos kept back peddling, splashing through the water of the moat, bursts of flame from his sword growing shorter and feebler until his back was to the wall of the castle.

In horror, Kenya watched as the beast closed in on Marcos.

He will be killed.

"Marcos." Kenya pulled out the burning brand, the only thing she could think of. *"Catch—put it to your blade."*

Heaving with every ounce of strength in her body, Kenya threw the wood in the direction of Marcos. He looked, saw the brand flying end over end his way, and leaped up, grasping the wood in his fingers as the torch flew over his head.

The suddenness of the blazing stick flashing across the beast's field of vision from nowhere halted the monster briefly. The huge head swung in Kenya's direction, snout up, searching the air for her sight or scent.

Marcos clasped brand to sword, doubt clouding his features, but a determined look in his eyes.

The blade exploded with incandescent fury.

Marcos swung the weapon on the creature and advanced, kicking through the water of the moat, and relying on his speed to evade any attack the monster made. This time the fire engulfed the body, clinging hungrily to the flesh. Screaming in pain the monster back up, biting at the flames burning its skin, howls of anguish reverberating off the castle walls. Marcos held the blade steady, allowing the inferno to wash from the head to the tail as if channeling the flow of a waterfall with a glowing pipe.

With a convulsive shudder, the demon fell to its knees, withering in death throes. Smoke belched out of nose and mouth, the skin glowed with an internal white light of fire, and melted as the circle of combustion spread farther. The next instant the beast exploded in a shower of burning flesh as the gas within the belly ignited in a detonation of fury.

The force of the blast hurled Marcos backward against the wall. He bounced off the barrier and slumped to the ground, stunned.

Before Kenya realized what she was doing, she flew down the steps from the battlement, screaming at the top of her lungs to the gatekeeper, *"Lower the drawbridge, Marcos is hurt!"*

The men threw her a startled look and then leaped to their windless. Slowly the portcullis rose and the drawbridge lowered while Kenya hopped anxiously from foot to foot in worry.

Before the iron barrier was fully up and the drawbridge down Kenya darted through, leaping from the edge of the wooden planks and landing in the dirt at a dead run. Marcos lay unconscious when she reached his side. Coughing, with the acid stench of burnt meat and black smoke filling the air, Kenya gasped at the blood covering the warrior.

Oh, no. Is he dead? Please don't be dead.

Terrified, Kenya knelt beside Marcos, snatching up his wrist and feeling for a pulse. She found it, strong and throbbing under her fingers. *He's alive, thank God. Marcos lives.* "Marcos," Kenya shook him. "Marcos, wake up."

Marcos sat up, coughing, and glanced around, confused. "The beast...?"

"Dead," Kenya replied, wrapping her arm around his shoulder and helping him to his feet. "You killed it."

Still dazed, his eyes landed on the smoldering remains of the demon and then wandered to his sword and burning torch next to him. "It was the brand," he muttered, bending and picking up the torch and presenting it back to Kenya. "When I touched the wood to my blade I felt the power drain out of me and sucked into my sword."

Kenya nodded and held him steady. "The magic was always in you. The brand brought the power dwelling inside you out." She tucked the torch into her pouch.

Blood flowed down Marcos's face and a ragged gash in his shoulder oozed scarlet. Red stained Kenya's hands. Marcos slumped and sank down suddenly, groaning. "Let me bring you back inside. You're bleeding." Kenya wrapped an arm around his shoulder and attempted to lift him to his feet.

"He saved us."

Kenya glanced around. Villagers and the refugees surrounded the two. More sloshed out of the ocean where they'd run for safety.

"Indeed he did." Harold stood there, sword in hand. He strode forward and knelt, clasping Marcos in a hug. "A brave deed, lad. Quick witted, too," he exclaimed. His voice lowered, until it was hardly above a whisper. "Now I truly feel ashamed for how I treated you all these years, never seeing the worth within you. Would be you were my son instead of my nephew. Forgive me." The king motioned to the villagers standing around them in a circle. "Take this brave warrior into the castle so his wounds may be tended too."

Two of the men stepped forward. "Here, we will take him." Together they picked up Marcos on either side and carried him back into the castle.

Chapter Thirteen

"I do not understand how something so large snuck past our scouts." Randall paced back and forth in the healer's room, hands behind his back, while he stroked his short black beard furiously. "Impossible."

Marcos reclined on a table, the surgeon applying a poultice of herbs to his shoulder and bound the bandage tight with a long strip of cloth. Kenya sat next to him, eyes darting from one face to the other in worry as she listened to the two men talking.

"You saw the demon, the beast was here." Marcos winced as the surgeon patted the poultice tight to his wound. "I saw no wings on the creature. It did not fly over our scouts and to the keep at night."

Randall frowned at Marcos and waved a hand in his face. "You know as well as I do we search the sky for flying danger. The question is, how did the creature reach the castle unnoticed without flying? *How?*" Randall continued his aggravated striding, shaking his head, and muttering wordlessly to himself.

"I didn't see many scouts when I chanced upon you," Kenya said for the first time. "A few fires in the night. If the creature managed to evade those...."

Randall issued a sour laugh. "You did but see two or three, yes, Lady Kenya, but I assure you plenty more were scattered where you did not see. Our patrols are checker boarded in a wide arc, also. The chance is possible an invader might sneak through one line, nevertheless, it would hit the next, or the one after."

"He is right, Kenya," Marcos affirmed, sitting up. "I helped devise the pattern myself from volunteers."

"Could someone intentionally allow the monster to pass through?" Kenya wondered aloud. "A traitor, perhaps? Someone who doesn't like Evertree or the king and wishes to see our downfall?"

Randall paused in his pacing and glanced at Marcos. "It is possible, but…."

Marcos scowled. "I handpicked all, most from the king's own soldiers and Galvin's men. To fill out the ranks I selected refugees who know the terrain, and who are known to me to be loyal subjects of the king. These men have farms out there and wish the end of the war as much as the people of the castle do." He shook his head in denial. "I see none of these betraying the kingdom to demons. Besides, to allow attack at Evertree is to invite death."

"That's something else," Kenya said slowly, thinking of the beast. "The monster was not a proper demon at all, was it?" She glanced from Marcos to Randall to see if they understood. "The creature reminded me of animals from the past existing on earth before man."

The two warriors exchanged sharp looks. "We find bones, from time to time," Marcos said slowly, thinking, "but how would…?"

"Could whatever evil releasing the demons on the world again have also drawn these monsters from the past?" Kenya wondered aloud, searching Marcos's face.

"It would mean someone has breached the Arch of Time," Randall said. "In this case we are sorely beseeched indeed. What foul creatures could be thrown against us? The dead themselves would rise."

"If they wished they could summon the wielders of evil magic we thought long since gone to other realms." Marcos's face was dark with worry.

Kenya sensed the tensions in the room grow. She said cautiously, "Summoning beings from the past is a relative thing. Perhaps animals, demons—but people? If I left this land, I don't think it would be an easy matter to bring me back if I didn't want to, and held the ability to resist the summons."

"True, Lady Kenya," Randall said after a minutes thought. "Still, who or what would do such a thing?" He glanced at Marco. "Is there one in this world who has the ability and desire to bring ruin to us all?"

Marcos said nothing.

A deep suspicion arose in Kenya's mind.

***

Speculation ran riot for the next few days within the castle walls debating how the demon managed to draw so close or who might have sent the beast. Harold ordered more men out onto the prairie to patrol until protest arose from Marcos and others he was stripping their defense bare.

After a week, Randall left to rejoin his companions, telling Marcos and Kenya, "If there be a traitor among the scouts I will speedily discover who it is. I will not finish seeking until I root him out, whoever he may be."

Marcos and Kenya watched from the battlements as the warrior disappeared into a small dot, swallowed up into the dark forest. "I wonder if we shall ever see him again," Kenya said sadly, turning away to the stairs. "For the short time I knew him he seemed like a noble man."

"Most noble," Marcos agreed. "We have been friends since childhood. He has stood by my side when all called me useless, because of my failure to use the magic within me."

Kenya bit back a reply. She knew in her heart this wasn't his shortcoming. When the need arose, so would the power within him. He'd shown his strength already, and even the king took notice of his worth now.

He must learn to believe in himself. It's so simple, why can't he understand?

Marcos paused at the head of the stairs. "I hope he discovers the traitor, if there be one, but I think it wise to look to our own defenses here at Evertree in case there is not one. If by some chance the dark forces have discovered a way to circumnavigate our ring of warriors, we are sorely undermanned, with our warriors scattered across half the plain."

Kenya stopped also and gazed out at the wide vista of sea and sand surrounding the castle. She nodded in agreement. "I thought the same thing. Have Galvin's men been training ours in the manufacture and use of the fire rings as he promised they would? With all the turmoil since I've returned I forgot to ask."

Marcos released a sigh speaking his growing aggravation of the defense of the castle. "Training, yes, but the manufacturing of the rings occurs slow," he explained. "The sulfur is brought from the South, a land of volcanoes and steaming pools that few but the bravest men transverse. The miners must dig the rock out of the smoking earth, and then transported the material overland across the burning desert on camelback. We used what small supply we possessed here at the castle right away. Now we must wait for more to arrive. King Harold has sent messengers to seek traders, but how long the seeking will take, no one knows." Marcos gestured along the walkway. "This is why I used some of Galvin's men for the scouts. Come, they practice in the rear of the castle on the sea side to stay out of the way of our soldiers standing guard on the battlements, and protect against any prying eyes watching from concealment in the forest."

They set off along the causeway to the back of the fortress where a dozen soldiers gathered under the supervision of four men. The soldiers paired into twos, six groups, where they practiced tossing the rings over the side of the castle under the watchful eyes of their instructors. On occasion, one of Galvin's men would stop a pair, and explain something with a throwing motion and a stabbing finger at the hoop.

Kenya surveyed one group as they stooped, lifted a heavy ring, and tossed the loop over the battlement. "They don't light the rings?" Kenya questioned. "Seems like a waste of time, the dangerous part is doing the throwing when the circles are flaming."

A smile touched Marcos's mouth as a pair of the warriors lifted a ring. One released a moment earlier than the second man let go of the loop. The circle flopped against the battlement and sprang back, causing the two warriors to dance out of the way. This evoked a harsh remark from their instructor and gruff chuckles for the rest of the soldiers. "No. These are for practice only. Galvin's men tell us the lifting, aiming, and throwing are the hardest part, not the flame. The men must learn to act as a team so their efforts are coordinated." He pointed a finger at the two soldiers who picked up the loop again sheepishly. "See what I mean?"

"Hmm…. Perhaps you are right." Kenya continued to watch the men tossing rings over the wall, and then trooping down the stairs to retrieve the hoops. "I still feel something is wrong," she said slowly to Marcos. "Mistakes will happen, and the men are plainly bored with this exercise. After all, how hard is it to go 'One—Two—Three—*Throw*?" Kenya executed a heaving motion to illustrate the point. "What they're doing now is useless."

Marcos chuckled. "The training might be for all I know. Many of us feel the same way, but Lord Galvin's men insist this is how the exercise must happen. The king backs the warriors on this so…." He lifted his shoulders in mock despair.

Kenya shook her head wearily. She should have realized the king would be unsure of something new, and decided to listen to Galvin's soldiers instead of his own advisors. Kenya swung to the battlements and gazed out across the ocean. "Is there anything to fear attacking from the water?" She shivered. "Sea demons? Water monsters? Perhaps pirates who have aligned themselves with evil?"

Marcos frowned. "I think not." He swept his hand over the bay. "Our navy has us well protected in that direction. In olden times, the battles have always been on the land, and pirates have never troubled us this close to the coast. In years past, they tried and their fleets destroyed. They know better. No. If an assault occurs, it will launch from the land."

Kenya's lips shut into a thin line. "Then in an attack the villagers and refugees from the country will be the first to die?" She searched the along the side of the castle where people were seen wading in the water.

Marcos followed her gaze and nodded sadly. "True, but there is no place else for them to go. If they return to their farms it is certain death."

Kenya switched her vision back to the ocean and studied the ships at anchor. "We must evacuate any who will go," she said at last with certainty. She waved to the boats. "Put the people on the ships, at least the women and children. A few on each one for safety."

"It could work," Marcos admitted slowly, thinking of the logistics of such a move. "We would have to convince the king, but...."

Kenya spun around on her toes, marching toward the front entrance of the castle, determination in each step. When Marcos didn't follow right away she yelled over one shoulder, "Well, don't stand there gawking, let's ask."

They located the king in an anteroom adjacent to his chambers pouring over a map in heated debate with his war councilors. Harold glance up, annoyed, when Kenya and Marcos barged in. "Well, what do you want," he snapped, glaring at the two, as his fingers clutched the parchment on the table before him. "Do you not see we are busy at the moment?"

Before Marcos could utter a word, Kenya said, "The women and children from the village. They must be evacuated to the ships in the harbor at once."

"What?"

Kenya continued in a rush, "All will be killed in an invasion if they are left out there in those hovels. A few on each ship so none may be overburdened. These are your people, Sire, who have fled here for your protection. Surely you cannot let the citizens of your kingdom die."

Harold's mouth moved wordlessly, stunned by Kenya's words and the fact a woman would criticize his judgement. His face clouded over red. Before he exploded in anger one of his advisors whispered urgently in his ear. Harold swallowed, nodded slowly in agreement, his eyes taking on a shrewd look. He said to Kenya, "Aye, perhaps it would be a good idea for the people to understand I think of their welfare at a time like this. The men will fight harder if they know I am a righteous ruler." He glanced past Kenya to Marcos. "This will be a good job for you. Women, children, the old and sick, anyone who cannot defend themselves will be evacuated to the fleet. We will keep the able-bodied men here to defend the castle and fight, although I do not know how much good they will do in a battle."

Marcos bowed, and murmured, "As you will, Sire." He turned to the door.

"Wait," Kenya said laying a hand on his shoulder. While the king spoke she'd studied the map laid out before Harold and recalled the terrain approaching the castle. Walking the landscape, Kenya never noticed the shape of the land. One feature leaped out from the drawing. She pointed to a narrow spot on the peninsular the fortress stood on. "Most of the refugees are farmers, right? They are used to digging. Why not have these people dig a deep trench from here to here." Kenya drew an imaginary line with her finger across the narrow point. "Reinforce the two ends with wooden stockades, dams if you will, and if an army approaches," she made a jerking motion, "we destroy the dams and let the water flow in." Kenya watched Harold's face to see if he understood what she meant.

The king stared at his map blankly. The councilors did the same with interest. One murmured to another and a third took out a stylus and made quick calculations on a piece of parchment, showing the results to Harold. His lips broadened into a smile and he studied the map again. "Your plan might work," he said carefully to Kenya, "but we must move swiftly if this is to be accomplished. No one knows the day or time of the attack. In any case, the project will give the men something to do other than stand around worrying and keep their minds occupied." Harold cleared his throat. "Perhaps this also will stop the grumbling I have heard lately about how I conduct the defense of the castle."

Kenya took the task upon herself to walk through the village, stalking from shack to shack, explaining the new orders from the king and urging the people to escape to the waiting boats as soon as possible. Some of the women grumbled at leaving their husbands, especially the younger ones, but Kenya was insistent, saying, "This is for your own good, and the king has ordered the evacuation."

Before the day was finished, Kenya lined the evacuees up at the beach waiting. Well into the night, ship after ship docked at the castle, taking on loads of people carrying bundles of their belongings on their backs. By sunrise, the women and children were gone, village and shantytown deserted. Marcos and the castle's engineers surveyed the peninsular and as the sun rose, the remaining men waited, prepared with mattocks and shovels in hand. Marcos marched the workers out to the designated area for the trench and the work began.

***

Kenya sat in her chamber, idly plucking at the lyre, attempting to select a combination of notes to produce some magical effect. No matter what she attempted, however, failed to produce a response, other than a chorus of sounds. Kenya began to wonder if she'd imagined the strange occurrences, perhaps some other force outside her range of knowledge stirred to deliver her from danger. But the torch resting on the table still glowed brightly, throwing off light and warmth without burning or displaying any decay of the wood.

There must be magic in this instrument. I know some enchantment rests inside, but how to unlock the power. How?

Boredom was setting in also. The digging of the trench was well under way with Marcos driving the men into the night, and besides a quick nod of gratitude for her suggestion, King Harold made no demands for her presence, or asked for any suggestions about the defense. Marcos rarely returned to the fortress during the day, his supervising of the men occupying all of his time. The rest of the castle personnel contented themselves with preparations for an assault and possible siege, each one knowing exactly what tasks needed completing in their own sphere of occupation. Her dubious title as wordsmith forbade her the privilege of helping with any of these jobs other than those assigned by the king himself, nor was she skilled enough to be of much use.

Kenya set the lyre down with a sigh wondering what to do to pass the time. She stretched out on the bed thinking of taking a nap. The room was too light, and her mind kept running over the problems facing the defenders of the fortress. Kenya rose and strolled to the window. In the distance, the men labored at the trench. *Might as well go down and watch. Better than sitting here all day. Marcos will be at the site. Maybe together we can devise some new suggestions for the king.* With fresh resolution she stood, and pushed the boredom away, tucked the torch into a pouch while stringing the instrument over her back. Before Kenya exited the castle, she left word with the guard of her whereabouts in case Harold decided he needed her and headed for the diggers.

As Kenya passed through the wreckage of the village, soldiers tore down the remains of the homes and the shops of the town, along with the crude shacks of the refugees and leaving the rubbish in big piles for the workers to haul away by oxcart and dumped into the ocean. *Place certainly was destroyed by the demon. Maybe when the war is over they can build a new town with permanent homes and shops for the people that doesn't look like the bottom of a latrine.*

"Ho, Lady Kenya," Marcos shouted out a greeting with a wave as she approached the trench. He scrambled over a pile of rocks and wiped his brow with the back of one dirty hand, leaving a long muddy streak on his cheek. "What brings you out here?" He scanned the length of the dug out channel. "Checking up on your construction project?"

"Mine?" Kenya watched men shoveling sand and rock, while still more hauled the soil away in ox carts. She handed Marcos a hesitant smile of confusion. "Since when has this project become mine? I think since you started I've only been down here twice."

Marcos's lips broadened into a smirk. "The men have already named the channel 'Kenya's Trench," in your honor, since it was your idea to dig the waterway in the first place."

Kenya's face burnt hot with embarrassment. "Very flattering—I think. A hole in the earth with my name." She studied the long cavity with new interest. A temporary wooden bridge spanned the depression from one side to the other, while long poles with buckets attached acting as levers rose and fell hauling dirt from the lower levels of the trench for emptying by workers above. The men operated as teams with precision, each group trying to outdo the others in deepening the hole to the encouragement of their foremen. "How soon do you think this will be done?"

Marcos waved a finger in either direction where land met the sea. Massive logs drove into the ground by means of pile drivers, logs weighted with boulders and allowed to run down a slide, acting as giant hammers banged away. "We construct retaining walls now so the water will not rush in until we are ready. When they are finished, the digging is completed." He rubbed his cheek and glanced at the blue sky, estimating the time. "I have instated a series of rewards for the team of workers who haul the most dirt in one day so construction moves quickly. Four more days?"

"I see they are destroying the remains of the town," Kenya commented gesturing back toward the castle.

"I know. Since the demon demolished most anyway, the king has ordered the complete flattening of the area. The building might provide cover by an invading army. This way the archers and our rock throwers have a clear field of fire if the enemy approaches our walls."

"Any word from Randall or the other scouts," Kenya asked idly as she watched a cart roll away with dirt.

"Nothing. A rider arrived this morning from Lord Galvin carrying word from King Goron. It is a wonder he made the journey through the central plains at all. The evil stalking the land has disrupted communication with the king and the Western Mountains for many days. The rider was lucky demons did not eat him alive." Marcos stopped talking abruptly and looked past Kenya toward the castle. A soldier on horseback pounded their way. "It appears the rider has brought weighty news. The king would not dispatch a rider here in such haste unless the information was vital and could not wait until tonight."

The rider drew up before Marcos. "The king has summoned you back to the castle for a council of war. You also, Lady Kenya." The warrior added to Kenya, "Now."

"What news?" Marcos asked striding for his horse. He shouted brief instructions to the foremen and then vaulted onto his mount. He offered Kenya a hand and hauled her up before him.

"I know naught," the man replied as the three rode back to Evertree at top speed, "other than to fetch you and any who might be here of the king's court."

The main hall was crowded with the king's advisors and any warriors not on duty. A sweat-soaked warrior stood next to the king. When all assembled from their tasks, Harold spoke. "A messenger from Lord Galvin has arrived, bringing word from King Goron. He and the other mountain lords are gathering a force and marching to the plains in order to confront the evil massing there. Evertree is asked to muster as many troops as possible and join their company."

A low rumble of talking broke out in the assembly. The king allowed the comments to continue for a moment unchecked, and then raised his hand for silence. "He has asked me to hasten as fast as possible and meet him five days hence." He surveyed the men watching him intently. "I have agreed."

More murmurs erupted. One of the warriors, a captain, asked in a loud voice, "The plains are closed to us. How are we to reach King Goron?"

Mutters of agreement sprang up. The warrior standing next to Harold stepped forward and spoke. "I brought the message from Lord Galvin and King Goron. I faced danger on the plains, yes, but traveling here, I saw naught of the great evil we have grown to fear. For a large company the dangers would be slight." He took a step backward and resumed his position next to Harold.

The king raised his hand for silence. "My scouts report the demons have withdrawn, perhaps to confront this new force of Goron's. I do not know. In any case, for a short span of time we are free of danger if we move quickly. I have ordered our scouting parties to return except for a few spotters. When all is assembled we march."

As the hall emptied, Marcos wore a worried expression on his face. "If for some reason we are defeated," he said to Kenya as they walked back outside, "Evertree will surely fall. There will not be enough warriors left for another assault or to defend the castle."

Kenya's eyes opened wide. "Are you so sure of defeat, then?" the stark fear in Marcos's voice shaking her. He would not say such a thing if he believed otherwise.

Marcos rubbed a grimy hand across his forehead, worry still rumbling in his voice. "I hope not, however, I have a bad feeling about this message. Why did Lord Galvin send it instead of King Goron himself?"

Kenya had no answer.

The troops Galvin sent to Evertree volunteered at once, declaring, "If our Lord goes into battle so shall we."

The following day small clusters of scouts began arriving at the fortress, pulled back from the plains surrounding Evertree. All bore the same message. The demons that plagued the kingdom for months had withdrawn, always to the West and North, never quickly, but surely as if pulled by an unseen force.

On the third day, King Harold summoned Kenya informing her she would travel with the troops, to record the battle and compose songs of the warrior's valor when they defeated the ancient foe once and for all. Kenya bobbed her head solemnly, collected clothes into a traveling kit, and the next day the party set out, tramping across the temporary bridge constructed over the trench.

The day was overcast, grey clouds drifting across a sullen sky with the ever present threat of rain in the air.

Except for the creaking of wagons and the clomping of the horse's hooves on the dry earth, the party rode in silence, King Harold, his standard-bearers marching before him as he headed up the column. A cloud of dust rose behind the troops, a dark spirit tailing the soldier's every twist and turn on the lane.

Kenya rode at the rear of the king's retinue with Marcos and the rest of the cavalry keeping herself busy scribbling notes on parchment, studying the men's faces, and attempting to devise songs to match their temper and mood as the thoughts of the coming battle flashed through their minds.

Kenya noticed a heavy weight pushed down on the men, a shroud of wool deadening spirit and joy as the soldiers trudged along. Grim lines creased their features, more so, she thought, than the prospect of going into combat would warrant. The dust raised by the horses covered the soldiers marching behind until they appeared to be grey ghosts. *They act as if they tread on a death march from which none will return.*

The pressure filling the column descended on Kenya also, and she found no reason for the anxiety weighing on her spirit. She asked Marcos, "Do you feel it, too? The despair?"

"Huh?" His jaws muscles tightened, shoulders hunched over the saddle. "Perhaps it is the thought of the upcoming fight," Marcos mumbled. "Once the battle starts the men will be too busy to worry."

"Are you sure?" Kenya shot a hard look at him studying Marcos's face. "I see the disquiet in your eyes too, desolation of the soul."

Marcos released a long shuddering sigh and straightened with start. "Yes, you are right," he admitted, and spit the words out with a groan. "If I did not know better, I would say an evil spell has been laid upon this host to sap will, spirit, and strength." He glared upward and checked the gloomy sky and joked, "Perhaps our mood is caused by the weather. This is not the day to march to battle. Too depressing. Men need to march to war in bright sunshine, with maidens waving and birds singing."

"I wish I knew something to do to wash the fear away," Kenya muttered. "A simple song, a joyous song of cheer and happiness to lighten everyone's spirits." Her eyes lit up and she snapped her fingers. *"That's it."* Kenya held the lyre gently in her hand and plucked out simple notes.

"I wish there was a melody,
To wash the fear away.
A simple song, a joyous song
Of cheer and happiness today.
The warrior spirit flows bold and strong
In everybody here.
Undaunted men of bravest heart,
No demons will they fear."

The tune wasn't good, she admitted to herself with a wry grin, certainly not one she'd try selling to a publisher or producer, but she kept plucking strings and singing, fiddling with the words and melody. Kenya rode up and down the line of men, throwing the tune at the soldiers with a wink and quick laugh.

A light breeze sprang up, pushing away the hot, humid air. The same breeze shifted the dark clouds and a shaft of sunlight fell upon her, making her black hair sparkle with shimmering motes. Kenya kept singing and more light shone down on the company until it seemed as though they marched in a blaze of glory under the sun.

Men started joking and laughing. Those closest to Kenya picked up the tune and began chanting the song themselves. She continued to play, but stopped singing, allowing the men to continue, improvising and making up new verses as they marched along.

"Was it your tune, or the magic of the lyre," Marcos asked, his face a mask of astonishment, watching the changed expressions on the warrior's faces.

"I don't know," Kenya replied, awed herself. "Maybe both, or the change of the weather. Songs *can* work magic, though, you know."

The good feelings persisted through the rest of the day and night, carrying over to the next day. The weather stayed cleared also with a warm sun in their faces and a balmy breeze at their backs.

Kenya continued writing new songs and creating different melodies attempting to keep the spirit of the marching warriors up. When she ran out of ideas, she substituted new words for the old songs she knew.

Harold kept patrols out ranging far ahead to the West, North and South, and a constant stream of riders continued riding to the column and galloping off again after delivering their news. The clusters of scouts still on the plains reported no sign of the ancient evil afoot. On the fourth day of the march, the king called a halt in a desolated stretch of the savannah surrounded by low hills. The king held a council of his retinue, advisors, and captains.

"I do not understand," Harold started, puzzled. He cupped his hands by his eyes as if by cutting off the sunlight he could see the gathering armies marching their way. "This is the spot the message indicated the armies to join, but…" the king surveyed the area again, helpless as he raised his palms and dropped his hands again, "none have appeared yet. Our scouts report nothing in sight for a day's march in any direction."

"We are early," one advisor offered aloud for all to hear. He turned to Kenya. "Your tunes made us march too fast." This brought a raft of chuckles from the assembly.

"Or late," a captain said seriously, "The armies have marched to war without us?"

Marcos studied the terrain since the halt. He spoke up with authority. "I see no sign an army of any size has camped here. The land is undisturbed. Also," he added, thoughtfully, "this is a place I would not care to linger in too long with an army. No water, and while the spot is secluded from sight, so to you cannot see what is approaching. To my mind, this is a foolish place to wait for anything, especially an enemy. I wonder why Goron choose this location."

Harold waved a hand in dismissal and answered loftily, "No doubt he had good reason. For the time being, we will camp here and wait. Post sentries on the hilltops. They will provide ample warning of any approaching danger or the arrival of King Goron and his host. I doubt attack will come to this spot any time soon since we have seen no sign of our enemy. If by tomorrow King Goron has not appeared we will push on toward Cliffward and meet him."

Marcos erected a small pavilion for Kenya to sleep in. More tents popped up like mushrooms around the shallow bowl of hills. After eating, they sat around the campfire talking before the two retired for the night.

"Something is amiss, I feel sure danger is brewing," Marcos muttered as he threw dried brush into the fire and watched sparks drift upward into the night sky.

"But the scouts reported nothing wrong, nor does King Harold appear concerned. Do you fear an attack anyway," Kenya replied nervously, peering into the darkness.

"I do not know what I fear," Marcos groused savagely, standing. "Perhaps the message was garbled by Lord Galvin and the meeting place is somewhere else." He stretched, yawned, and stared off into the night. "Anyway, the time is late. Tomorrow arrives early. We should rest."

Kenya entered the pavilion and laid down. Her eyes barely closed when yelling erupted from outside. She sat up with a start. Sunlight filtered through the cracks of the tent flaps. *Must have slept all night.* Kenya yawned and stretched.

More yelling from outside and the drumming of running feet passed by the pavilion. Kenya stood hastily, throwing the tent flap open wide and stepped out to see what the commotion was.

Warrior carrying swords drawn and at the ready ran in every direction. Chaos reigned supreme. Kenya grabbed the arm of one soldier as he hurried by. "What has happened?" she demanded.

The man panted, eyes unfocused, and shook her hand off his arm. "We have been betrayed during the night," he gasped, striding away. "The camp is under attack."

Chapter Fourteen

Marcos pounded up to her and thrust a short sword into her hands. "Here take this. Collect whatever you need, but hurry and go to the center of the camp with the horses where it is safe. Wait for me there."

"What happened," Kenya gasped running into the tent, scooping up lyre and torch. She tumbled back outside. Marcos still waited impatiently. "I thought the king posted guards."

"Murdered in the night. So was their relief." Marcos pushed her along glancing over his shoulder toward the perimeter of the camp. "No one realized anything was amiss until first light when we found the bodies and saw we were surrounded." He kept hurrying Kenya toward the center of the camp where the king's retinue of advisors waited. "Now go," he commanded with another frantic look to his rear. "I run to battle in hopes of stemming the tide of enemies and we might still live."

Harold himself was there in the center. He shouted orders to his men and deployed his troops as best he could, while cursing himself, the enemy, and whoever betrayed the army to the demon horde.

Marcos gave Kenya a final shove to the back. "Stay here," he shouted as he swung around and dashed after the rest of the troops.

"Wait," Kenya shouted, but it was too late. Marcos disappeared into the mass of sprinting warriors.

Along the ridge of the valley flames erupted. Dark shapes surged over the top with animal screams of hate. Harold's warriors responded with blasts of power from their flaming swords and arrows shot with deadly accuracy by archers. The two forces clashed in a wild melee and the soldiers started a slow retreat, pressed inward by the overwhelming number of the enemy. Large numbers of the ikkitousen led the assault, howling in madness. Intermixed with the dog demons moved more of the armored creatures such as the one that attacked the castle. Bull-like, they made lunging attacks, spewing their horrid yellow gas before them.

Farther back, other dark shapes loomed, strolling and floating, driving the front ranks forward in a frenzy.

Oh, God, they are all going to die. Kenya searched desperately for Marcos among the swirling mass of battling warriors, scanning in the direction he'd run. She spotted him, his sword sputtering flame, but flaying away as he attempted to hold at bay a pack of the dog demons single-handed while his comrades form a hasty skirmish line.

Frantic to help in some way, Kenya held the brand against the lyre. A surge of energy flowed through her fingers. Concentrating, she drew upon the power, channeling the magic with her mind, and hurling the force toward Marcos in pulsing waves.

The sputtering fire from Marcos's blade steadied, assumed new life and flared with a clean white brilliance. With renewed fury, he lashed the ikkitousen back where they tangled the rush of demons surging forward. Marcos destroyed half of the monsters in the process and then raced to his fellow warriors screaming at the top of his lungs. Others joined him and for a few brief moments, the advance of the demons halted in confusion and fear as the soldiers made a furious counter-attack.

Despite this repass, the demons pressed in from the right and left quarters and the ring of death tightened around the circle of King Harold's company.

The ikkitousen were cunning, slipping around either side of Marcos's small band of warriors while a pack kept the men occupied in front. Before he was outflanked completely, Marcos realized what occurred and beat a hasty retreat backward rallying his men in a semi-circle. Kenya attempted to spread her magic in a wider circle to encompass more of the line in her sight, but to no avail. Whatever force she drew upon, other world or not, or could not, be leveled at more than Marcos.

King Harold was everywhere at once attempting to plug gaps in his line and rally his faltering troops. He passed Kenya and his retinue with a troop of grim-faced warriors, shouting to his people, "*Mount.* We will hold the devils off as long as we can. Some of you might escape." He kept moving down the line, waving his sword in the air, and ordering men to their horses.

Kenya ran to the picket line, leaped onto a mount, and gathered a handful of reins in one fist. Kicking the mare in the ribs, she galloped forward, leading the other horses to where Marcos and his men made a last stand against the demons.

"*Marcos*—it's our only hope," Kenya yelled pulling up sharply to the rear of the fighters. Across the horizon, more monsters appeared creating a dark line along the lip of the valley.

His men saw the horses and vaulted onto their backs. Marcos looked around, dazed. "The king?"

Kenya was busy trying to hold her mount still among the dying men and raving demons. She glanced quickly left and right, saw the king to her left, and pointed. A score of demons surrounded Harold and his troop, his men dragged down as she watched. The king's sword blazed as a dozen ikkitousen leaped on top of him and Harold disappeared from view. "Gone, and if we do not move swiftly so are we."

The battle disintegrated into individual battles, the warriors quickly overwhelmed by the invading horde. Those who could make their way to the horses galloped back in the direction of Evertree.

"Marco—Watch out."

Demons converged on Marcos.

The warrior struck out with his sword. Flame blazed and monsters flared into nothingness. He stood there, clothed in sweat, splattered in blood, dust rising from the approach of more demons. Around Kenya and him only a few warriors remained.

Marcos took this in with one swift look and mounted. "Let us ride."

A running battle commenced. Those who possessed the power fell behind. Like tigers at bay, they turned to give battle to the demons as they approached, lashing with their swords to allow their comrades time to put distance between them and death. Marcos led this group. His teeth gritted in pain. A wild gleam shone in his eyes as if he wished single-handedly to destroy every monster in sight. After the fiends halted, he and his men would turn and flee, only to stop and wait to fight again.

Kenya continued to pour her remaining strength into him, gasping for breath and shaking with each surge of magic as her stamina drained. Before the last of her will power disappear, she yelled to Marcos. "Halt, I have an idea," before he answered, Kenya leaped off her mount.

Marcos galloped up, anger flashing across his face and in his voice as he exclaimed, "What? Get back on your horse before the demons reach us and attack again. We have no time…." He reached down to yank her into his saddle.

Kenya ignored him. Instead, she broke away, ran forward and then down the line of their retreat, touching the burning brand to the dry yellow grass as she went. Small flames appeared accompanied by faint lines of twisting grey smoke. Kenya hurried back to her mount and leaped into the saddle. "Be careful. Let's see if this works." She ripped the lyre off her back and hit the strings.

The small flames in the grass exploded into geysers of fire, spreading until they joined, a wall of blaze separating the fleeing humans from the demons and racing toward the advancing monsters. Kenya nodded in satisfaction. "There, that should hold them for a while." She collapsed in the saddle, barely able to hold the reins in one hand, the torch and lyre grasped in the other.

"Kenya." Marcos rode forward and reached out a hand, holding her in place until she'd recovered enough to sit upright. "Here," he passed his water skin over, "drink." Marcos scanned the burning vegetation with satisfaction. "This will stop the beasts until we make a good escape." He smiled at Kenya. "Whatever magic you worked has saved us. By the time these flames die down enough for the chase to begin again we will be far away and out of reach. Rest now."

Marcos's prediction proved true. Although he continued to send warriors to their rear on scouting missions, no pursuit followed the company. They kept riding throughout the day and into the night, the blaze of the prairie fire to their rear throwing grey shadows into the air. The company finally halted, Kenya tumbling out of her saddle and fell on the grass, clutching herself and shivering.

The men surrounding Kenya were in no better shape. Hollow faced, vacant eyed, with groans of despair issuing from their lips. Marcos dropped beside her and threw one arm around her shoulder. "I did a count. Two-thirds of our army is dead or missing." His face was bleak. "We were betrayed from the start of this adventure." Marcos rubbed his hand over his dusty face, leaving a long smear of mud across his chin. "The false note led us into a trap, our sentries killed in the night. Who...? Who...?"

"Isn't the person obvious?" Kenya pressed a palm against her forehead fighting a throbbing headache. "Galvin. Our betrayer must have been him. His man brought the note, and the note was written by him." She scanned the faces of the beaten warriors. "Where are his warriors who rode with us? I see none, and I don't remember any of them fighting either. If I were to guess, I'd say they are the ones who killed the sentries."

"You must be right." Marcos categorized the lord's sins. "So eager to volunteer his soldiers from the first, setting vipers in our midst when he was ready. His men then *volunteer* to ride with us, so they will not be at Evertree to receive our wrath, and are able to play us false at the right time. Your dreams about him attempting to use you to enter the other world against your will was an omen of evil to come. He has leagued himself with the forces of darkness somehow, perhaps even reaching into the other world to bring the monsters out and lead the devils here in order to rule over the land."

"Do you think your cousin Jessica is in leagues with Lord Galvin? She was drawn to him from the start," Kenya pointed out. "If not, how does the princess play into this game? A pawn of Galvin's? His queen? Prisoner? Would Jessica betray her own people in order to please Galvin? She refused to return to Evertree also. Was this by her own free will?" Kenya spat out her doubts in loathing detail, thinking over the princess's attitude toward the people of the kingdom and herself.

The vehemence of Kenya's tone brought Marcos up short. He shook his head in bewilderment. "I do not know. Maybe Galvin has enchanted her somehow, but my cousin always possessed an evil streak inside waiting to be unleashed at the slightest cause." He licked his lips, the questions too much to fathom in his state of confusion. "In any case, of her own free will, or enchanted by magic, Galvin will receive Evertree, if not by invasion and conquest," he scanned the defeated men around him, "then by inheritance. With Harold dead, Jessica is rightful heir to the throne."

The ring of truth in Marcos's voice shook Kenya. Fear coursed through her stomach. "All is lost, then," she whispered bleakly. "Galvin wins either way."

Marcos squeezed her shoulder and muttered angrily to himself, "Where there is life, there is hope. I will not release Evertree to Galvin without a fight. I hold claim to the throne also now the king is gone. Perhaps my right is not as strong as Jessica's, but still I have a duty to the people to protect them from harm."

"Me too," Kenya replied. Whether this was a dream turned nightmare, or not, she would see the war through until she woke or died. "Will the men follow you or Jessica?"

"After the princess I am next in line to the throne, at least for now," Marcos replied cautiously. "Until matters are settled, they will listen to me. Afterwards," Marcos raised his hands, palms up, "who knows? We shall see. In any case, I need you to stand with me for your good council." He gave a self-depreciating chuckle. "I never thought the throne would descend upon me. I will need help, and yours is the only advice I know will not be clouded by divided loyalties."

Realization swept over Kenya. For so many years, Marcos was treated as a lesser noble, an object of pity by Harold's court as one who's magic was not equal to theirs. Now he must assume the mantle of Prince in truth, or perhaps king, never trained by the king, nor had he trained himself, not even given the idea much thought.

What can I possibly tell him? I'm a waitress, bartender, wannabe song writer. I think I was anyway. I know as much about ruling a kingdom as he does.

The party pressed on. The only food, the emergency rations in their saddlebags and water in short supply. The host lost another score of men to festering wounds pulsing a putrid green, inflicted by the demons no surgeon could cure or cut out. The men screamed in pain, begging for death as the malignant sores crept up along their limbs and across their bodies.

Sheer exhaustion took more. Warriors stopped in their tracks, or dropped from their saddles, too weary, hungry, and thirsty to forge on. Their faces reflecting the horror they'd witnessed. Marcos pleaded with these, but no amount of coaxing would make the men resume the torrid pace he set. In the end, he was forced to leave the soldiers with a small amount of food and drink, hoping their courage would return and they'd make their way back to Evertree on their own before the demons pursuing the company found them.

"This should not be," Marcos raged to Kenya, swinging his fists in the air as he stalked back and forth. "There is magic at work here, a spell to sap our strength and will."

Kenya saw his despair, and knew he was right. She felt it, an oppression of the spirit weighing down on the company like a smothering pillow. Kenya received the same sensation as when they'd marched out on this ill-fated adventure, but before the feeling appeared natural. Now? "A spell, are you sure? Who do you think…?"

"Who else?" Marcos flashed her a haggard smile. "Galvin." He spat the name out as if uttering the word were a curse.

The remains of the army reached the fortress tired, half-dead, and hungry, riding over the makeshift bridge spanning the completed trench. They reached the remains of the town, weaving through the ruins with heads hung down. The cheers of welcome died on the lips of the population when they saw the ripped clothing and haggard expressions on the warrior's faces.

The first thing Marcos did when his troops were settled and resting was call the remaining soldiers from the castle together in the main hall. "Bring the townspeople also, and the women who remained behind," he ordered. "All have a stake in our defense. All must hear what I have to say." He said to Kenya, "Remain by my side. I will need your council." He attempted a feeble grin and clutched her fingers in a tight squeeze. "I am new at this."

After the citizenry of Evertree assembled, Kenya stood beside the throne, a nervous smile on her face, one hand resting lightly on Marcos's shoulder. The hall was quiet, too quiet, expressions of fear showing on the people as they waited for Marcos's speech. The mob of advisors, councilors, and courtiers, usually surrounding the king were missing. No captains with their flaming swords strolled about, boasting of their prowess. The few who remained acted as apprehensive as the commoners were. They gathered apart from the rest of the people as if closeness to one and other was their greatest protection.

The great mass of farmers, villagers, and a few warriors stood watching her and Marcos, dread on their faces, terror of the future showing in their stance.

A voice called out from the crowd, "Where is Princess Jessica? Why does she not sit where her father once sat? Are you then the ruler of Evertree?"

Marcos explained to the people what happened, from the false note sent by Lord Galvin, to the murdering of the sentries, the attack, and what he surmised of the lord traitor's ultimate plans. He ended by saying, "As for Princess Jessica, I do not know if she has given herself over to the dark forces, or is held against her will and is a prisoner of Galvin's. This we must wait on. For sure, though, a strong demon army marches this way only a few days behind us. If any of you wish to leave, do so now, or take refuge on the ships in the harbor, for I can make no guarantee Evertree will not fall." He stopped speaking, allowing the people to digest the information he'd given them. After ample time passed he said, "For the time being, I rule, as best I can. How say you, follow me or flee?" He paused tensely for a reply.

Kenya waited also, anxious, unsure of what the response would be. Would these people desert Marcos in his hour of need? If so, should she urge him to give up his defense of the fortress and escape by sea while there was still time? Kenya tried to read their faces, the stance of their bodies.

They are desperate. So is Marcos. They could do anything.

When Marcos heard no answer, he asked again in a voice almost too low to hear, "How say you? We are all in this together."

A mutter arose from the rear of the hall where the common folks gathered, spreading forward to the soldiers and castle personnel.

"*We will stay,*" one warrior shouted.

"*...and fight.*" This from a farmer holding a shovel over his head.

"*And I,*" another yelled with a mattock.

More voices joined the farmers and the hall rang with "*Aye—Aye-AYE.*"

Marcos stood and yelled back, "I will do my best to protect you all."

Shouts of agreement resonated within the chamber from the crowd, growing into a roar until Kenya found herself screaming with her eyes shining, "*Marcos—Marcos—Marcos,*" pumping her clenched fist into the air. The people took up the chant until the hall reverberated with Marcos's name. Sentries outside guarding the walls ran inside to see what the explosion of shouting meant.

Marcos shot Kenya an incredulous look of disbelief, his lips curling up into a grin as he saw her working up the crowd. With a nod to himself, he turned back to the people and raised his hand for silence. Cupping his hand, he murmured out of the side of his mouth to Kenya, "Now you have the men all excited and expecting me to perform a miracle, any suggestions? Ideas? We have the populous and soldiers with us, but I do not have the faintest idea of how to defend ourselves." His eyes swept the crowd waiting on him. "Should I dismiss the people and we can discuss this later in private?"

Since the return to the castle, Kenya was thinking the same thing. How to protect the fortress during an assault from the demons and safeguard the inhabitants at the same time? She remembered the debris from the town's buildings and the prairie fire created by her torch and lyre. Kenya whispered back to Marcos, "The wood and straw from the town, what if we fill the trench with anything burnable? When the army arrives, set the wreckage on fire. The inferno will stop the advance for a short time and the fire will burn through the supports for the dams, causing the trench to flood as we planned in the first place. This will slow them down more." Her eyes clouded over attempting to think up something else. She found nothing and shrugged. "Well it's a start."

Marcos sat down on the throne with his fingers moving restlessly on the armrest of the chair as he thought over what Kenya said. He nodded. "Good idea. I had not thought so far ahead." He issued orders to the men standing before him, and the crowd dispersed, the warriors and farmers to fill the trench with whatever rubble remained from the town and would burn. The castle personnel hurried to resume their tasks, and in addition, carrying anything not essential from the fortress to the village, adding to the wreckage the villagers and soldiers hauled to the trench.

As the men and women streamed out, one of the sentries from the main gate ran in and whispered into Marcos's ear. Marco's eyes widened and said eagerly, "Send him in."

"What is the problem now?" Kenya was alert to the change of expression on Marcos's face. "Good news? Reinforcements?"

"Maybe both," Marcos replied.

The guard escorted a dark man with a grey beard into the hall. His long flowing white robes swishing on the floor as he strode forward. The man stopped and bowed low with a wave of his hand before Marcos. "I am Ben-Salin, a trader, from Mavareen in the far South. A merchant friend of mine told me of the war you fight here in the North, and I received word you seek brimstone for your defense." He straightened up, beaming from Marcos to Kenya, and pressed his hands together. "I have brought as much as you wish, Oh King Harold." His benign smile centered on Marcos and stayed there.

Brimstone—Sulphur. *What we need to complete the hoops.* Kenya broke out into a grin, as did Marcos.

"We thank you," Marcos replied graciously returning Ben-Salin's bow. "I am not King Harold. He is dead, but…"

"Dead?" The trader's happy expression bent into a scowl and he shifted nervously from foot to foot. "There is no need then? You must understand, master, I have traveled a long way, facing attacks from bandits, wild animals; storms such have not been seen since the beginning of time swept the desert I crossed in order to bring your brimstone." He waved his hands in the air, mimicking a sand storm raging over his head. I…"

"We still have need," Kenya replied before Marcos said anything. "A small one. I am sure *King* Marcos would agree." She swung to Marcos, her eyes boring into his. "*King* Marcos, perhaps we will be better served if we let your steward dicker over price instead of us, so this good man can unload his burden, collect his money, and be back on his way." Kenya nodded to the trader. "I am sure he must be in a hurry to return to his home country."

"Huh? Oh, yes, of course." Marcos acted bewildered and shot Kenya a puzzled look, waving over one of the sentries standing by. "Summon the Chief Steward to discuss with this man payment for his goods."

He again smiled benignly at the trader, attempting not to appear as confused as he felt. "Uh, we thank you for the brimstone, and hope we can continue to do business with you whenever we have a small need." He glanced quickly at Kenya who nodded back.

Ben-Salin bowed low waving his hand again. "Your servant. Whenever you have a requirement, all you must do is send for Ben-Salin." He threw the hem of his robe over his shoulder. "I will be outside with my caravan, waiting. You steward can find me there with my men." With another bow, he twisted on the balls of his feet and sauntered out of the chamber.

After the trader disappeared, Marcos asked, puzzled, "Why did you interrupt me? I know enough the steward pays for our goods." He crossed his legs with faint ire. "I am not so inept I do not understand the basic operations of this castle, and you acted as if the Sulphur was not important." He grimaced. "Whether Lord Galvin knows it or not, the loops are the one means we may have of saving this fortress and our kingdom. You know we need brimstone to complete the fire hoops." He tapped his fingernails nervously on the armrest of the throne waiting for Kenya to supply him with an explanation.

Kenya smiled at Marcos with a smile one might hand to a child when the answer is right before him. "Exactly, but he doesn't know we need the brimstone so bad. The price would double, triple, or more if he did." She giggled and laid a hand on Marcos's shoulder. "You're too honest and would have agreed to the first price he stated. Let your steward handle the dickering, or me when it comes to dealing with salesmen."

Marcos's eyes sparkled in delight when he realized she spoke the truth. "As you wish, *Lady* Kenya. I see you are wiser in such matters than I." He clasped his hands together. "Perhaps I should locate the keys to the castle just in case and hand them over to you also." When he saw the surprise on Kenya's face, he reached out and squeezed her hand. "Nevertheless, for now we must prepare and hope your wisdom and our luck are enough." He rose and began issuing orders to the sentries.

The castle leaped into a frenzy of activity. Those not engaged hauling wood to the trench, stripping the fortress for burnable material, or carting baskets of Sulphur to the men pounding the brimstone into fine powder for the construction of the fire hoops, were set to work digging pits on the outside of the trench. At the bottom of each hole, sharpened sticks, pointing upward, nestled. Afterward, a thin layer of leave and dirt concealed each pocket.

On the near side of the ditch, Marcos ordered large pointed stakes dug into the earth with the tips jutted outward, pointing toward the trench, each a long spear meant to impale the unwary, and break up the demon formation once the enemy breached the castle's first defense.

The men worked through the night, dropping in their tracks when they grew too exhausted to continue, only to stagger to their feet and continue after a few hours' sleep.

None labored harder than Marcos did. When a man stopped working to rest, Marcos was there to take his place. Kenya toiled beside him, but even she found it necessary to rest, wrapping her sweaty, stained cloak around her and curl into a ball during the early morning hours.

"Our efforts will not be enough," Marcos kept muttering to Kenya as they supervised the busy warriors. "We need more people, or more time. We have neither." With a groan, he snatched up a blackened wooden beam and tossed the shaft over his shoulder. "You might as well go back to the castle in case one of us are needed there." He grunted to Kenya, "Someone must be available if our presences is called for." He took in Kenya's sorry appearance with a shake of his head. "A warm bath would not hurt either. Before the day is out I will need your head clear and fresh. I fear mine will be befuddled. I will stay here and attempt to make one man do the work of two."

"But..."

"Go. A single person here will make no difference. Perhaps you can devise a more effective use of our people."

Kenya trudged along the beach back toward Evertree, eyes wandering over the harbor as she worked on their problems in her mind. A group of men rowed out to one of the ships moored in the water where the evacuated women and children were. This was one of her suggestions to Marcos. The men rotated on regular bases for short visits to their families. A way of keeping morale up. The men labored harder and faster knowing what they worked for and hoped to protect.

Why not. Ain't nothing happening at the castle that can't wait for a couple of hours.

On impulse, Kenya located another boat preparing to leave. "Mind if I ride along," she asked the helmsman. "Neither Marcos or I have visited the ships yet. I'm curious how the inhabitants fare."

The sailor's eyes widened and he hastily shouted to the other men in the boat, "Move over. Lady Kenya wishes to join us." He extended his hand to Kenya. "Of course. Now mind, yah may get yourself wet. Just warning yah."

Kenya allowed herself to be helped aboard and took a seat. "A little water never hurt anyone," she assured the helmsman, "but make sure we don't sink. I'm a terrible swimmer."

The sailor gaped unsure whether she joked or not until he saw Kenya smiling. He guffawed back and replied, "I've never lost a lady yet."

While the boat made the trip to the ships, Kenya studied the faces of the other inhabitants of the craft. Each held a haunted look. The expression of defeat or a mule forced to work long after the time the beast should have died.

They're already beaten and the demons haven't arrived yet. How are we going to survive?

As boat docked against the ship's side, a rope ladder lowered for their party. The men climbed up, eager hands of women and children pulling husbands and fathers over the side onto the deck. Kenya clambered up the ladder last, the corners of her mouth flickering upward hearing the squeals of joy and greeting as families met and united once more.

An officer, she assumed the first mate, strolled over. "Lady Kenya, what brings you out here? Is there a problem?" Concern echoed in his voice and he automatically glanced toward shore. "Is the invasion about to occur? We have received no word since the army returned to the castle."

"No, nothing yet," Kenya denied. She forced herself to remain calm, refusing to allow the worry show in voice or manner. "I wanted to see how the women and children fared on board. The attack approaches, be sure, but not yet." A thought occurred to her. "Do you have spare men to send to Marcos? He needs extra hands to complete the fortification of the cape." Unconsciously her eyes swept to Evertree. "So much must be done. Even a few sailors would help. The men work day and night, but...."

The sailor bobbed his head in understanding. "Of course. We are at anchor and the duties are light." His gaze flickered to the seamen standing around idly moping the deck and wiping down the railings. "I think they would enjoy a break in the routine. Boredom sets in easily." He searched over the heads of the passengers, lips moving soundlessly, counting. "I will see who we can spare and pass the word along to the other ships."

One of the woman with two small children in tow who stood nearby with her husband said, "If you need extra help, I will gladly volunteer. It's better doing something than squatting on this ship waiting for the end." Three of the women standing close overheard her remark and muttered agreement.

"But your children," Kenya protested in surprise, searching the woman's face. "You can't bring infants into danger, and who will watch them?" What the woman said was absurd. The reason these people were here in the first place was to keep the noncombatants safe. What kind of a mother would willingly abandon her children?

The woman grimaced and waved a hand. "Posh. I see plenty of old women here who can watch my brood," she replied after considering what Kenya said, glancing around at the growing crowd surrounding her and Kenya. "I have worked all my life in the fields, cooking and cleaning, too, I might add. Helping my man and Evertree will be a holiday compared to farm life."

"Me, too," another woman, younger, with a baby clutched to a breast added. "My mother is here and can watch this one. I need to be with my man." She stared down at her feet and murmured, "Especially at this time, I may never see him again."

"But...." This was ridiculous. Kenya attempted to think up an argument to quell this foolish nonsense. She couldn't. She felt the same way about Marcos. "I understand your point," Kenya said at last, giving up. She said to the ship's officer who watched the growing argument with a grin on his face. "As long as the ships are sending sailors, can transport be made for any woman who wishes to join and help in the defense of Evertree?" Kenya scanned the crowd, and tried to estimate how many more women on the other ships desired to join their men. "I'm not positive how...."

"I am sure enough boats can be arranged," he replied, still smiling as he saw the chagrin on Kenya's face.

Kenya swung back to the women. "No children," she lectured sternly, "do you understand? Arrange for their care, but realize you are returning to your deaths." With a deep breath, Kenya said to the mate, "Can I be taken back to land? I must inform Marcos what has transpired here."

As a sailor rowed Kenya back to shore, she kept repeating to herself, *what am I going to tell Marcos. Oh, he will be so mad at me.*

Chapter Fifteen

"Where were you all afternoon? I returned from the trench to see if you needed me here and you never arrived." Marcos stifled a yawn with the back of his hand. The puffiness beneath his eyes showed his lack of sleep.

He'd halted the construction of the defense for the night, deeming the men needed a good rest. Otherwise, they would not be fit to fight when the demons arrived. "I asked everyone but no one knew where you were." Marcos crossed his long legs and regard Kenya with interest and a bit of concern. They sat around a table in Kenya's chambers discussing the day's events.

When Kenya arrived from the ships, the time was late and the main hall already jammed with men wolfing down food. A large crowd surrounded Marcos, anxiously asking questions which he deflected or tried to make light of to allay the people's fears. Kenya was unable to talk to him during supper and impatiently waited for the crowd to disperse. As soon as it was seemly to do so, she motioned with her head toward the staircase to the upper reaches of the castle, still unsure what she was going to say.

"I—I took a ride out to the ships." Kenya fiddled with a goblet of wine, making small circles with the bottom of the glass on the tabletop. "I wanted to see how the women and children were doing."

Marcos took a sip of his wine and nodded gravely. "Good idea. Something I should have thought of earlier. Their welfare is as important as the men. In all this haste, I forgot about the evacuees. I am glad you did not." His vision focused on the wine goblet, the problems he faced still plaguing him. Marcos finally asked absently, "How are they doing? Everything is fine, I trust."

Kenya nodded vigorously, not daring to stare Marcos in the eyes. "Oh, yes. Uh—the captains are sending sailors from the ships to help with the work…"

"Great." Marcos looked up, face brightening as he heard the news. He nodded enthusiastically, turning his attention back to his goblet again, commenting, "We can use all the extra hands we can find." He took another sip of his wine.

"…and women," Kenya added lamely.

"What?" A garble of noise issued from Marcos's throat as he slammed his goblet down, splashing liquid on the floor while he sputtered in disbelief, spraying more on the table from his lips. "Why? Once the attack starts, the demons will kill them all. What can they do? Whose idea was this?"

Kenya finally looked up from her goblet and glared back defiantly. "*My idea.* The women want to help…and fight as much as the men want to. As for what they can do," she drew a deep breath and leaned forward, "Look. For most of the things we are doing a woman can do as well as any warrior is able to. They can dig your mantraps, and lay stakes as well as a man does. You need your Sulphur pounded into dust? Your fire rings constructed? Does it matter whether a man does the work or a woman? As for carrying wood and thatch to *my* trench," Kenya drew another deep breath, "maybe they can't lift as much weight as a man, but they carry something, and that's more than we had before."

In the following stillness, Marcos opened his mouth, and then shut it quickly, face frozen. His only comment was, "I hope you told the people they will die in the most horrible way."

"I told them," Kenya replied simply.

"And still they wished to leave the safety of the ships?"

"Yes."

Marcos rubbed his lips, eyes closed. "So Mote it be."

Kenya relaxed. "I couldn't deny the women since I am staying also."

***

A hazy, blood red sun rose over the ocean. Kenya and Marcos leaned on the parapet of the keep and watched the red orb make a lazy ascent into the sky. The last remains of stars disappeared, leaving dark clouds drifting above to replace them—black fists with ripples reminding Kenya of knuckles clenched to strike.

Whatever work needed competing was finished. The trench filled to overflowing with wood and thatch, stakes set firmly in the earth, pits dug into the ground and covered. A thin line of scouts covered the approaches to the cape through the forest from the plains waiting to rush back to Evertree with the news of the approaching attack.

Marcos wore his armor and sword. Kenya wrapped herself in a green cloak to keep the morning chill from her body. The smell of the ocean was in her nose, a gentle breeze ruffled her long black hair.

"Today will be the day," Marcos whispered. *"I feel it. I feel the evil approaching."*

"You have received no word from our scouts?" Kenya asked continuing to watch the sky darken with sullen anger. The sun vanished behind the thunderheads drifting in from the south, changing the morning into twilight.

"Not yet," Marcos acknowledged, "but soon." He turned his gaze on Kenya, but his eyes held an otherworld look as he peered into the future. "Don't you feel it? In the air?"

She *did* feel an oppression. Kenya didn't know if the impending storm sent shiver up along her back, or the anxiety from the wait, but a queasy, fluttering engulfed her stomach into a knot and traveled to her chest, the air packed with electric charges, invisible sparks pricking at her skin. "Maybe," she hedged. "The sensation is the same as followed us from the defeat on the plain."

Kenya found though, the strength to throw off the discontent if she concentrated on the malaise. Kenya closed her eyes, humming, and then snatched off the lyre from her back, strumming to the same song she hummed. The sky didn't lighten, but the weight hanging on her soul slowly dissipated, and those around her threw back their shoulders and determined expressions replaced those of despair. Kenya kept plucking at the strings, eyes tightly locked, imagining the notes as little bubbles floating over the cape, soothing the warrior's fears.

A shout rang out from the direction of the trench and the watchers there swung in the direction of the keep waving their arms frantically in the air to gain the attention of the soldiers. A troop of horsemen pounded in from the mainland, crossed over the makeshift bridge and sped toward the castle. Kenya and Marcos leaped down the steps and met the men in the courtyard.

"What news?" Marcos yelled. Fear consumed Kenya, dreading the answer she felt sure would return.

"They come," replied the leader out of breath. "A great host. They will arrive within the hour. We rode as swiftly as possible."

Marcos nodded dourly. "You have done well," his voice cold. "Go. Rest your horses and yourselves. We have a long day ahead, and you must be prepared to do battle in a short time."

Kenya called to the gatekeeper, "Have the trumpeters sound the alarm. The enemy approaches." She swung about in a swirl of her cloak and started into the castle. "Be right back," she yelled over a shoulder to Marcos.

"Where are you going?"

Kenya glanced behind her still striding forward. "Why to get my torch and a sword, of course. I can't fight without them now can I?"

She returned a few minutes later, a sword belt clasped around her waist, firebrand and lyre clutched in her hands. "Let's go greet the enemy," Kenya said to Marcos, mouth set in a grim line of determination.

His eyebrows raised, but he said nothing other than calling for two horses, and ordering three companies of archers along with infantry to follow the pair out to the trench.

The crashing of the ocean and a stiff wind blowing off the water replaced the stillness of the morning and the gentle breeze as the two rode across the cape. A light cold mist filled the air. Grey clouds rolled their way and the ominous booms of thunder accompanied the dark sky. "In for a tempest," Marcos commented gaging the speed of the gloom sweeping in from the sea.

"Will a storm help us, or the enemy?" Kenya wondered aloud.

Marcos bellowed a laugh and pushed his slack hair off his face. "Hopefully us. We can retreat to the dryness of the castle. They must sit in the mud. No one wishes to fight in the rain, right?"

Cheers arose as Kenya and Marcos approached the thin line of soldiers guarding their barrier. "Since you wish to be a warrior princess, Lady Kenya, you take the right side." Marcos waved a hand toward the line. "I will take the left."

Warrior princess? Like what's her name? I like that. "As you will m'Lord." A gentle rain began to fall, replacing the mist and splattering the dust. "Will the rain effect the burning of the lumber?" Kenya asked Marcos. "Maybe we should light the wood now to be sure."

Marcos studied the sky and the trench. "I do not believe so. Too soon, and the flame may burn out before the enemy arrives. I ordered the men to drench the material in oil. The wood will burn, wet or not unless the rain turns worse."

A low grumbling shook the air. At first, Kenya thought the sound was the noise of more thunder, then before her, a black line emerged in the distance growing steadily larger from the forest. Soon she made out the shapes of individual figures advancing boldly toward the cape.

Lord Galvin marched in the lead accompanied by Princess Jessica at his side. Behind, a host of demons, some running on all fours, others sprouting horns on the misshaped heads, lumbered in their wake. Sickly purple-green clouds floated overhead, neither matter nor energy, but a horrid mixture of both, shot electric red sparks within their bodies to strike the earth from tentacles dangling below.

"Now it is time to light the wood," Marcos called out as he waved his arm toward the ditch. Soldiers holding torches sprinted forward from the ranks touching straw and hurling their brands into the middle of the wood filled trench.

Smoke curled up, and then flame, but as quick as the fire leaped up most was extinguished by the rain.

"So what is this? A welcome fire for my bride and me?" Lord Galvin stood on the other side of the ditch, arms a jumbo, a smirk on his face as he surveyed the smoldering pile of wood. "I would think you could make a better reception for your new rulers than a smoking heap of rubbish."

Jessica covered her lips, yawning in boredom and called out to Marcos, "You are forgiven, cousin, I know you have tried your best." The princess waved a finger negligently toward Kenya. "Perhaps the scullery maiden sitting over there on the horse, who pretended to be a wordsmith, led you astray in the proper way of greeting rulers with bad advice. But thank you for watching over my kingdom. I now claim Evertree as her new queen."

Kenya ignored Jessica's insults and kept one eye on the men, waiting to see their reaction. She didn't have long to wait. A captain of the infantry stepped forward with his men trailing in his wake. "We will have no ruler who consorts with demons and monsters," he cried, staring pointedly at Galvin, "or their friends." The warriors to his rear banged javelins on shields to show their agreement and shouted war cries in defiance. He glared at Galvin and Jessica and shook his fist. "Go back to your cold mountains and may the ice dragons who abide there eat your souls."

More shouts of contempt arose from among the ranks, promising death to whoever dared to cross the smoking trench in the dirt. Galvin listened patiently with a smirk on his face and laughed contemptuously at the men. "So be it. My companions will chew the meat off your bones and suck out the marrow for dessert." He strolled forward to the edge of the trench, the demons crowding behind him eager to leap across and attack the army.

A few flames managed to catch in the trench, but most of the wood smoked or refused to ignite at all. Marcos rode over to Kenya and said, "The fire is not working. Be prepared to retreat back to the castle." The rain splattered harder making small craters in the dust and ash. The odor of wet burnt wood filled the air. In the distance a clap of thunder rumbled.

My firebrand. I wonder…?

Kenya scrambled off her mount, tripped, and caught herself. She spotted one of the small flames still flickering on a beam, stumbled forward, and threw her torch into the fire. A *whoosh* exploded in the air as smoke and wood ignited into a fiery blaze of light, spreading the length of the trench and creating a shimmering curtain of heat.

Galvin and Jessica screamed, leaping back in fear and rage. *"In the name of Evertree I defy your horde!"*

Kenya screamed. When she spied the shock on the lord's faces, Kenya smiled sweetly at the two over the blaze, curtsied, and sauntered back to her horse. Marcos rose in his stirrups and shouted, *"Archers—forward."*

The three companies of bowmen stepped in front of the infantrymen, holding their weapons at the ready. Marcos called out, "On your mark…set…*fire.*"

The archers bent their bows, arrows pointed at a forty-five degree angle. At the word fire, they loosed their bolts. The arrows flew upward into the air and over the fire, peppering the ranks of the demons lined up on the other side with deadly effect.

Galvin yelled a word of defiance. The purple clouds drifted over the trench, shooting red sparks from their hanging tentacles at any soldiers who were near. More arrows shot, passing harmlessly through their translucent bodies.

Fire blazed from the swords of the warriors, lashing the demons, exploding the creatures into sparkling motes, which faded into nothingness. This did not stop the attack of the other demons. In a ravishing pack, they leaped ahead, ignoring the blaze and burning themselves into black husks until Galvin ordered the monsters to halt the assault. Smirking, he joined hands with Jessica and the two started chanting in a strange archaic language. The rain, which fell in a steady drizzle, commenced to fall in long sheets. Smoke and steam bellowed upward from the trench in huge swirling clouds, and the burning inferno separating the two armies slowly died.

The fire, however, did its job. The wooden supports holding the dams at either end of the trench burnt away. As the blaze died, sand and dirt crumbled and the ocean rushed in, a swirling tide of the sea meeting the water from the bay in a froth of blackened debris.

A deformed bird, two heads with one blazing red eye in each, swooped down from the sky shrieking in deranged hate to attack Kenya. In reflex, she drew her sword holding the blade upright over her head and the creature impaled itself, ripping the weapon out of her grasp.

More of the demon army leaped forward into the turbulence, many swept away by the sharp current flowing through the channel. The ikkitousen clawed onto the backs of the less fortunate along with hordes of rats, scrambling over the drowning demons to reach the other side.

Marcos circled his blade over his head, flame trickling in the sword's wake. "We must retreat," he shouted to his men. "Back to the fortress." He, and the rest of the lords of power, fought a rear guard action, holding off the increasing horde of creatures that scrambled out of the water, while the balance of the warriors ran to the safety of the castle.

Kenya hesitated whether to fight with the men or not, and then fled with the rest, galloping to the fortress and pulling up sharply in the courtyard. Before the mount fully stopped, she vaulted off, and sprinted to the top of the wall, watching in intent fear as Marcos and the rest swung about, lashing fire at the demons, galloped away, only to stop and attack again.

Each time the ravenous pack of demons approached the retreating soldiers, one warrior stood out before the rest, Marcos. Even from the distance of the top of the battlements, Kenya saw the blaze of his sword, the determined expression on his face, and heard his screams of rage.

"Be prepared to raise the drawbridge and lower the portcullis the second our men are safely inside," Kenya commanded the gatekeeper in a hoarse whisper.

In a final burst of speed, the warriors sprinted ahead of the monsters, crossed the drawbridge, and escaped to the security of the courtyard. Marcos lagged, slashing with his sword of power to make his comrades escape good.

His sword failed.

Ten of the dog demons leaped. Marcos wheeled his horse and sped for the fortress, throwing a curse behind him.

"Run—Run," Kenya breathed, watching. As Marcos neared the drawbridge, she raised one hand, switching her attention from the gatekeeper to Marcos and back again. As the horse's hooves touched the wood, she dropped it. *"NOW."*

The bridge rose. Marcos's horse slid on its haunches and made a frantic dash into the courtyard as the portcullis slammed down, barely missing the tail.

Kenya breathed a sigh of relief. Safe. They were all safe…for now.

The demon dogs skidded to a stop at the edge of the moat, yapping in frustration as they prowled around the edge attempting to bridge the gap. The archers on the wall loosed a volley of arrows and the ikkitousen backed up out of bow range still snarling in rage.

Marcos stomped up the stone steps out of breath to stand beside Kenya. "Close one," he exclaimed as he ran his fingers through his tousled hair, grinning. "Thought they were about to catch me."

"You're a fool. They almost did," Kenya replied with a frown. "You shouldn't have waited so long. What if you'd been killed or captured? What would Evertree do then?"

The rain beat down harder as the wind picked up. Kenya pulled the hood of her cloak closer over her head. At her remark, Marcos stopped smiling and scowled at the sky. "You are right," he growled. "In the future, if we survive, I will attempt to be more careful."

Thunder boomed louder. A streak of lightning flashed far out at sea, lighting the dark. Abruptly the weather brought Kenya back to the events around her. "It's time to signal the ships to put out to sea," she said. "When the fighting starts, I don't want those children anywhere near this castle to see the carnage happening." Kenya shouted to the gatekeeper, "Have the trumpeters signal for the fires to be lit."

Horns blared and smoke rose in the air, informing the captains of the moored ships to set sail for safety.

The demon dogs prowled around the edge of the moat, howling, dodging arrows fired, and casting forlorn glances behind them as they waited for the rest of Galvin's army to arrive. They didn't have long to wait. The lord and his lady approached astride beasts, which reminded Kenya pointedly of armored dinosaurs, *Talarusus*, except they showed pointed teeth more suited to a shark or tiger. More of the behemoths plodded behind, while other demons loped between their feet and in their wake.

The fortress rock and bolt throwers commenced a heavy bombardment of the approaching army. Many fell, crushed or impelled, but more surge forward.

Galvin and Jessica stopped their beasts well out of range of the castle's artillery, and the lord put his fingers to his mouth issuing a sharp whistle and waving his hand over his head. The armored demons lumbered forward. The castle's artillery concentrated on the monsters and flattened three by carefully aimed boulders hurled by rock throwers until the creatures plodded under the depression of the weaponry. The rest of the monsters splashed into the shallow water of the moat, and scrambled up the opposite bank to the foot of the castle. With determined grunts, they dug at the base, heaving dirt and rock between their legs as they attempted to undermine the fortress walls.

Bowstrings snapped and arrows flew. Women and men hurled rocks over the parapet or dumped red-hot sand on the monsters' heads. All bounced off the tough hides. Kenya looked furiously around, saw the soldiers standing by with the fire hoops ready to light and toss on command. She nudged Marcos and pointed in their direction. "They are our only hope," she whispered. "Given time those creatures will bring down the walls around us."

His face went sober and he nodded in assent, signaling to the soldiers to commence the barrage of flaming death. "Let us pray they are enough."

Kenya and Marcos stepped out of the way as the warriors took up position along the wall carrying hoops and braziers of flaming coals. The men began lighting, heaving the loops as quick as they could stoop, lift, and toss. After a minute's assault, Marcos halted the counter-attack and he and Kenya peered over the wall to see what damage occurred on the demons below.

Two of the hoops made direct hits on the creatures, spreading flame along the length of their bodies. The demons shrieked in pain, but continued to dig as their bodies caught fire and burned. The other hoops missed their targets, but the burning fabric flared in the breeze clinging stickily to legs, tails, and the side of the beasts.

"More," ordered Marcos, licking his lips nervously and pulling Kenya aside. The soldiers heaved again with renewed vigor encouraged by the screams of their victims. The fires spread, creating a line of flames around the base of Evertree. Fumes from the burning brimstone covered the earth swirling upward with the smoke, causing the soldiers on the battlements to choke.

The monsters backed off, repelled by the heat and fumes. Others took their place in waves of flesh regardless of their own lives. Pandemonium erupted on the battlements. Sergeants shouted orders and messengers flew along the battlements directed by captains attempting to cover areas under their command with too few men. Women and older children scurried up and down stairs carrying more arrows to the archers, or hauling rocks to rain down on the attackers.

Marcos waved to the towers where the catapults were mounted. The *thud-thud-thud* continued in earnest with five-foot bolts tipped with iron shooting into the mounting horde of demons assaulting the walls along with fifty-pound boulders crushing anything they came in contract with.

"It will not be enough," murmured Marcos as he raised his eyes and gazed out over the peninsular. A heaving mass of flesh covered every inch of the earth on both sides of the trench, which rapidly widened into a canal. This did not stop the flow of demons. They leaped on the backs of those who floundered, willingly sacrificing their lives, a living bridge of flesh for their comrades to cross over. The sole obstacle stopping the final rush of the monsters was the thin line of flames from the hoops surrounding the fortress walls.

A cold flash of fear surged through Kenya's body quickly replaced by incomprehensible fury engulfing her soul. *We will not die like this. We can't. I will not allow us to perish.* Kenya traced Marcos's gaze and his vision rested on Galvin and Jessica.

The two wore maniacal expressions on their faces. Galvin raised his hands and began chanting again. Jessica raised hers and entwined her fingers with his over their heads. More rain fell, harder, dousing the ring of fire surrounding the fortress walls.

Kenya's rage crystalized into clarity.

Two can play at this game.

Kenya clutched her lyre close to her breast, strummed notes, and started to sing.

"Storm and sea,
Surf and foam,
Lightning flash,
And thunder roar!
Pile high and higher still,
Until the ocean drinks its fill!
We beseech you gods on heaven high,

Let your wrath fall from the sky!"

I've never tried this before. Work. Please work.

Kenya concentrated on the cape and the brewing tempest, forming a picture in her mind of the storm raging, rain pelting down in torrents. She threw this image into the air drawing all the power within her. Kenya didn't know where the words came from, but kept singing and hitting the strings of the lyre furiously until she found a beat. Marcos's eyes widened and he placed his hand on her shoulder, chanting along in his deep bass. Energy flowed into her from him. A confused babble of voices and images appeared in her mind, Marcos's memories and thoughts. As if she gazed into a foggy mirror, the mist evaporated and the power within him surged. Kenya grasped the force eagerly and merged his magic with her own strength and for a time they were of one soul and mind.

The sky, already dark with clouds, blackened into night. A shocked look passed over Galvin's face. He shot a startled glance at Kenya and Marcos standing on the battlement singing, and started a chant of his own, attempting to quell the building storm before the tempest grew out of hand.

The wind continued to rise until the gale was the howl of a beast. Lightning streaked across the heavens, detonating on the ground with explosions of cannon shot. Savage combers morphed into towering waves, crashing onto the beach and sweeping inward with increasing wrath. The ocean rushed through the trench from one side to the other carving out large sections of the wall, broadening the gap from a channel into a river.

The fury continued. Gigantic waves hurtled over the land, swirling around the base of Evertree. Demons flounders in the wake, attempting to hold their ground against the surf, only to be tossed up like corks and sweep away into the pounding ocean. Unceasing thunder blasted earth, sea, and sky in a crescendo of world shattering explosions shaking the very stones of the castle itself.

Kenya stopped singing, appalled at what she wrought. The lyre dropped from her bleeding fingers.

"Oh-My-God."

Where the demon army once stood now remained only flotsam and broken bodies washed rapidly away in the tide. Evertree was an island amidst a sea of death.

Incredulous, Marcos whispered in a small voice, *"We won."*

"Yeah, I think." Kenya cringed as another clap of thunder erupted over their heads, the electric charge causing her hair to stand straight up in the air.

The storm showed no signs of abating around them. Waves continued to lash the coastline throwing foam as high as the battlements. On the beach, the surf reached fingers across the sand, crashing into the forest, sweeping inland for miles.

The tempest lasted all night and the following day. When the storm abated, no trace of the peninsula Evertree once stood on remain. The keep rested, a towering structure on an island, a monolith defying the assault of the sea.

Chapter Sixteen

It was the time of the Summer Solstice again. A crew rowed Kenya and Marcos to the mainland from the castle to celebrate the longest day of the year and bring good fortune, the joy of life, back to the kingdom once more.

Kenya sighed and threw back her head, drawing in a deep breath of the salt air. The water was calm, the sun warm, a gentle breeze ruffled her long black hair. Peace flowed through her soul, a harmony with the world she'd never felt before in her life.

It's been a whole year already? Seems shorter. I always thought this was a dream, and I'd wake up one day to the reality of my real life. Not so sure now. Maybe my former existence was the dream, and I'm waking up to what is real. Can't even remember the young girl Kenya was anyway.

She swung around in her seat and gazed at the receding castle. *Home. My home now. How could I ever think of leaving this place?*

Kenya glanced surreptitiously at the man sitting beside her in the boat with a faint smile on his face as he concentrated on the shore drawing rapidly nearer.

Marcos.

The type of man Kenya always dreamed of, kind, understanding, tall and handsome. He made her laugh, stood beside her when she needed reassurance, laid back and let her have the lead when she wanted to make her own decisions. Sure, they argued at times, but never out of hate. The debate was always on tactics, not strategy. They both strived to make the situation they found themselves in better for themselves and the people around them, no matter at what cost or how long the crafting took.

Every day brought a new revelation in their relationship. He'd grown into the type of man Kenya always knew he'd be. So had she. In the months since the defeat of Galvin, he'd turned into a benevolent ruler. When they rode out into the new village growing along the rocky shores of the castle, Kenya saw the adornment in the people's eyes, hear the shouts from the people she knew weren't forced. He listened to their complaints, no matter how small or great, consulting each person as to their needs. More often than not, at the end of the day Marcos and she would hurry away to his chamber or hers and fall into deep conversation on how to solve the problems, which presented themselves in fewer numbers each day as the king and subjects fell into a new routine. Evertree prospered under his rule, as it never had before.

Kenya changed, too. No longer was she the timid person who was too afraid to try new things. In her heart, Kenya knew she could overcome any challenge if she tried hard enough. Her lyre was a weapon, but the power derived from within her soul, the strength of will, hopes, and desires.

The gentle rocking of the waves made Kenya sleepily, the sun beating on her head didn't help. She stretched out and let the heat bake her chest, and relax the muscles, imagining a life with Marcos as his queen and partner. The thought sent small electric shocks speeding up into her throat. He hadn't said a word about marriage, but Kenya knew the day was drawing close when he would. She saw the love and desire in his eyes. Perhaps even tonight under the moon, by the sea, as the waves lapped the beach. Kenya wondered how he would say it, and what her reply would be.

The bow of the boat grounded in the sand of the beach. Sailors leaped out, dragging the craft farther up onto the shore. Marcos stepped over the edge and offered his hand to Kenya. "If you will, my Lady Kenya, I will gladly escort you to the party." His mouth broadened out into a smile and his eyes laughed as he gazed into her eyes.

Kenya giggled, covering her mouth with one hand, and offering her fingers to him, allowing to be helped out of the boat even though she didn't need assistance. She hopped lightly over the side and landed in the sand, making a curtsy. "Why, thank you, sir. You are most kind." They smirked at each other.

More skiffs pulled up beside their boat. The sailors disembarked and hurried to unload the contents, while others rushed from down the beach, passing Kenya and Marcos and carrying casks of wine, ale, and mead to the site of the party.

Kenya and Marcos allowed the sailor wide berth as the two strolled hand-in-hand along the beach enjoying the day out without the problems of state to bother them. "Any word of Galvin's castle or the horde he commanded," Kenya asked suddenly, as a premonition of uneasiness struck her mind. All this was far too simple; girl meets boy, girl loses boy, girl gets boy. This was like a fairytale, a book with a happy-ending read in primary school. Not real life. Something would go wrong.

"Our scouts reported back yesterday," Marcos replied as the two danced nimbly out of the way as a wave splashed up on the sand threating to engulf their boots. "Sorry. I forgot to tell you with all the planning for the celebration," he apologized. "Fierce fighting has broken out in the mountains and the passes are closed by warring clans. Our men could not reach Galvin's fortress, but were told by those fleeing the battles the castle is sealed off from all comers, but not by any natural force or men." Marcos kicked at a stone in their path and watched the pebble splash into a wave. "A pale of enchantment hold his land, befuddling the senses of those who try and enter, and no one is sure if Galvin is alive, or still rules, or who does."

Kenya breathed a sigh of relief. After the storm, bodies of demons and monsters aplenty had strewn the shore of the mainland and castle, some floundering in the surf, barely alive. Those the warriors dispatched quickly. More drifted in the water washing out to sea, but no trace of Galvin or Jessica surfaced on the shores of Evertree or the mainland. Marcos dispatched ships to scour the ocean to discover if their remains floated on the surface, but the ships returned empty-handed. Events became chaotic after the war, and Marcos sat uncertain on the throne. Kingship was new to him, and only with Kenya's advice was he able to learn the more intricate inner workings of how to rule a kingdom. More time was lost resettling and rebuilding the homes of the displaced and farmers of the plains, which both Kenya and Marcos felt was a top priority. Marcos was forced to dispatch half his remaining troops to the task of rounding up runaway herds of horses, cattle and sheep, escaped from their pens, or wandered off when the ranchers evacuated their lands.

After the homeless returned to their farms with a minimum of provisions to see the people through until crops were replanted and animals fattened, the construction of the new town began. Finally, the kingdom settled into a new routine. Marcos decided it was time to send out a strong party of warriors and learn what transpired in the rest of the world.

Contact was made with King Goron who reported the demon army never attacked his kingdom in any number and confirmed Kenya's suspicion Galvin was the writer of the message they'd received. A clever plot to draw Evertree's forces out into the open where they were vulnerable to attack. "He meant to destroy one kingdom at a time," Marcos declared after he received the news. He smashed a fist into his open palm. "Attack the farthest one first so his treachery would not be known to the rest until it was too late." The scouts also reported they'd seen no sign of demon or monster armies on the great plains. Small clustered wandered, dazed and confused, easy picking for the soldiers who dispatched the devils with swords and arrows. All was quiet in the land.

Kenya and Marcos arrived at the stretch of beach she left a year ago. The site already decked out for a celebration with red ribbons and white bows, garlands of flowers, and banners fluttering on poles. Hastily assembled wooden benches and tables rested in a wide circle with the center left empty for dancing or standing and talking. In one part, the musicians set up their area with drums and chairs, while in another, casks of drink and cooking fires took up residence waiting for the call to use.

"Tonight we will dance for joy again," Marcos exclaimed as he waved to people scurrying by. They waved back, broad smiles on their faces and shouts of recognition. Marcos sauntered to one of the casks and pouring drinks for Kenya and himself. He handed her a goblet. "Not only do we celebrate the longest day of the year and a good harvest to come, but also to rejoice in the peace and security descending onto Evertree once more." He lifted his cup in a salute.

Kenya raised her goblet. "May your reign be long and prosperous," she acknowledged and took a sip of the heavy liquor. Immediately she felt the drink go to her head. Sweat beaded on her forehead as the alcohol clawed down her throat. "Whew. I'd better not drink too much of this," Kenya gasped, laughing, and passed the tankard back to Marcos with a shake of her head. "Otherwise I'll never make it to the evening and you'll have to carry me back to the castle."

"Hah, we cannot have you drunk. We have too much to discuss tonight." Marcos winked.

A thrill of anticipation ran through Kenya.

The soft strains of a song filtered in the air as one of the musicians strummed his lute. Another performer took up the tune and beat on a drum to the rhythm. The sound throbbed within Kenya, her breath quickened, heart beating faster with the pounding of the drum. Handing a swift smile to Marcos, she pulled the lyre off her back and started playing along with the entertainers, tapping a foot and attempting to match the beat and tempo.

People drifted over and surrounded Kenya and the other musicians, clapping or stomping their feet with hoots of approval. An arm reached out holding a tankard. Without thinking of what she was doing or missing a beat, Kenya snatched the container, tipped the cup back and gulped quickly, passing the vessel to waiting hands.

More musicians joined the party. People danced in circles. The songs changed, the beats faster, more demanding.

The hour grew later with the sun disappearing leaving pink fingers rippling across the sky. Stars and the moon appeared overhead. Kenya noticed none of this as more dancers swirled around her in merriment. The pace of the music quickened and Kenya released herself to the joy of singing, music, and the Summer Solstice.

The grinning face of Marcos appeared before her with a bow. Kenya slung her lyre over her back and took his hand in hers. He snatched her up around the waist, spinning her in the air, and set her down on her feet again.

Laughing, the two intertwined their fingers and Marcos twirled Kenya away in a circle. They danced, whooping and singing along with the rest of the partiers, tossing their hands in the air and gazing into each other's eyes. Marcos stopped dancing and watched Kenya weaving in joy. He slapped his thighs in time to the music and her movements, sweat from the dancing dripping down his face and staining his tunic under his arms.

Kenya threw her arms upward in one last final spin, staring at the moon in joy, which gazed at her with a gibbous smile.

257 • A Kingdom by the Sea

The moon reached down and lifted her up and away.

***

"Miss, are you alright?"

Kenya's eyes flickered open. She squinted against the bright morning sunlight shining in her face, the pounding of the surf roaring in her ears.

"Marcos?"

Kenya focused on the face above her; light chocolate skin with deep brown eyes, right now crinkled at the edges in worry. "Who—who are you?" She dug her hands into the soft sand underneath her and struggled to rise.

Vertigo hit Kenya, setting her head to spin, a static grey haze flashed across her mind. She gasped, sinking down toward the sand again until a strong arm slipped behind her back helping her into a sitting position.

Curious bystanders surrounded her whispering, mostly in bathing suits, strangers she'd never seen before. Beyond, the grey ocean lapped on the shore, with a blue sky beyond. Seagulls floated in flocks swooping and diving after fish.

Is this a dream within a dream?

The wooden tables and benches set out for the celebration were gone; the musicians playing their music disappeared; the partygoers, casks of drinks and platters of food departed as if they'd never been on the beach.

Where was everyone? Who were these people?

"Marcos? *Marcos.*"

Kenya struggled to rise, body knotting in fear, swaying uncertainly on weak legs. With a gasp, she sat down abruptly.

"I'm right here, Lady. It's okay. Simmer down, you'll hurt yourself." The hand was on Kenya's shoulder again. What was this person doing touching her? Did Lord

Galvin somehow attacked the celebration? Killed everyone and taken her captive? Kenya tried to think, clear her mind, and remember the events of the night before.

We danced, drank, ate. We played music—I played music, strange wonderful tunes. I saw the moon.

The happenings of the previous evening blurred in her mind, but one face remained, a smiling adoring face she'd grown to love.

Kenya pulled away from the arm, looking at the man who spoke to her. "You're not Marcos," she accused, fear turned into panic.

This man can't be Marcos no matter what he says. Marcos looked...he looked...how did he look? Kenya strained to remember the face she knew so well.

He laughed deeply. "Sure am. Marcos McDuffy is the name. I'm a medical student at the school." He hooked a thumb over his shoulder in the direction of the college up the road. "You must have passed out here on the beach sometime last night. At least, that's what we think. I walked this beach myself about five o'clock last night and you weren't here. We came back this morning to swim and discovered you laying on the sand unconscious."

Kenya's vertigo passed. She focused her mind and tried to think of what happened. "I—I walked down to the beach last night," she muttered, scrubbing at her face as memory returned. "A party. Noise." Kenya glanced around. No sign of the bonfire showed on the sand, not even the burnt out remains of wood indicating one existed at some time. She groped for the lyre. Kenya still remembered the musical instrument, and located a rectangular piece of plastic—her cellphone half buried in the sand where it dropped from her fingers.

"Do you think you can stand," asked the man who called himself Marcos. "Do you live nearby?"

Kenya waved vaguely toward the sea oats and trail. "I'm staying at the inn." She wavered to her feet again with

Marco's strong hands on one shoulder and waist holding her steady.

"I know Kay," Marcos replied. "I'll walk you up there to make sure you arrive in one piece. Can't have you passing out on us again." To the crowd he said, "Show's over, folks. She's going to live." He released Kenya's shoulder but kept one arm around her waist as they walked up the beach to the inn.

Kenya gazed about her in wonder. The waving grass was so green or yellow. The sky a sapphire blue above her head.

Is this another dream? The other place—Evertree? Was that a dream too? Real? I can't remember.

A terrifying sense of abandonment overwhelmed Kenya and she felt lost and bewildered. The sensation passed as they emerged from the sea oat and the inn rose into view, leaving her sad but not knowing why.

Kay glanced up sharply from behind her desk, relief passing over her face as Kenya and Marcos entered. "Well, there you are. I was worried about you," the old woman exclaimed walking around the desk to stand before the two. Kay placed hands on hips and surveyed Kenya critically searching for signs of her ordeal. "When you didn't come down for breakfast this morning and the time grew so late I checked your room." She added quickly, "I hope you don't mind, but as I said, I was worried. You weren't there, and the bed hardly looked slept in. I didn't know what happened to you. I was about to call the police if you didn't show up in another hour."

"I...walked down to the beach last night. I thought I saw a beach party happening and wanted to investigate." Kenya glanced at Marcos. "I don't remember what happened. I must have fainted."

Marcos guided Kenya into the parlor and set her in one of the plush red chairs by a window with Kay hovering close by. "Thirsty? You must be freezing, too," he said, stepping over to the coffeemaker and filling two Styrofoam cups. He loaded each with creamer and sugar. Kenya wondered how he knew she drank coffee that way. He handed over one cup.

"Thank you." Kenya sipped slowly, warming her hands against the cup, and savoring the taste of the coffee. She'd never drank anything this good. Kenya glanced from Kay to Marcos. "How do you know each other?"

Kay was busy gathering pillows and stuffing them behind Kenya's back. She smiled at Marcos. "Oh, one of my guests, the daughter, stepped on a Sailcat's spine," the woman said with a nod. "Nothing serious, you understand, but *Doctor* McDuffy happened to be at the beach and fixed the girl right up. The parents were so grateful. They took *Doctor* McDuffy and myself out to dinner."

"Not doctor yet," Marcos replied with a shake of his head, grinning. "A few more years yet, but soon."

Kenya's stomach rumbled loudly. She giggled, her face burning hot, and remarked, "Sorry. Haven't eaten today and all I ate yesterday were cookies."

Kay put her fingers to her mouth, appearing contrite, and exclaimed, "I can fry you up some eggs in no time at all, dear. You must be famished." The woman looked toward the dining room door. "The kitchen is closed but…."

Marcos raised his hand. "I think this calls for more than fried eggs and toast." He winked at Kenya. "There's a diner up the road. How about I take you to breakfast and you can tell me all about yourself?"

Kenya stared him in the eye. It was a long shot but…. "Do you like music? In particular, country western music?"

Marcos broke out in a grin and said in a deep western drawl, "Why Ma'am, you're lookin' at the original Pecos Marcos." He threw out his chest and hooked his thumbs in his shirt. "Back on my grandparent's ranch in

Texas, I even have my own horse. Got thrown from a bull once." He leaned forward and whispered, "Of course, I was at a bar in Dallas, but…." He took her hand. "C'mon. Let's feed some vittles inta yah."

Kenya rose, wondering if she'd fallen into another dream.

The End

About Arthur Butt

Army Veteran, graduate of Florida State University, former police officer and plant manager. Native Long Islander now living in Florida was wife, two puppies and SnoopyCat. (and yes, a coffee drinker!)

Social Media Links:
Twitter – https://twitter.com/artyny59 @artyny59

Facebook / Author Page –
https://www.facebook.com/pages/Arthur-Butt-The-Fantasy-SyFi-Author/1528729850734703

Amazon link:
http://www.amazon.com/s/ref=nb_sb_noss?url=search-alias%3Ddigital-text&field-keywords=Books+by+arthur+butt

Goodreads link:
https://www.goodreads.com/search?utf8=%E2%9C%93&query=Arthur+Butt

Instagram: https://www.instagram.com/artyny59/

Acknowledgment:

Editor K.C. Sprayberry and all the people at Solstice Publishing.

263 • A Kingdom by the Sea

If you enjoyed this story, check out these other Solstice Publishing books by Arthur Butt:

Gail is Gaea

To the people who enslaved her she is a priestess trained in the art of prophecy. To the new land she escapes to, she is an outlaw. To the natives she leads in revolt, she is a goddess.

https://bookgoodies.com/a/B0193QH2SE

Dragonkiller

Hope is a monster killer, First Family of her town, and condemned to death if people knew she is the mother of a half-human, half-dragon child. When summoned to another dimension, she discovers love, and a man who accepts her son. In order to stay, however, she must vanquish a demon army that threatens to destroy this new land, and the old world she is leaving behind.

https://bookgoodies.com/a/B00USNA7TI

The Girl Who Rode Dragons

All Jackie wanted was equal treatment and to ride a dragon. When her cruel brother-in-law takes over as head of household, and makes her quit school, she is forced to do all the chores, and collect wood in the forest. Jackie finds a dragon's egg, and although law forbids girls to ride dragons, she secretly hatches the egg, and dons boy's clothes. After she brings the gift of fire to the dragonriders, she becomes an accepted member of their band.

Civil wars breaks out, dragonrider against dragonrider. Jackie leads the loyalist faction against the rebels. The stakes—the fate of the kingdom and the life of her and the man she has grown to love.

https://bookgoodies.com/a/B0117QI24Q

Caitlyn

A father and husband commits suicide for a murder he never did. A wife devastated by the death of her husband and sister. Two families left wondering why.

https://bookgoodies.com/a/B01N0KCSO5

Troubleshooter for Earth

Sometimes smuggler and full-time Space pilot Don Weiss teams up with Puddlefoot, a mischievous fairy, to defend Earth. Their greatest challenge, locate and subdue the Vas, an evil race of spider aliens bent on destroying our solar system, and turn them into peaceful non-belligerents.

The problem: The Vas do not exist.

http://bookgoodies.com/a/B01434A8SM

2050

The end of civilization as we know it

http://bookgoodies.com/a/B01HSOSY26

30

When the Gaea manifests herself on Earth, she seeks one man who feels the planet's pain. She finds none, and the human race pays the price.

http://bookgoodies.com/a/B01C37Z8WC

The Ultimate Weapon

A father and husband commits suicide for a murder he never did. A wife devastated by the death of her husband and sister. Two families left wondering why.

http://bookgoodies.com/a/B01M318FZ9

www.ingramcontent.com/pod-product-compliance
Lightning Source LLC
Chambersburg PA
CBHW051147030726
47504CB00004B/1077